COURTNEY MILLER

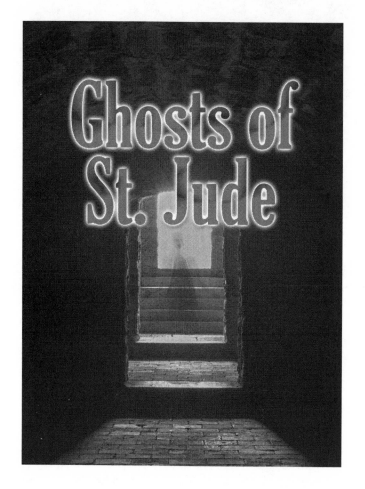

Courtney Miller

Books may be purchased in quantity and/or special sales by contacting the author or publisher at: **Popul Vuh**
www.PopulvuhPublishing.com **Publishing**

Book Design: Nick Zelinger, NZ Graphics
Book Consultant: Judith Briles, The Book Shepherd

Published by Popul Vuh Publishing

ISBN: 978-1-949742-02-2 (Hardback)
ISBN: 978-1-949742-03-9 (Paperback)
ISBN: 978-1-949742-04-6 (e-Pub)
Library of Congress Control Number: 219915206

1. Native American—Fiction 2. Cherokee—Fiction
3. White Feather (Fictitious Character)—Fiction 4. Murder Investigation—Fiction 5. Wet Mountain Valley—Fiction

First Edition Printed in USA

Acknowledgments

I am so thankful for all of the great friends, authors, and professionals who helped with this book.

The idea for "geezer lit", that is, writing about old geezers by an old geezer was inspired by the trend-setting author, Mike Befeler.

I owe a great debt of gratitude to Sheriff Shannon Byerly of the Custer County Sheriff's Office for helping me understand the procedures and dynamics of a real, rural mountain valley Sheriff's Office.

Once again, the great publishing team has put together a beautiful book. The team was led by Dr. Judith Briles, The Book Shepherd. The cover and interior were designed by Nick Zelinger, NZ Graphics.

And a special thanks to my wife, Lin, whose support, help, and advice is invaluable.

*This book is dedicated to all the old geezers
unafraid to love again.*

Other Books
by Award-winning Author Courtney Miller

The First Raven Mocker
Book 1 of The Cherokee Chronicles
> Has received a Beverly Hills Book Award,
> International Book Award, and NIEA Excellence
> Award for Historical Fiction

The Raven Mocker's Legacy
Book 2 of The Cherokee Chronicles
> Has received a Book Excellence Award for
> "Literary Excellence in Faction" [Fiction based
> on Fact]

Gihli, The Chief Named Dog
Book 3 of The Cherokee Chronicles
> Winner of the 2019 CAL Literary Novel Award
> Finalist in the 2015 Extravaganza Draft to
> Dream Book Competition

Ludwig's Fugue
Book 1 of The White Feather Mystery
> Rated "Outstanding" in all categories by
> *Reader's Digest*

It's About Time
Book 2 of The White Feather Mystery
> Winner of the 2016 Extravaganza Draft to
> Dream Book Competition

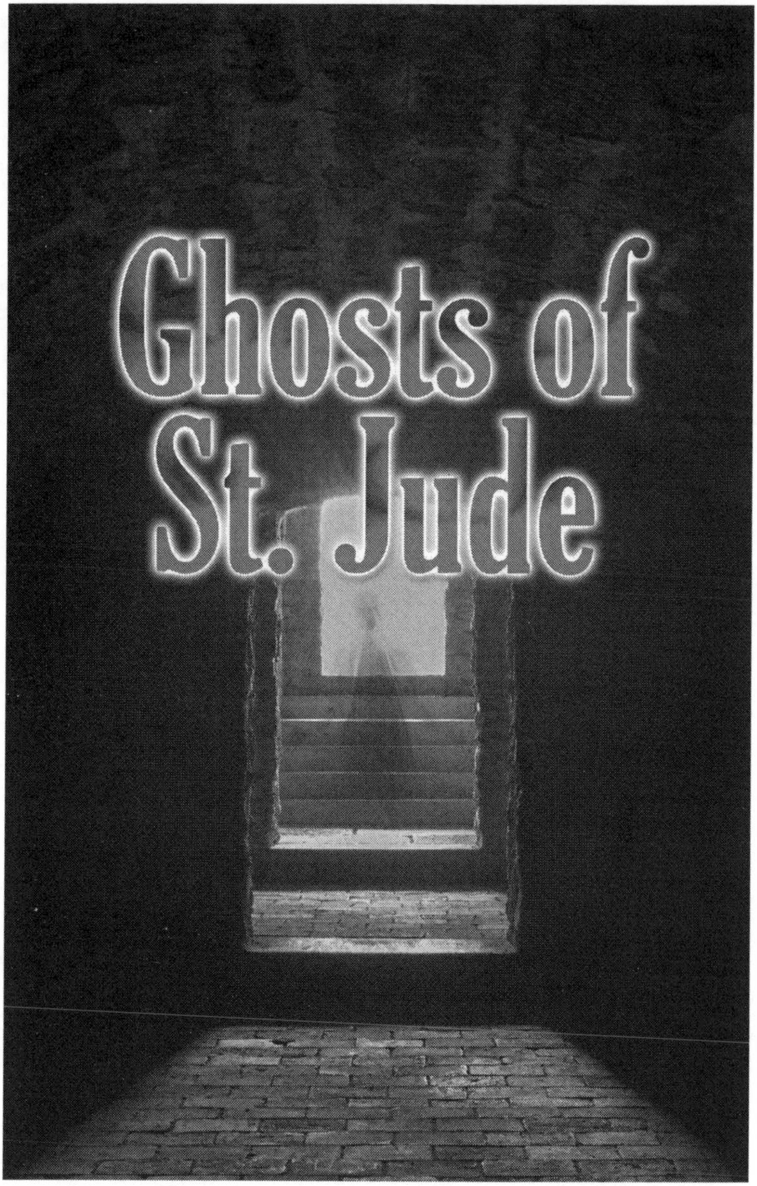
Ghosts of
St. Jude

Prologue

The Letter

To My Love,

For ours is lost; what we were is lost; what we had we've lost; what could have been we've lost except for what is in our hearts. For that which is locked in our hearts is ours alone and cannot be taken from us.

Words cannot aptly express what I feel in my heart, but still I offer this, my most sincere lamentation:

For you, my last encomium, to sing my amative requiem.

Vast the distance between our hearts, once interstitially apart.

Lives destroyed with deft celerity, ravaged by such harsh severity.

Left by cruel vicissitudes, to languish in our lassitude.

Excluded from a proud society, like ghosts who've lost their ubiety.

Love's inheritance in rapturous gestation, fouled by a feckless ablation,

Penitence wrapped in sad regalia, buried in its penetralia.

Immure me in your heart, so that we shall never be apart.

Stephen

A tear released from the old woman's eye and raced down her cheek. She had read and reread the tattered letter so many times she knew the words by heart, yet its meaning still confounded her. But, because it was written by his hand, it was the emotion, not the meaning; it was the connection, the feeling that she understood and clung to.

Wednesday

For ours is lost; what we were is lost; what we had we've lost; what could have been we've lost except for what is in our hearts.

Chapter 1

Fires of Contention

FRANKLIN DAMON ROBERTS RODE THE claustrophobic elevator down to the second floor. The elevator bell dinged; the haunting coffin like room stopped, shuddered and paused for an unsettling moment. Loud, echoing chatter greeted him as the elevator doors opened. Something was afoot, something big.

Frank found his best friend, Albert Stein, sitting quietly beside his neighbor, Ralph Jacobs just inside the door of the noisy parlor. It appeared as if all of the residents of the center had crowded into the room and were arguing among themselves.

Across the room, the enigmatic old Native American, White Feather, was standing alone, eyes closed, in front of the windows. He was whispering some native chant as the morning sun was rising above the Wet Mountains in the distance. His pale thin skin suggested that the old Indian might be a hundred years old or more. But the old man was not frail in any way. He moved agilely, never showing signs of the stiffness or aches and pains that Frank felt in his own octogenarian body. White Feather carried many youthful characteristics. He was deceptively strong for an old man: his vision was sharp; his hearing was precise; and his senses more sensitive than any man's should be.

From the neck down, White Feather looked more like a cowboy than an Indian. He wore a plaid shirt, Levi's, cowboy boots, and a belt with a turquoise stone centered on a large silver buckle. From the neck up, he was indisputably Native American. His long white hair was braided in back, but the top was threaded through a hollow deer bone that made it look like a white fountain spraying out of the top of his head. A single white feather dangled beside his bronzed face with the hilt tied to the deer bone.

Rabbit skin pouches on his belt, Frank knew, were filled with native potions. A gourd rattle was tucked nonchalantly in his belt. But a modern cell phone bulged in his shirt pocket and he carried cash and credit cards in his billfold. He seemed to be comfortable with both ancient traditions and modern technology and he mixed the two with an eccentric flair.

Frank slipped into a chair next to Albert and Ralph. "What's up?"

It was difficult for Frank not to call Albert, "Woody," because of his remarkable physical resemblance to actor Woody Allen. He was short, thin, had a long, hooked nose and wild hair. But Albert's reserved, soft-spoken, and dignified manner was nothing like the famous actor and Albert detested the moniker. Albert was a scholarly man whose many years spent as an investigative reporter for *The Denver Post* had trained in him a refinement and eloquence.

Albert answered, "Elizabeth has leaked some confidential information she overheard our administrator, Mrs. Barkley, and Nurse Nujent discussing. She claims that St. Jude has received a grant that will be used to replace the old boiler system with a new, modern heating system. The news has set off Elizabeth into a tirade prompting all of this noisy and enthusiastic argy bargy."

Frank was surprised by such an ambitious project. Although comfortably appointed, St. Jude Methodist Retirement Center for Indigents seemed to squeak by on a sparse budget dependent upon support from the Methodist Church, donations, volunteers and efficient spending.

The majestic but ancient four-story red brick building sheltered a storied past. It was built in 1891 as the State Institution for the Insane. In 1945, it was closed amid accusations of abuse and scandal. It was then converted into a multi-county hospital and served in that capacity until a new hospital was built about forty miles away in Canon City to replace it.

In 1975, the Methodist Church purchased the vacant building and eventually turned it into a charity retirement center. St. Jude Methodist Retirement Center for the Indigent only accepted residents with no financial means of support, mostly homeless or church members fallen on hard times. Residents were recommended by a sponsor and approved by a board. It was an assisted living facility, so most of the residents were relatively healthy for their age.

The room suddenly hushed as the young facility administrator, Mrs. Edith Barkley, stepped in. She smiled and calmly pushed through the tentative crowd to stand before the grand floor-to-ceiling windows through which a spectacular view of the Wet Mountains looming in the morning haze provided a stunning backdrop. Off to the side, White Feather continued his quiet chant undisturbed.

"My, aren't we busy this morning?" Nervous laughter rolled around the room. The scary old woman, Lizzie, had everyone on edge.

"It seems our little secret has gotten out. Let me share what I know and I'll try to answer your questions. We have heard from the board that St. Jude will receive a generous grant from the Weltie Foundation that will enable us to replace the dreadfully inadequate and outdated boiler system with a new central heating system. We could begin the replacement as early as next month and hopefully finish in time for the worst of winter."

Crazy Lizzie charged forward and shouted, "No! You must not disturb them!"

Frank's petulant friend and next-door neighbor, Ralph, turned to smirk at Albert and whispered, "This'll be good."

Diana Elizabeth (Lizzie) Austin Dawson had wild white hair and wrinkles born of a permanent scowl that were entrenched in her pale skin covered with a powdery white makeup. Her piercing eyes seemed to be searching for anyone to dare challenge her. All eyes turned to the administrator for her reaction.

Frank shivered. Lizzie was the spookiest person he had ever met, and apparently, he was not the only one who was afraid of her. The room was deathly quiet. Administrator Barkley took a deep breath and addressed the crazed woman, "Who, Elizabeth? Who will we disturb?"

Elizabeth closed her eyes and clasped her hands as if reciting a line from a play, saying, "Lives destroyed with deft celerity, ravaged by its harsh severity, left by cruel vicissitudes, to languish in our lassitude ..."

Edith Barkley forced a smile and stared back at Elizabeth. Most everyone knew that Lizzie had a history with this building. She had also been a resident when St. Jude was the State Institution for the Insane. Barkley seemed to be searching for a tactful response, but Lizzie's eyes grew distant and she spoke as if reminiscing, "Penitence wrapped in sad regalia, buried in its penetralia."

Frank instinctively turned to his retired journalist friend, Albert, hoping for a translation. But Albert appeared to be lost in some distant thought. He was repeating in a whisper, "Penitence wrapped in sad regalia, buried in its penetralia."

Frank whispered, "What does that mean?"

Ralph concluded, "It's a bunch of crap."

Albert blinked as his consciousness returned to the present. "I'm not sure, but I've heard it before."

Ralph shouted out, "You talkin' about ghosts again, Lizzie?"

The group laughed. They had heard it before. Recently Lizzie had warned the obnoxious resident, the late Benjamin Cook, that the ghosts would strangle him if he continued to taunt them. When he had a violent seizure and his convulsions appeared to be the result of invisible hands strangling him, Lizzie quickly gave credit to the ghosts. Although the investigation had proven his death was the result of strychnine poisoning, she had held fast to her belief he had offended the ghosts and they had gotten their revenge.

Lizzie glanced around searching with her angry eyes, "You'll see, fools!" She stomped out of the room leaving everyone stunned.

Edith Barkley nervously interjected, "Are there any other comments or questions about the new heating system?"

No one spoke, so Mrs. Barkley made another announcement, "Okay, then, I'm not sure this is a good time, but I have an announcement. We think it would be fun to celebrate the news of the furnace with a dance this coming Saturday night! We will be contacting each of you to get your size for a new dress or suit for the event. In the dining room there is a box to put your requests for music selections."

Barkley glanced around the room and then raised her eyebrows as if sharing a secret. "And Saturday is Elizabeth's birthday, so we thought it would be nice to celebrate that, too."

Ralph protested, "Won't do no good. She'll still hate it."

The room filled with laughter followed by noisy conversation as Mrs. Barkley flowed with the noisy crowd out of the parlor. Ralph grumbled and cursed as he tried to push his way through the mass.

Frank and Albert remained seated. Albert was in deep thought and whispered the curious line again, "Penitence wrapped in sad regalia, buried in its penetralia."

Frank frowned and asked, "What?"

Albert gripped Frank's arm, smiled brightly and declared, "I remember where I heard that riddle. I heard it from the former administrator of the institution."

Frank was confused. "Before Mrs. Barkley?"

Albert smiled and responded, "Oh, yes. It was from Dr. Weisman when this was the Colorado Institution for the Insane."

Frank pressed, "What does it mean?"

"He wouldn't tell me. I interviewed him on a story I was researching on the closing of the institution. Ironically, he was in an institution himself at the time. He was a tormented soul and his answers were cryptic, like riddles. That one stuck in my head."

Chapter 2

Why Not Four Trees?

AFTER THE MEETING, FRANK decided to forego the invitation to play pool with Ralph and Monty and headed downstairs to take a walk around the pond to get some fresh air and clear his head.

In back of the massive St. Jude building was a wide grassy lawn separating it from a tarn ringed by a decaying asphalt path. To the right, a curved wooden bridge reached like a dull rainbow across the babbling brook that fed into the pond. A park bench faced the pond and the majestic Sangre de Cristo Mountains where the light of the morning sun was glistening off the snow-capped peaks. In the valley, the first snowfall of early autumn had already melted.

After one lap, Frank retired to the park bench where his weary eyes closed and his mind began to shut down for a nap in the warmth of the sun cutting through the thin high-altitude atmosphere. Suddenly the bench lurched. He opened his eyes to find the old Indian, White Feather, settling down next to him, arms folded, eyes gazing straight ahead.

Frank and White Feather sat on the teetering bench staring

at the gnarly trees whose roots reached out like bulging veins to make the ground all around them uneven. Frank wondered if sitting perfectly still to keep the bench stable bothered White Feather as much as it did him. He crossed his legs and the bench lurched back to the right. He glanced at the old man expecting to be scolded. However, White Feather remained undeterred with his eyes focused on the trees. Frank shook his head, jealous that nothing could disturb the Native American's tranquility.

White Feather was a mystery to Frank. Everything about him prompted questions. The old man was stoic and often sat with his eyes closed as if napping, but never missed anything happening or said around him. He spoke slowly and deliberately and with an efficiency of words, but was quick witted and could be quite eloquent. He was calm in a crisis, decisive, bold, and unafraid. Nothing ever seemed to disturb him. But this morning, something was engaging White Feather's curiosity. He at last declared, "Three trees."

Frank frowned. He did not want to rehash this old argument. White Feather had once asked him if the junipers growing in front of the bench were three trees or one tree repeated three times. Before the question, Frank had assumed that three trees had sprouted from the same spot and had grown up fighting for space. But after White Feather had pointed it out, he realized that the three trees were exact copies of each other except that they were different sizes, progressing large to smaller, left to right.

They had already covered this, but he was willing to cut the elder some slack and answer the question again, "One tree repeated three times."

White Feather chuckled. "Why not four?"

"Four?"

"Should be four now."

Frank was confused. "Why four?"

"Time quake."

Now Frank got his point. White Feather had told him that the reason that the one tree was repeated three times was because there had been three "time quakes" in that spot. He had told Frank that occasionally there would be a quake that enabled certain people to step through a time portal and go back in time. White Feather had told Frank that he was convinced that Frank was one of those people with the ability to reenter a point in his past.

Since that conversation, there had been a mild earthquake and the building had been evacuated. As they were standing in the yard waiting for the "all clear," White Feather had suddenly grabbed his arm and dragged him around to the bench convinced that it was not an earthquake but rather a time quake.

They had sat on the bench for over an hour waiting for the portal that never appeared. They had not spoken of it since, but obviously White Feather had not forgotten nor given up on the idea.

"I guess it wasn't a time quake after all," Frank suggested.

White Feather appeared to be mildly perturbed. "Humph."

Frank tried to console him by telling him, "Did I tell you that Stacie looked up that 'seeing time' thing?"

White Feather did not respond. Frank continued, "Remember, you told me that people like me can 'see time.'"

White Feather still did not respond. Frank was not surprised since White Feather was the epitome of brevity when it came to speaking. Frank continued, "Well, I told Stacie about it and it sounded familiar to her so she looked it up, and sure enough there is a condition called synesthesia in which the brain is wired differently. Some people with synesthesia can taste colors or see numbers as colors—-funny stuff like that. And some are like me. They see time as a giant circle, like a vinyl record."

He turned to look at his friend for a reaction, but White Feather was steadfast. Frank nervously continued, "Of course, you knew about the circle thing."

White Feather's lack of response made Frank uneasy. He worried about offending the strange man, or irritating him, or coming across as condescending. White Feather was a mystery with a long-hidden past. So little was known about him, even by Albert.

Frank was equal parts afraid of and attracted to White Feather. The old shaman was equal parts scary and endearing. Frank would trust him with his life, but feared for his life if he might inadvertently offend the man.

Finally White Feather spoke, saying, "We were too late."

Frank thought about his take on it. No question, he had not given up on the time travel idea. But Frank was skeptical. Nothing in his eighty-seven years on earth supported something as farfetched as time travel. "So why aren't there four trees?"

White Feather nodded his head. "That is the question."

The pond had turned almost white with the late morning sun. The brightness hurt Frank's eyes so he looked down. He wanted to be White Feather's friend, so he offered, "Perhaps, it takes someone passing through the portal disrupting matter around it and that is what causes the tree to be distorted."

White Feather's eyes opened, widened and turned toward him. It was the first time Frank had ever seen a glimmer of excitement on the Indian's face. Then White Feather's eyes squinted skeptically. "You know something?"

Frank swallowed hard. "No! I was just ..."

White Feather looked at the trees again and then closed his eyes as if the matter was resolved. Frank stole a peek at the trees and concluded, *Time for a nap.*

It was as his eyes closed that he noticed it. "What about that, White Feather?"

He pointed to the three new leaves at the base of the smallest repeat. "Is that a fourth tree sprouting?"

White Feather stared at the sprout. "Humph."

Chapter 3

The Black Firebird

DEPUTY SAM MORRISON IDLED down the alley in his newly issued Dodge Durango SUV. Chief Buster Crab had shaken his hand and declared, "Time to take the training wheels off," meaning his initial training period was over. He was now a full-fledged deputy of the Wet Mountain Valley Sheriff's Office and could now take his deputy vehicle home with him.

The vehicle ran quietly compared to his personal vintage Dodge Charger. Even idling, the big Hemi engine loudly echoed off the cedar fences lining the backyards of his neighbors' townhouses when he drove down the alley. With the Durango, maybe he would no longer disturb his nosy neighbors when he came home to his center unit.

As he pressed the button to raise his garage door, his mind dwelled on the previous evening's visit with his family. The newness of his move to Rockcliffe had worn off. His son, Jerry, had been more interested in the games on his X-box than on his father. His daughter, Tammy, was more interested in her boyfriend David and painting her nails. But they were his kids and that was forever. He was not so threatened by them taking him for granted.

What bothered him was that his ex-wife, Samantha, seemed distant and distracted. She was pleasant and courteous but that sparkle in her eyes was not there. When she looked at him, he sensed passiveness and disinterest, a reminder that they were divorced. He had hurt her so deeply that the love they once had might be gone forever. Their marriage was over and maybe she had gotten used to it, although he had not.

His heart suggested he move their relationship to the next level and ask her for a date. His mind told him it was absurd. His logic told him that it would not work. What they had was gone and he needed to accept it and accept their new relationship. But his heart stung and craved her affection. She was the only woman he had ever loved or ever would love.

It took a precision maneuver to fit the Durango alongside his Charger in the small garage. There was barely room for him to squeeze out of the SUV. He pushed the button by the man door to lower the garage door and then crossed the small yard between the garage and townhouse, entered through the kitchen door and locked it before making his way through the darkness past the dining room table, the living room recliner and couch. He stopped to check the lock on the front door. Now he gazed through the flimsy, shear curtains of the front window at the dimly lit street. His was a sad and lonely existence here. Rockcliffe did not provide the busy, exciting life he had become accustomed to as a homicide detective in Denver. Murders in the sleepy little mountain town were rare. His days were filled with uneventful patrols: ticketing disrespectful visitors from out of state; chasing cattle off the highway; and controlling traffic at the many town events aimed to draw in tourists.

As he drew the heavy drapes across the window, he heard it! The familiar sound that evoked fear and dread into his heart. He checked the front door again to make sure it was locked and then peeked through the drapes to watch for it. The deep rumbling of glass pack mufflers grew louder as the black Firebird with heavily tinted windows slowly rolled down the street drawing closer and closer. Thank goodness he had not turned on any lights. Thank goodness the drapes were drawn. Thank goodness the doors were locked.

The classic sports car with the gold firebird painted over the entire hood pulled over to park in front of his townhouse. "Damn!"

The deputy's heart began to race as he pinched the drapes shut and slipped up the stairs to his bedroom. The drapes on the front-facing bedroom window were open.

He ducked and sneaked up to the window and peeked out. The driver door of the 1968 Firebird opened and long, slim legs in a tight, short black dress swung out. The provocative woman stepped out, stood, tossed her long, dark hair and looked up at him. He ducked hoping she could not see him in the darkness. He sat on the floor in front of the window: waiting for the knock on the door; waiting for the insistent doorbell; hoping she would not start yelling at him to open up; hoping the neighbors would not be disturbed again.

Once before, a nosy neighbor had reported one of Darla's visits to Samantha. Rockcliffe was a tiny town where everyone knew everyone and secrets could not be kept. Samantha had seemed to overlook that episode. But if it happened again?

The first knock was soft, almost imperceptible. Morrison stood to look down at her but she was too close to the house for him to be able to see her. He sat on the bed and remembered how he had tried confronting her and demanded she leave him alone, but she had just smiled playfully and taken it as a joke or, perhaps, a challenge.

She began pounding on the door. Darla had completely misinterpreted his kindness. He had met Darla his first day on the job at the Wet Mountain Valley Sheriff's Office. His new partner, Jessie Calhoun, had taken him to Maggie's Restaurant for lunch where Darla worked as a waitress. She had seemed so shy and insecure; he had felt sorry for her. Her timid nature was alluring in a strange way and he was attracted to her. He remembered feeling that she was the type that one just wants to take care of—-like a little child. But he was not attracted to her in the way one might actually act upon.

Darla began ringing the doorbell incessantly. Morrison remembered the first case he worked at the Wet Mountain Valley Sheriff's Office—the Jon Ludwig family triple-homicide. Jon Ludwig, his wife, and son had been found murdered in their home. Deputy Jon Ludwig had been the crime scene photographer for the sheriff's office. But he had also used his camera for elaborate blackmail schemes. Their investigation had turned up nude pictures of Darla. That is when he had learned that she had been Ludwig's mistress. Feeling sorry for her, he and Sheriff Bailey had decided to give her the pictures and destroy the digital images. The gesture had turned her grief over Ludwig into affection for him.

He had tried to let her down gently, but she continued to misinterpret his actions as advances. Now she was convinced he was just playing hard to get and she was up for that game.

Morrison sat on the bed in agony as the desperate woman grew more and more impatient. "I know you're in there!" she yelled.

Morrison took a deep breath. Perhaps he should go down and try once more to get rid of her. "Open up, Sam, it's cold out here."

His heart went out to her. Before Ludwig, she had been a shy, lonely, sheltered girl. Then, when she met Jon Ludwig, she found him exciting and domineering. In a crazy, fearful world, she liked to be told what to do, not to have to make decisions. She probably felt safe when she was with him. Now, with him dead, she wanted that feeling again.

"Sam!" she screamed as she pounded on the door again. When he had questioned her during the Ludwig murder investigation, he had asked her if she had ever wished she could get away from Ludwig. Her revealing answer had been, "Jon was my life. He gave me a life."

Now she had turned to him to rescue her and give her a life. How could he be cruel to someone so fragile and desperate?

"Sam, please," she pleaded, "let me in."

Let her in? Did she mean let her into his life? Morrison rubbed his face with his hands. He was all she had now. It was so pathetic, but heartbreaking. Darla needed someone to replace Jon Ludwig in her life: someone to lean on; someone to take charge; and ...

Sometimes, under pressure, the mind can get creative. Suddenly, he had an idea! Calhoun! His deputy partner needed someone like Darla to dote over him and depend on him. They would make a perfect couple.

He was getting excited. This could kill two birds with one stone. He could set up a double date with Calhoun and Darla. It would be an excuse to ask out Samantha. With her big heart, she was sure to love the matchmaking idea.

He jumped up and ran downstairs. "Darla, can you quiet down?"

In a whimpering tone she cried, "Please, Sam, open up."

Morrison spoke through the door, "Not tonight, Darla. Can you meet me tomorrow night at ... the Feedstore Restaurant?"

"I work tomorrow."

He opened the door and stepped outside. She tried to throw her arms around him but he grabbed her wrists and held her back. "Sit down, Darla, we need to talk."

Reluctantly, she sat on the steps and leaned her shoulder into his side. Morrison took a deep breath, "You can't come over here like this, Darla. Please think of your reputation."

"I don't care about my reputation, I just ..."

Morrison held up his hands to stop her. "Well, I care about mine. I'm a deputy in this town. I need the people's respect and trust."

"That's what you think of me? You think I'm a slut?"

"No, I don't, not at all! But it looks bad, you know?"

Darla did not respond, so he tried to get back on track. "You know Deputy Jessie Calhoun, right?"

Darla pushed her hair back from her face. "Jessie? Yeah, I know Jessie."

"Jessie has been trying to get me to go on a double date. Maybe he and I could stop by the restaurant tomorrow and see if we can set something up."

"A double date?"

"Sure! It would be fun."

Thursday

*For that which is locked in our hearts is ours alone
and cannot be taken from us.*

Chapter 4

Restless Morning

Morrison had tossed and turned all night rehearsing his call to Samantha to arrange the double date with Jessie and Darla. Maybe he would say, "Sam, do you know Jessie Calhoun, my partner?" *Assuming she does,* he'd say, "I think Jessie may have a crush on Darla down at Maggie's restaurant, but he's too shy to ask her out. I thought maybe we could help him out and arrange to double date with them."

No. It sounds too much like I'm using her, or taking advantage of her.

And so it went and every time he came up with something, it wound up sounding ridiculous to him when he repeated it. The time dragged on throughout the night and he kept vowing to clear his mind and get to sleep, but then he would realize that another hour had passed and he was still wrestling with his quandary.

He did not know when his thoughts finally slipped into a dream until the alarm clock went off, waking him from a deep sleep. He dragged himself out of bed and got ready for work.

He sat down at his desk with a mug full of strong, black coffee and placed his feet on the desk. He really needed some sleep. Today would be rough. Jessie Calhoun was already on a computer inputting a report. Morrison had also rehearsed how he would approach Jessie about the double date idea. At this point, he wished he had not already proposed the idea to Darla. Now it seemed like a really bad idea.

"You look terrible." It was his boss, Chief Buster Crab. The large man was standing in the doorway of his office grinning. "You have a hot date last night?"

"No!" Morrison felt his face heat up. He was embarrassed by his overly defensive response. "Sorry, Buster, just couldn't sleep."

"Wanna talk about it?"

Buster Crab was a good man and a good friend. When Morrison's zealousness had gotten under the skin of his coworkers at the Denver Police Department and they had plotted to get him fired, Buster Crab had come to his defense.

Crab had once worked in the burglary division in Denver and they had gotten to know each other on burglary cases that overlapped with homicide. Several years back, Crab had retired and moved back to his old hometown of Rockcliffe and had run for sheriff against two very competent opponents. One was a young energetic policeman from Pueblo and the other was the Wet Mountain Valley undersheriff, the previous chief. When the younger candidate, Sean Bailey, won the election, the previous undersheriff had taken the defeat badly and resigned. To Buster's surprise, Bailey had asked him to take the position.

Then when Morrison was fired from homicide in Denver, Crab had recommended him to Sheriff Bailey. It had been a godsend when Bailey had called to offer him a deputy position.

Morrison considered Crab's offer to talk about why he was sleep deprived. Maybe it would be good to discuss his worries with his good friend. It would be nice to hear what a third party might advise. But he just was not ready to talk about it.

"No thanks, Buster. It's just some family stuff."

Chief Crab saluted him with his coffee cup. "My office is always open."

Jessie's sharp ears had picked up on the conversation. He swiveled around in his chair, crossed his arms and gave his colleague a knowing look. "Trouble with the family, eh?"

Calhoun puffed up. "Wanna talk about it, pardner?"

Morrison took a deep breath. Jessie meant well, but he was the last person on earth he wanted to share secrets with, although it provided him with a lead in. "What'd ya say we have lunch at Maggie's today?"

Calhoun beamed. "You really like that 'Full of Bull' hamburger I talked you into, don't ya?"

"Yeah, it's pretty good. You game?"

"Sure. I told you that Full of Bull hamburger was the best."

Morrison dropped his feet off his desk and scooted up to his computer. "You did. You truly did."

Chapter 5

When Ghosts Attack

FRANK DRUMMED HIS FINGERS on the table absent-mindedly as he stared at the crazy woman, Lizzie. His four best friends sat with him quietly finishing their meals. His drumming irritated his grumpy old friend, Ralph. "You ever gonna stop doing that?"

Frank was startled. "Doing what?"

Ralph drummed his fingers noisily to demonstrate. Frank apologized. "Sorry, Ralph, didn't realize I was doin' it."

Ralph glanced at Lizzie. "You got a crush on that old hag?"

Frank realized he had been staring at Lizzie. "Oh, no, just thinking about her obsession with ghosts."

Ralph looked back at the pale, chalky-faced woman dressed in a silky white gown. "Hell, she looks like a ghost."

Walter "Monty" Montgomery, a tall hefty man with a cheerful disposition, tried to be humorous. "Maybe she is one." Then he chuckled happily.

While Monty chuckled, Frank shook his head. "Albert, didn't you tell us that she lived here back when it was an insane asylum?"

Albert put down his fork, blotted his mouth with his napkin, and cleared his throat. "Oh, yes, she first lived here decades ago as a young teen when it was the Colorado Institution for the Insane. She was released from the institution when it was shut down in 1945. Now, ironically, Elizabeth has returned as an indigent resident."

Ralph shoveled corn in his mouth and commented, "I told you she's crazy."

The comment shocked the gentile senses of soft-hearted Monty. "Oh! Th-that's a mean thing to say, R-Ralph."

The fifth friend, the old Cherokee, White Feather, startled his friends with a rare comment of his own. "Tormented maybe, not crazy."

Albert agreed. "Yes, Elizabeth has had a very hard life. I interviewed her a few years after she left the institution for an article I was writing. She had married and was trying to live a normal life."

"What's she muttering?"

Lizzie's lips were moving and then stopped. Her face reflected resolution, as if she had talked herself into something.

The five old geezers watched Lizzie leave her table and slip across the room toward the exit. Unlike her usual confident glide, she seemed tentative, glancing back and forth as if worried she was being watched. They found it very curious when she turned right at the corridor instead of going left toward the elevators.

"Where's she goin'?" Ralph carped.

Monty whispered, "W-Well, I'll say."

Frank proclaimed, "Let's find out."

The five men scrambled after the mysterious woman. The chill of autumn lurked in pockets of dank air caught in the recesses of the ancient castle like structure. It was more proof that the old boiler-style heating system was inadequate for the drafty four-story brick building. The five nosy elderly residents shivered as they passed from the warm dining room into a pocket of the damp air in the wide corridor and stopped to watch, from a safe distance, the departure of the home's scariest resident.

White Feather looked on with stoic calm beside Frank. Albert was poised and dignified in stark contrast to his flustered friend, Monty. Stooped, wrinkled, and grumpy, Ralph glared from the front.

The eccentric friends fancied themselves the amateur detectives of St. Jude. They were amiably referred to as the "Five Sleuthkateers," a moniker awarded them by the head chef, LaWanda "Birdie" Boudreau. Their claim to fame came from solving the case of the mysterious poisoning of resident Benjamin Cook. Although each had played a role in the resolution, White Feather had actually been the one to put the pieces together.

It was not White Feather's first venture into crime solving. Before coming to St. Jude, he had helped a young teenager suspected of murdering his family—-the case of the Ludwig triple homicide. The boy had suffered a head injury during football practice and contracted temporary amnesia. While in his fugue, White Feather hid him in an abandoned train terminal while he secretly investigated the homicide. White Feather's assist left him in good stead with the Wet Mountain

Valley Sheriff's Office. It was because of their recommendation that he had been accepted into St. Jude.

As they stood in the drafty corridor, they were mesmerized by the crazy lady's wild white hair and long white gown that appeared to be dancing around her as if in a swirling breeze. She glided along the wide corridor as if floating on air, pushed by the drafts like a phantom sail.

Lizzie was headed for the door to a narrow hallway housing the emergency stairway and the exit to the south end of the building. Stepping into the hallway, suddenly a white cloud materialized around her and engulfed her like a ghostly shroud. Her arms flailed as she fought the churning apparition that appeared to be attacking her. As the five elderly gentlemen watched in horror, the door to the hallway slammed shut.

Frank gasped as Monty clutched his chest and staggered backward. Without hesitation, White Feather rushed to the hallway door inspiring his skittish friends to follow. The elderly Native American threw open the door and knelt to examine the silk clothing on the floor. Monty, a retired veterinarian, joined his friend and touched the pile of white silk and gasped. White Feather turned to his friends with concerned eyes and informed them, saying, "She's gone!"

Frank and Ralph were stunned but Albert found words for the occasion. "May she rest in peace. She warned us this could happen."

Monty clarified, "N-No, sh-she's disappeared. The d-dress is empty."

Chapter 6

Double Jeopardy

As the morning dragged on, Morrison busied himself with old reports, but his mind was on his double date scheme. He agonized over whether to call Samantha before or after lunch. He decided that it must be before. He slipped outside for privacy.

"Hi, Samantha."

"Hello, Sam."

"Sorry to bother you at work, but I need your help."

"That's okay. We're not busy right now."

"Do you know Deputy Jessie Calhoun?"

"Jessie? Yes, we've met."

"Oh, okay. Well, Jessie is a great guy and I was thinking that, well maybe we ought to double date some evening."

"With Jessie?"

"Yeah, you know, Jessie is so shy. He never goes out and I thought maybe we could, you know, help draw him out?"

"Who else?"

"Oh, well, I was thinking about that waitress over at Maggie's restaurant, Darla."

Samantha was slow to respond. "Darla? Oh."

Samantha got quiet. Morrison felt very awkward. "I don't know, what do you think? Want to help him out? I'm thinking Saturday evening, maybe at the Feedstore?"

Samantha did not respond. Morrison pressed on. "Shall we say six o'clock?"

He could hear Samantha take a deep breath. She was considering. He waited fully anticipating bad news, but after what seemed like a long time, she quietly responded, "Fine," and hung up.

Morrison tapped his cell phone and dropped it back in his pocket. His heart was pounding and he was out of breath. It's a date! He paused to let it sink in. For the first time in so many years, he and Samantha would be going out again. He gasped in the cool morning air. It was a done deal but he was concerned that Samantha had been so reluctant. Her lack of enthusiasm was disconcerting. He was on trial; the date had better go well.

He looked at his watch as he returned to his desk. It was already eleven-thirty. "Jessie, ready to go get some lunch at Maggie's?"

Calhoun swelled up. "Maggie's, eh? So you really like that Full of Bull hamburger I talked you into."

Calhoun was a chatterbox as they drove the few blocks to Maggie's. Morrison was lost in thought remembering his conversation with Samantha. She had accepted a date with him, but it hurt that she was so reluctant to agree. He had hoped that things were going better between them, but now he wondered if she had only been cordial because of the kids. Maybe she was not warming up to him the way he was hoping. But maybe the date would kindle old feelings.

As they pulled into the parking lot of Maggie's, Morrison decided to break the news to Calhoun. "Hey, I've been thinking. Maybe we should double date some time."

Calhoun's eyes bulged and Morrison could almost see beads of sweat pop out on his forehead. "Double date?"

"Yeah, sure, what do you think?"

Calhoun shrugged and shifted nervously. "Well, you know I ain't been dating anyone lately."

"That's okay. I think I can help you out."

Calhoun's eyes widened. "You got somebody in mind?"

"Sure. And it would really help me out as well. You've met my ex-wife, Samantha, right?"

"Oh! Samantha? You're ex-wife?"

"And I was thinking about the waitress here at Maggie's. You know, Darla."

Calhoun grinned. "Darla, eh?"

Morrison smiled. "She's kinda cute, don't you think?"

Calhoun smirked, "Oh, yeah, she's cute all right but kinda shy, though."

Morrison smiled. "I was thinking the Feedstore, Saturday."

Calhoun parked and turned off the ignition. "Sounds good to me, if you're sure you are okay with it."

As they stepped up to the door of the restaurant, the nervous deputy stopped and looked at Morrison with shear fear displayed on his face. "What do I have to do? You're gonna set everything up, right? I don't have to ask her out or anything?"

Morrison chuckled. Calhoun was even more bashful than he had thought. He put his hand on the nervous deputy's shoulder. "Okay, I'll ask her for you. Just leave everything to me."

Chapter 7

The Frantic Search

W HITE FEATHER'S EYES DIRECTED Albert to the small alcove at the end of the hallway where two exit doors opposing each other lead outside. Albert got the message and rushed out. Frank hurried to the stairway and scuttled up as fast as his eighty-seven-year-old legs would carry him in hopes of catching up to Lizzie if she had taken that route. Ralph plodded down the hall to join Albert outside while White Feather stood to examine the hallway leaving Monty whimpering by the dress.

"Lizzie!" Frank called out as he bounded up the stairs to the second level. There was no answer. There was no sign of Lizzie on the stairs or in the second floor corridor where a ditsy old woman stood motionless, clutching her fingers in front of her lips and staring at Frank with fearful eyes.

"Did you see Lizzie come up these stairs?"

The poor woman's eyes flared and she shook her head nervously.

"Thanks." He muttered to himself, "Where did she go?"

The old woman overheard and whispered, "I don't know."

She looked as though she might cry. "It's all right. Don't worry; we'll find her."

At the bottom of the stairs was TJ, a young assisted-living aide drawn by the commotion to the hallway, screaming her head off. Monty stood and tried to comfort her by explaining that it was only a dress on the floor.

Albert returned with Ralph in tow. They had searched in vain for any sign of a half-naked Elizabeth outside. Frank sat on the bottom stair panting from exhaustion. Naomi, the receptionist, burst in and took over comforting TJ while glaring at the very guilty appearing White Feather and Walter Montgomery. The corridor started filling with curious residents from the dining room.

White Feather calmly held up the empty dress. "She has disappeared."

Wet Mountain Valley Undersheriff, Buster Crab, pulled into the St. Jude Methodist Retirement Center's parking lot, not sure what to expect. Gabby, the dispatcher, had told Crab that all she knew was that the St. Jude administrator was very excited and wanted him to come out right away because someone was missing.

When he entered the reception room, his cousin and St. Jude receptionist, Naomi Jefferson, was waiting for him. She rushed up to hug him and then explained, "It's just dreadful, Buster. They found Elizabeth's dress she'd had on in the south entryway and she has disappeared."

Buster recognized the name of the home's most notorious resident. "Maybe she just decided to drop the dress and go in the buff."

Naomi slapped his chest in disgust. "Really, Buster, you shouldn't make jokes. Elizabeth may be in grave danger."

She led her cousin into the corridor where Mrs. Barkley was trying to get the crowd of residents to return to their rooms. Buster pushed in, stood beside her and raised his hands to quiet the noisy crowd. "Please, folks, please return to your rooms so we can investigate Mrs. Dawson's disappearance. Go on now."

Reluctantly, the curious residents began to disperse. Crab turned to Mrs. Barkley. "Tell me what happened."

Mrs. Barkley led the chief into the narrow hallway. Crab surveyed the cramped area of the south entry noting that the hallway ran beside the stairs and led to opposing exit doors. She pointed to a crumpled white dress on the floor. He noticed his old friend, White Feather, standing with his four friends who together had been nicknamed "The Five Sleuthkateers." Buster nodded. "Good Morning, White Feather, gentlemen."

The five sleuths spoke in unison, "Chief." Undersheriff was his official title, but almost no one called him undersheriff. He was commonly known as "Chief." Mrs. Barkley pointed at the dress. "White Feather and his friends saw Elizabeth enter this room. They said that ..."

She paused, raised her eyebrows and stared at the five old residents apologetically. "They saw a ghost attacking Elizabeth just before the door closed. When they rushed in to save her, they found only the dress and no sign of Elizabeth."

The chief glanced at Albert Stein. He remembered from the poisoning incident that Stein was a very good witness. Stein was an investigative reporter before retiring and had been impressively articulate when questioned. "Mr. Stein, what can you tell me about this?"

Stein seemed embarrassed as he stepped forward. "Well, Undersheriff Crab, I'm afraid that it is pretty much as Mrs. Barkley described. We were curious when we noticed that Elizabeth turned right leaving the dining room instead of turning left to go to the elevators. So, from the dining room exit, we watched her enter this hallway. Before the door slammed shut we saw what appeared to be ghost-like white smoke attacking her. When we got to her, all we found was the dress."

Albert glanced at the floor and then continued, "Ralph and I searched for her out back." He pointed toward the south exit. "Frank checked upstairs. But, she had just simply disappeared."

Chief Crab had been watching White Feather while Mr. Stein gave his account. White Feather's face had not betrayed any emotion as he listened with his eyes closed as he was apt to do. "What do you make of this, White Feather?"

White Feather slowly opened his eyes and shrugged.

Chief Crab chuckled. "Okay. Edith, besides this door," he pointed to the door to the corridor, "those doors," he pointed to the outside exits at the end of the hall, "and the stairs, is there any other way out of this hallway?"

The administrator paused to think and then glanced around the narrow hallway. "No, I don't think so."

Buster rapped his knuckles on the wall opposite the stairs, "What's behind this wall?"

Mrs. Barkley pictured the next room over. "That's the kitchenette for the staff lounge."

Crab glanced around. "Is there a closet or anything under the stairs?"

Mrs. Barkley shook her head. "Not that I know of."

Crab felt the wall that covered the area below the stairs. The top two-thirds was stucco; the bottom third was wainscoting.

"Why would she come to this nook? Where would she be going?"

Stein spoke as if thinking out loud. "Buried in its Penetralia."

Crab frowned. "Say what?"

Stein explained, "At our meeting regarding the new heating unit, Elizabeth recited a curious riddle, 'Penitence wrapped in sad regalia, buried in its penetralia.' I think she was referring to something in the basement."

"Is there a way to the basement from here?"

The engineer in Ralph prompted him to answer, "This vestibule does not have stairs to the basement. The stairs in the corridor next to the elevators go to the basement. And the little hallway on the other side of the building has a stairwell, also. It's possible there are stairs to the basement there. Maybe she thought this one did, too."

Crab found the anomaly interesting. He looked at the blank wall under the stairs again. If there had ever been stairs to the basement, it had been boarded up.

"Edith, have you checked her room?"

The administrator raised her eyebrows apologetically and shook her head.

"Then let's start there."

Chapter 8

Searching for Lizzie

Chief Buster Crab was not surprised when they found Elizabeth Dawson's room empty. He suspected there was something more going on. Mrs. Barkley seemed horrified by the clutter, smell, and disarray of the room, but he was not surprised by that either.

As he and Mrs. Barkley examined the room, they were joined by the Five Sleuthkateers. Other curious residents were starting to collect in the corridor all eagerly awaiting the results of their search. Crab was accommodating. "She ain't here."

Mrs. Barkley pushed her hair up with her fingers clearly overwhelmed. "What are we looking for?"

The chief began rifling through the clutter on a small white vanity-style desk. "Have you noticed Elizabeth acting strange lately?"

Everyone laughed. Crab realized the absurdity of his question. "I mean more so than usual?" He pulled open one of the drawers.

Mrs. Barkley smiled reassuringly. "Lizzie was very upset about the grant."

Crab closed the drawer and tilted his head to one side questioningly so Barkley explained, "We have received a grant that will enable us to replace our antiquated heating system. When Lizzie found out she was very upset."

Ralph dropped into a chair near the window and added, "She went ballistic."

White Feather quietly sidled up to Crab to look over the vanity. Crab stepped aside and frowned. "Why do you think that upset her?"

Mrs. Barkley shrugged. "Elizabeth seems very protective of the basement."

Crab still appeared to be confused.

Ralph explained, "Ghosts."

Albert offered his take on it. "Elizabeth was a patient when this building was one of the Colorado Institutions for the Insane. It may be that awful things happened while Lizzie was a patient. I think maybe there are ... secrets ... buried down there. Perhaps there are bad memories for her."

Crab was intrigued. "Secrets?"

Albert repeated Lizzie's curious riddle, "Penitence wrapped in sad regalia, buried in its penetralia."

Crab did not understand a word of Albert's statement. "Whazzat?"

Ralph Jacobs offered his perspective. "She's crazy as a loon."

Frank clarified, "That's what Lizzie said at the meeting yesterday. Remember, Mrs. Barkley?"

Mrs. Barkley drew a blank. Albert tried to explain, "I had heard the same riddle from the old institution's administrator when I interviewed him years ago. 'Penitence,' which is regret for sins. 'Penetralia' is the deepest recesses of a place, perhaps the basement of this old building."

Ralph persisted. "Like I said, she's crazy as a loon."

Albert glanced around at his friends and then looked to the chief. "I think there may be answers buried down there or perhaps tender memories."

Ralph chimed in again. "Tender? Lizzie? More like a tender box."

Crab was catching on. "Do you think Elizabeth is afraid something will be found when they replace the heating system?"

Barkley raised one eyebrow and nodded omnisciently but Albert had a different take on it. "Or, perhaps she just doesn't want things disturbed."

Crab opened up his hands. "Maybe we check out the basement?"

Before he could take a step, he noticed White Feather pointing a cell phone at a piece of paper. He was snapping a picture with his smart phone.

Crab and Stein glanced at each other thinking the same thing—*White Feather is always full of surprises.*

"What have you got, White Feather?"

The old Cherokee elder replaced the phone in his shirt pocket and replied, "Riddles."

Crab and Albert rushed over to the vanity which drew the attention of Frank and Monty. The letter was wrinkled and ragged from age and apparent frequent use. Albert finished reading the letter with the chief. "You know, Buster, when I interviewed the old institution administrator, he rambled on and on in riddles. I recognize many of those riddles in this letter."

Buster nodded and pulled out his cell phone to take a picture for himself.

There was murmuring in the hallway. Someone shouted, "Lizzie is back!"

The crowd in the corridor parted to reveal Elizabeth Dawson dressed in her gown.

"Damn!" Ralph exclaimed.

Frank muttered, "How's that possible?"

"What's everybody lookin' at!" Elizabeth scowled as she scampered into her room.

Chief Crab turned to Mrs. Barkley who declared, "Well, that's Lizzie for you."

Lizzie scowled at Ralph. "Get out of my chair!"

Ralph crossed his forefingers as if shielding himself from a vampire. Lizzie turned to Crab pointing at the door. "Everybody get out of my room!"

Crab held out his hands defensively. "Okay, Mrs. Dawson. We were just concerned about you. We're glad to see that you are all right."

She turned to Mrs. Barkley. "Out! I demand everyone out of my room."

Mrs. Barkley stepped toward Lizzie and put her hands on her shoulders. "Calm down, Elizabeth; please sit down." She gently led the hysterical woman to the bed.

Nurse Nujent barged in. "You found her?"

Nujent was small in stature, but most prominent in character. If Lizzie was scary in a freakish way, Nujent scared everyone with her belligerence and domineering behavior. She quickly checked Elizabeth's vitals and then stood studying the fuming woman while fiddling with her stethoscope. "She should be fine," Nujent concluded.

Mrs. Barkley sat down on the bed beside the angry old woman. "Elizabeth, can you drink some water?"

Elizabeth pushed away the glass in disgust. "I'm fine; leave me alone."

Crab put on his official face. "Lizzie, I need to ask you some questions."

Elizabeth ignored him, but Crab persisted. "Where have you been?"

"None of your business."

"We have been searching for you, and we're concerned. Please answer my question."

Elizabeth squirmed. "Went for a walk."

"Without your clothes?"

She looked up at Crab and sneered, "You gotta problem with that?"

"It's pretty cold out there."

"You can say that again."

Ruth, Mary, and Katie burst into the room and raced to the side of their best friend. Ruth asked, "Lizzie, are you all right?"

Barkley moved away to let the fussy women gather around Elizabeth.

Ruth was the most responsible of the four; the one that

tried to keep her friends grounded. Addressing Mrs. Barkley, she asked, "Where did you find her?"

"She just came back all dressed and everything. She seems fine."

Ruth nodded omnisciently. Chief Crab stepped up. "Hi, Ruth."

Ruth nodded and responded, "Deputy Crab."

Chief Crab did not bother to correct her. People were often confused by his title and position in the sheriff's office. "Ruth, do you have any idea where Elizabeth might have gone and why she would have disrobed?"

Ruth pursed her lips and replied with indifference, "Who knows."

Ruth turned away from Crab. "Are you feeling all right, Lizzie, dear?"

"I'm fine I said! I just want everyone to get outa here and leave me alone."

Katie and Mary tucked a blanket around her. Crab rubbed his face with his hand trying to decide whether there was anything more he could do.

Ralph yawned broadly. "What time is it?"

Monty checked his watch. "5:59."

Ralph plodded out noisily in his loose-fitting sandals flopping as he crossed the room heading for the door.

"Oh, d-dinner time, you c-coming, Frank?" Monty asked.

Frank nodded then looked at Albert who said, "You go ahead. I'll join you shortly."

Chief Crab checked his watch and inhaled deeply. "Well, I guess that about wraps it up for me. I don't see a good reason to go any further at this point. There is no evidence that a crime has been committed and Lizzie is safe."

Albert glanced back at Elizabeth. "I would have to agree with you."

Buster looked at Albert and White Feather. "I'll let you two join your friends for dinner."

Chapter 9

Possessed

Deputy Sam Morrison sat at one of the desks reserved for deputies to use in the sheriff's office open area. It was a slow day and although he had plenty of paperwork to do, he was procrastinating. In his mind, he was rehearsing the devious double date he had concocted to shift Darla's attention away from him to Jessie Calhoun.

The idea had seemed so perfect the night it came to him. *It would be like killing two birds with one stone.* It would give him an excuse to ask his ex-wife Samantha out on a date under the guise of helping out a shy friend. And it would throw Darla and Jessie together and, with any luck, shift Darla's attention away from him, especially when she saw him with Samantha and realized that he was still in love with his ex.

But now it felt like the most moronic idea he had ever had. Now he could see how awkward it would be to have his ex-wife, the woman he loved, sitting at the same table with a woman who was madly in love with him and bent on winning his affection.

Morrison rubbed his sweaty face with his palms and thought, *this is going to be a disaster! No wonder Samantha was so slow to agree to it.*

The phone on his desk rang startling him out of his nightmare. "Morrison," he answered.

It was Deedie Baker, lovingly nicknamed "Gabby," the young receptionist and dispatcher. "Sam, Mrs. Agatha Christopher, the author, is here. Can you ..."

Gabby paused and Morrison could hear a woman's voice in the background. Gabby needed to clarify. "Oh, actually Christopher is her pen name, Sam. Her real name is Agatha Phillips. Can you help her?"

"What's it about?"

He could hear a muffled conversation.

"She's very concerned about her son."

"Be right out, Gabby."

Morrison hung up the phone, collected his notes, stuck them in a drawer and crossed the large open area to the hallway in front of Gabby's desk. He nodded to her as he opened the door to the reception area. He smiled at the slightly hefty, well-dressed woman, who's disheveled, stringy graying hair was a contradiction to her demeanor that hinted of a refined upbringing. The wrinkled, sagging skin on her face did not hide the hint of beauty long faded.

"Mrs. Phillips?"

Mrs. Phillips crossed the room and placed her hand limply into his hand, while dabbing her nose with a tissue with the other. He shook her hand gently and then led her down the short hallway into the open area and offered her something to drink.

The office was empty and eerily quiet. Morrison pulled a chair away from the small conference table. Mrs. Phillips swiped the back of her skirt and sat on the edge of the worn chair. "Tea, please."

He crossed the room to the break room where he poured hot water into a Styrofoam cup, picked up a green box that dispensed four options of tea, and returned to the conference table. He handed her the cup and held the box out for her to choose a colorful packet. After she selected, he set down the box and got to the point. "What brings you to our office, Mrs. Phillips?"

She put the cup down as she glanced back and forth. Morrison explained, "Everyone's out today. It is very unusual for the office to be so empty."

He waited patiently for the flustered woman to rip open the packet of tea. She seemed to be searching for a way to begin. "It's my son."

She dropped the bag into the steaming water and glanced around the room. He asked, "Want sweetener?"

She flipped her palm up. "Blue stuff, if you have it."

He fished several packets of Equal out of a bowl sitting in the center of the conference table and handed them to her. She nodded her thank you and poured the sweet contents into her cup and he handed her a stir stick.

Her preoccupation with the tea was trying his patience. He prompted her, "Your son?"

Mrs. Phillips shook her head in disgust. "It's so complicated. I don't know where to begin."

Phillips stirred the steaming tea and stared into space. He pulled a chair away from the table, sat down, crossed his legs, clasped his hands in his lap and asked, "What are you concerned about?"

"Drugs."

"You suspect your son is doing drugs?"

"It must be that or alcohol."

"Why do you suspect that?"

"He has been acting weird."

"You've noticed a change in his behavior?"

"For some time now."

"When did you first notice a change?"

Mrs. Phillips' eyes rolled up in thought. "It started his last year in high school, I think."

"Anything happen then . . . maybe a family tragedy?"

She continued to stir her tea. "Actually, it all started after the death of his grandfather."

Morrison nodded his head. "He was upset with losing his grandfather? Were they close?"

"He didn't even know his grandfather."

Morrison was confused. Reading his confusion, she tried to clarify. "His grandfather was an evil, despicable man."

She blew on the steaming tea and attempted a sip. She winced and resumed stirring it. As she spoke, she began to shiver. "My ex-husband's father was an alcoholic; beat his wife; abused his kids. He loved to manipulate people. He thought he could charm people into doing whatever he wanted."

She glanced up for a reaction, and then resumed, "Too often it worked. He was a handsome and clever man."

She placed the dripping stir stick on the conference table and held the warm cup with both hands. "He would lie when the truth sounded better."

Morrison had seen the type many times in his line of work. The result was never good: broken families; tragic lives. But, he did not understand the relevance. "You say your son didn't know him?"

She sipped the tea. "Harold," she glanced at Morrison again, "my ex, hated his father and forbade him to contact us. Harold kept him away from our children and eventually the scumbag moved to Pueblo."

Morrison still did not get the connection. Phillips continued, "Several years ago, Harold called to tell me his father had passed."

She looked at Morrison. "Harold and I divorced years ago. The children stayed with me. Harold didn't want them and was struggling with problems of his own at that point."

Phillips glanced away. "It is awful to say, but Damien's passing was a great relief to me. Harold and I decided we would not tell the children since they had never really known him."

"So, your son didn't know that he passed away?"

Phillips began shivering again, then she closed her hands around the mug of tea and took a sip. "Almost immediately, I noticed a change in my son, Seth. He became moody and sarcastic. I started catching him in lies and I began to feel that he was trying to manipulate me, but I didn't put it together at the time."

"Put it together?"

She looked up. "The connection to Damien, I mean. That would come later. Anyway, Seth graduated high school and immediately moved out. He was always very intelligent and could make good grades when he tried. But Seth had a self-esteem issue. He ran around with the wrong crowd, thugs who were far beneath him. We would learn that his friends were doing drugs and alcohol. By then he was openly smoking. We would talk on the phone and he always claimed everything was going great. He bragged about how well he was doing at his job or whatever."

Phillips shook her head. "I could tell it was all exaggerations and lies, but I wanted to be supportive, so I let him lie to me."

She was unable to control her nerves and was trembling. She took a deep breath and tried to resume. "Anyway, that went on for a while. A girl moved in with him and I hoped she might bring him around, but she was a bigger druggie than he was. When they broke up, I was glad, but then he just hooked up with another ... and another."

Phillips' eyes widened. "Finally, we had a fight. It was horrible! He called me out of the blue and I got fed up with his lying and manipulating. He was clearly stoned and sounding crazy. I realized he was not going to listen to reason so I hung up. But he just kept calling and shouting at me and threatening me. I was ... I AM really scared. I don't know what he might do."

The traumatized woman shakily set down the mug and placed her hands over her nose and mouth as if praying. "It was like Damien all over again. It is as if Damien's ghost has taken over Seth's body and mind. He even looks more like Damien every day. He's gone from a sweet little boy with a round happy face to a long thin face with dark eyes, a low brow and thin smirking lips . . . just like Damien."

She picked up the tea again, trembled violently and spilled it on her dress. As she wiped off her dress, Morrison was thinking there was probably not much he could do for her. He asked, "Has he threatened your life?"

"No, not specifically, but if he IS Damien, I mean LIKE Damien, there's no telling what he might do under the influence."

Morrison, thinking out loud, said, "Probably not to the point for a restraining order."

She placed her hand beside her face. "Oh, no, John would never go for that. He thinks he can control him. He thinks he can protect me."

Morrison frowned and she explained, "John is my current husband . . . John Phillips. John didn't know Damien. He doesn't know what he is capable of."

Realizing that she was now calling her son Damien, Mrs. Phillips gasped and put her hand over her mouth. "Oh! I mean Seth."

Morrison tried to comfort her by offering, "I could go out and check on him--like a wellness visit. Where does he live?"

She seemed to be resigning to the truth. "Yes. It would be nice to know that he is all right. Unfortunately, I don't have an address. He moved to Oklahoma, I think, but I'm not sure."

"Have any idea where in Oklahoma? We could talk to authorities over there and I'm sure they would make a courtesy visit for us."

"He mentioned a job in Tulsa once."

Morrison made a note. "How about his friends, would they know where he is?"

Mrs. Phillips seemed distant. "Josh Hagen, Willie Madden."
She chuckled. "I doubt if they know where their own house is."

Morrison jotted down their names. She stood and blotted
her eyes with a crumpled tissue and then reached out to shake
his hand and attempted a smile. "You must think I'm crazy;
talking about ghosts inhabiting my son."

Morrison shook his head. "Oh, no ma'am, it's funny how
genetics works sometimes. I just wish there was more I could
do to help you."

"I'm sorry to have bothered you. Thank you for listening
to me."

He gave her his card and entered her phone number into
his cell. He reassured her that he would attempt to find
Seth and check on him. But secretly, he had a bad feeling
about it.

Chapter 10

Fogdog

ALBERT AND WHITE FEATHER entered the dining room. Albert waved to his colleagues and then headed to the carts to pick up a tray and a drink with White Feather following. When they arrived at the table, Albert could see that his friends, except for Ralph, had not started eating. Frank explained, "We waited for you. We're all curious to hear about your take on the letter."

Ralph scoffed. "What letter?"

"The letter that White Feather found on Lizzie's vanity table."

Ralph waved it off. "Oh, that crap."

White Feather put his tray on the table and pulled out his cell phone, pulled up the photo of the letter and handed it to Frank.

Monty was eager. "Read it aloud, Frank."

Frank read the strange letter aloud with some difficulty.

To my Love. Words cannot aptly express what
I feel in my heart, but still I offer this, my most

*sincere lamentation: For you, my last encomium,
to sing my amative requiem. Vast the distance
between our hearts, once interstitially apart. Lives
destroyed with deft celerity, ravaged by such harsh
severity. Left by cruel vicissitudes, to languish in
our lassitude. Excluded from a proud society, like
ghosts who've lost their ubiety. Love's inheritance
in rapturous gestation, fouled by a feckless
ablation, Penitence wrapped in sad regalia, buried
in its penetralia. Immure me in your heart,
so that we shall never be apart. Stephen*

Ralph summarized. "What a load of Hooey."

Frank turned to Albert. "What do you think it means?"

Albert paused to finish chewing. "Well, I think that it is a love poem that the administrator of the Wet Mountain Institution for the Insane, Stephen Weisman, wrote to Elizabeth. I think it speaks to the remorse he felt over the closing of the facility, the scandal it evoked, and the devastating impact it had on their relationship."

Frank reread the riddle to himself. "Hmm. I see what you mean, I think."

White Feather remarked, "Why send her a letter she could not understand?"

Albert considered his observation. "Hmm, an interesting point, White Feather."

Frank said, "Penitence wrapped in sad regalia, buried in its penetralia. That's the line Lizzie quoted at the meeting. It HAS to be referring to something down in the basement, doesn't it?"

Albert agreed. White Feather did not respond.

Frank thought about it. He was restless. "Whaddya say we go check out the basement tonight? May be our last chance before the crews come in and take it over."

Albert glanced up at White Feather. Without opening his eyes, White Feather nodded agreement.

Ralph pushed back his chair. "Let's go."

Albert reached out to his impulsive friend. "Wait a minute, Rudolph, we're talking about tonight, not right now."

Ralph frowned. "I heard you."

His friends gave him the look. "I'm not talking about that garbage, I meant enough of this crap, let's go play pool."

The details of the caper were hashed out in the recreation room. They would wait until eleven o'clock, an hour after lights out, just in case there was a bed check. No one brought up the fact that there had never been a bed check, but the old men were competing with each other to cover all contingencies.

Albert was nominated to be the alarm clock. He would go by Monty's room and then they would sneak up the stairs to collect White Feather, Frank, and Ralph. Together they would slip down the stairs to the basement to avoid the bell in the elevator.

It was going like clockwork until they discovered that Ralph was in bed with his pajamas on. They waited in Frank's room, which shared the bathroom with Ralph. It seemed like Ralph was taking too long so Frank started to go check on him, when he heard the contemptuous neighbor gargling in the bathroom. Frank doubled up his fists, hiked his shoulders but was stopped by 'Albert the peacemaker.' Albert whispered through the door, "We're not going on a date, Rudolph."

Ralph entered Frank's room momentarily, yawned, stretched and asked, "What are we waiting on?"

When they opened Frank's door onto the corridor, they were startled by a glowing white cloud. "What is that?" Frank whispered.

"A f-fogdog." Monty whispered back.

Ralph frowned at his rotund friend and repeated with disgust, "A fogdog? What's a fogdog?"

Albert shushed them and then whispered, "The light in the misty cloud that causes it to glow is sometimes called a fogdog."

Frank pointed. "That's a person, not a dog inside of it."

White Feather responded, "Dawson."

They squinted at the wispy, white cloud forming, building, changing around the wild-haired Lizzie Dawson. Lizzie was gesturing grandly as if fighting it off. "It's not my fault! I warned them!" she protested.

Frank questioned, "What's she wearing?"

Ralph responded, "Coveralls?"

Frank added, "She's talking to the fogdog? Does she think it's a ghost?"

Albert confirmed, "Apparently so."

Monty gasped. "I-Is it?"

Ralph growled, "There's no such thing as ghosts, Idiot."

Monty turned to the stoic Indian. "There are too, aren't there, White Feather?"

White Feather folded his arms across his chest and studied the fog like cloud massing around the ghostlike woman dressed uncharacteristically in a white jumpsuit. "Lost souls sometimes wander about while searching for their ancestors."

"Hogwash!" Ralph grumbled.

Monty reiterated, "L-Lizzie believes sh-she's t-talking to a ... l-lost soul."

Ralph was skeptical. "Looks like a steam cloud to me."

His comment drew the attention of his cohorts. Albert was curious. "That's interesting, Rudolph. You think it may be steam from the boilers in the basement? How did it get up here on the third floor? Are there vents over there?"

Ralph huffed. "Cracks in the structure. Shoulda' been condemned decades ago."

Albert pressed the retired engineer. "So is it possible we are seeing steam from the basement furnace?"

White Feather clarified, "Not from basement. Drafty hallway causing temperature inversion."

Ralph acknowledged begrudgingly. "That's possible."

Monty sighed with relief. "Whew. Th-That's good n-news."

White Feather posed the critical question, "She speaks to it as if she knows it?"

His friends grew quiet as they studied the old woman and the ghostly phenomena. As the crazed woman continued to battle the apparition, it slowly began to dissipate. Lizzie regained her composure and glanced around. Frank pushed the door to and they held their breaths.

Momentarily, White Feather squeezed in front and cracked the door open just in time to see the wispy woman enter the elevator. Ralph spoke for the group, "Where's she goin'?"

Monty observed, "It's after c-curfew. S-She should be in her r-room."

Ralph grumbled, "We should report her."

Albert placed his hand on the grumpy friend's shoulder. "If we report her, Mrs. Barkley will ask why we were out after curfew."

White Feather pushed his dangling white feather to the side of his face and ventured into the corridor toward the elevator. He opened the door to the stairway next to the elevator, pulled out his cell phone, clicked on the flashlight app and entered.

Ralph questioned, "What's wrong with the elevator?"

The friends followed White Feather. No one bothered to answer Ralph's question. They had discussed in the pool room that it would be safer to sneak down the stairs than to take the elevator and risk someone hearing the bell ding.

Frank and Albert ever prepared for a caper, produced flashlights. Ralph ever prepared with a snide remark, grumbled about the many steps to the basement from the third floor.

When they reached the ground floor and turned for the final descent into the basement, White Feather halted, putting up his hand. "What is it?" Frank asked.

"Door." White Feather tried to twist the door knob. "Locked."

Ralph summed it up, "Well, we ain't going to the basement tonight. Let's go to bed."

Frank could not give up. "Where did Lizzie go?"

The Sleuthkateers looked at each other questioningly. Ralph had a ready answer. "Who cares; let's go." He pushed his way into the corridor and headed for the elevator.

Frank tried the door knob, then put his shoulder to the door. Pain shot through his shoulder and arm. White Feather pulled him away from the door. "No good. Opens in."

Frank rubbed his shoulder. "Now you tell me."

Albert shook his head. "We have no way of knowing where Elizabeth got off the elevator or where she might have gone after that."

Ralph answered from in front of the elevator, "She got off on this floor."

The gang rushed to his side. Frank asked, "How do you know?"

Ralph pointed to the lights above the elevator doors. "The light is on one. That's the last place it stopped."

"So, she's down here?"

White Feather did not hesitate. He headed for the end of the corridor where Lizzie had vanished that morning. When he threw open the door, Frank commented, "No dress."

Albert reminded him, saying, "She was wearing a jump-suit."

Frank rushed past White Feather to the windows at the end of the hallway and tried to direct the light of his flashlight outside. The reflection on the dirty window pane temporarily blinded him.

"See anything, Franklin?"

"Yes, spots before my eyes."

The Sleuthkateers felt that the caper had come to a dead end until Ralph headed back down the corridor. "There's another stairwell on the north side."

The five sleuths hustled down the corridor to the vestibule at the north end of the corridor. With great expectations, they threw open the door and shined their lights down the hallway to find that it was a carbon copy of the vestibule on the south end. A stucco wall with wainscoting covered the lower third of the area under the stairs. Like the south vestibule, the stairs only led upstairs.

Forlorn they returned to the center of the corridor. The light for floor one was still lit. In unison they turned to look at the door blocking the entrance to the basement stairs.

"There must be some way to get that door open."

Ralph offered, "I have some C4."

Frank frowned and asked, "What's C4?"

Ralph explained, "Plastic explosives we used in the military."

Frank gasped, "Where'd you get that?"

"I was IN the military."

Albert tried to change the subject. "Perhaps we can find out where the keys are kept tomorrow."

Friday

Words cannot aptly express what I feel in my heart,
but still I offer this my most sincere lamentation.

Chapter 11

Preprandial

Frank walked beside his friend, Albert, on what he called his "preprandial." Albert had decided to start strolling around the pond behind the retirement center before breakfast every morning for exercise. Frank was attracted by his friend's enthusiastic and flowery description: cool, crisp air and vivid flora enhanced by morning dew.

But Frank found the morning air to be frigid. And he felt betrayed when Albert zipped up his jacket and stuck his hands in his pockets. Frank's breath crystallized into mist as he complained, "You didn't say anything about wearing a jacket!"

Albert chuckled. "Sorry, Franklin, I just assumed you would know."

Albert waved his hands referring to his surroundings. "It's autumn in the mountains. If you want to go up and grab a jacket, you can catch me on my second turn around the pond."

Frank shivered from the cold. "Yes, I guess I'd better."

Albert pointed to Frank's mouth and observed, "Fogdog."

Frank glanced about. "Where?"

"Your breath . . . the temperature inversion White Feather talked about.

Frank smiled, "Oh, of course."

Frank broke for the back door of St. Jude. "Catch up with you in a few minutes."

As Frank stepped off the elevator on the third floor, he spotted Lizzie at the end of the corridor gesturing with her hands as if in a conversation, but she was alone. He thought that maybe he could see the remnants of a steam cloud dissipating around her. As he approached, she stopped and then ran up to him with wild eyes and stuck her finger in his face. "Excluded from a proud society, like ghosts who've lost their ubiety."

She smiled with an eerie look, threw back her head to let out a demented laugh, then turned and scurried into her room. Frank was stunned and his skin felt tingly. He turned to find Ralph Jacobs standing in the narrow hallway feeding off the corridor between Frank's door and Lizzie's. He was sniggering in his childlike manner as he stomped past Frank and gave his analysis: "Stark-raving mad."

Frank let out his pent-up air. "I came up to get my jacket and then I'm going to join Albert on his ..." he held up his fingers to indicate quote marks "preprandial."

Ralph shook his head and grumbled, "Who talks like that?"

Ralph waved over his shoulder and continued down the corridor to the elevator. Frank checked his watch. The dining room would be open for breakfast soon.

When Frank stepped out the back door of the building again, he spotted Albert strutting around the far side of the pond. He decided to wait for him on the bench facing the three crooked trees, excited to share his encounter with Lizzie and get Albert's take on it.

As he sat down on the bench, he glanced over his shoulder half expecting White Feather to be approaching. He was not in the mood for another discussion about time travel.

Albert strode by the bench and Frank jumped up to join him. "Ran into Lizzie."

Albert was in the zone, gliding along, pumping his arms, eyes focused. He glanced over. "Oh?"

"She was having a rather heated conversation with herself."

Albert chuckled. "I hope you didn't interrupt her; that would be impolite."

"I'm afraid I did, but not intentionally. When she saw me she ran up and shook her finger at me and said the craziest thing."

Albert threw his hands out to the side as if to say, *Of course.*

Frank tried to remember the phrase. "I'm not sure but I think it was something about 'a ghost who has lost its you-bay-eh-tee?'"

"Yes, it means that it doesn't take up space; it doesn't exist in space."

Frank smiled. "Oh, so it IS a word. Then she said 'we're not allowed in their society.'"

Albert added, "Very poetic but not exactly in her vernacular is it? It's a line from the letter."

Frank smiled and added, "Then she laughed like a crazy woman."

Albert raised his eyebrows. "Yes, now THAT sounds like her."

They laughed as they crossed the bridge and followed the path to the far side of the pond. Frank persisted, "So, do you have the riddles figured out?"

Albert shook his head. "Not yet."

Frank suggested, "Maybe it is something the sleuthkateers could work on."

Frank looked around the table at his friends quietly eating their breakfasts. They were too quiet and it made him restless. He was in the mood for another caper. "How are we going to break into the administrative floor?"

His friends looked up and stared at him. Albert was the first to respond, "We don't know for sure where they keep the key, Franklin. It might be in the maintenance office."

Ralph suggested, "Maybe we could grab a couple of shovels while we're in there."

Monty gasped. "You th-think there m-might be bodies b-buried down there?"

Albert nodded. "I think there could be, Walter. But, it could be more complicated. Don't forget that the original boiler was replaced in 1963. If there were bodies buried down there that were not found during the original investigation, they probably would have found them then."

Ralph disagreed. "Naw. Wouldn't have done much digging. They would have just replaced the old one."

Albert questioned the retired construction engineer. "They did not remove the old boiler?"

Ralph shook his head as he stuffed mashed potatoes into his mouth. "They replaced it with a new one, but not the structure around it. Load-bearing walls."

Frank proposed, "Our mission today, gentlemen, is to find the keys."

Monty whispered urgently, "Th-there she is."

Elizabeth Dawson floated into the room in her usual silky white night gown. She appeared and acted no different from any other time, grabbing a tray and a drink and joining her friends at their usual table.

Frank had another idea. "How about a white board?"

Ralph glanced at the food trays and squinted. "White board? They doin' specials now?"

Even White Feather chuckled. Albert appeared to be interested. "A white board?"

Frank nodded. "You know, we could write the riddles on it and solve them one-by-one."

"E-Excellent!" Monty exclaimed, clapping his hands happily under his chin.

Ralph was unimpressed. "We could use the one in the

pool room. Then we could get something productive done while you guys waste your time on that malarkey."

White Feather countered with, "The hobby shop . . . more private."

Albert liked the idea. "Yes. No one ever uses that room."

Chapter 12

Solving Riddles

W HILE RALPH WAITED IN the pool room for his friends, Frank wrote the first riddle—the first line of the letter—on the white board in the hobby shop, next door to the pool room.

Albert dictated it to him, "For you, my last encomium, to sing my amative requiem."

Frank backed away to study the line and then remarked, "Three words ..."

Albert caught the implication. "Write above encomium, 'eulogy.'"

As Frank wrote the word, Monty was flipping the pages of his dictionary. He found the word and added, "Glowing and warmly enthusiastic praise." He looked up smiling proudly.

Albert suggested to Frank, "Put 'Praise' in parentheses."

Frank added the word "praise" in parentheses above "eulogy" and pointed to "amative."

While Monty was turning pages, Albert gave his definition. "Amorous."

Monty found the word. "D-disposed to love, a-amorous."

Frank wrote "love" in parentheses with "amorous" under it.

Albert waited for Monty to look up requiem. The large, lovable old gentleman declared, "A mass for the dead. A solemn chant for the repose of the dead. A musical composition in honor of the dead."

Frank turned to Albert hoping for a shortened version. Albert looked at the line again, read it and then suggested, "Maybe write 'chant of death.' I am not sure whether Weisman's requiem is for those who have been destroyed by the closing of the institution or for himself as he faces the end of his life. At any rate, I think he is describing the letter itself."

Frank nodded and then rewrote the line:

"For you, my last praise, I sing my loving song of death."

Albert translated, "His last words on the subject just for her."

Albert turned to White Feather who took a deep breath and offered his impression. "He is saying goodbye."

Albert's eyes brightened. "Yes, of course, he is stating the purpose of the letter."

Albert, Frank and Monty agreed enthusiastically. "Okay, next line."

Frank wrote the next line on the huge board as Albert dictated, "Vast the distance between our hearts, once interstitially apart."

Frank underlined "interstitially." Monty started flipping the pages of his dictionary while Albert offered a quick interpretation, "In between, or connected."

Monty added, "Relating to or s-situated in the in-interstices."

The jovial old man then provided the definition for interstice, "A space that intervenes between things; interval."

As Frank wrote in the definitions, Ralph came stomping into the room dragging his pool cue. Frank smiled to himself. The most apt visual of Ralph's walk was of a tall and skinny chimpanzee dragging a tree branch. Ralph found a comfortable chair to sit in and leaned his pool cue against his shoulder. "What's that crap?"

No one offered an explanation. Frank stepped back, studied the board and then announced his confusion, "Vast the distance between our hearts, once separated by an interval?"

White Feather put his spin on it. "Vast now, close once."

Albert and Monty agreed. Frank nodded and looked at the line again. "Oh, I see." Frank wrote White Feather's translation below the line.

Ralph blew out his disgust. "You geniuses through with Monty? He owes me a game."

Monty frowned at the grumpy old man and contested, "O-OWE you a game?"

Albert, ignoring the side conversation, added, "I think he's referring to the fact that he and Elizabeth were once very close, but now, or at the time of the letter, they were separated by a vast distance."

Ralph jumped up and declared, "Okay, that's settled. Let's play pool."

Monty countered with, "Th-That's only the s-second line."

Albert added, "There are seven lines, Rudolph."

Ralph dropped down into the chair expressing his disgust. "Crap."

Albert dictated the next line, "Lives destroyed with deft celerity, ravaged by such harsh severity."

Frank looked over at Albert sitting on the edge of his chair and raised an eyebrow. "See-lair-ee-tee?"

Albert crossed his legs and clasped his hands over his knees. "Celerity is swiftness. I would read that line to mean that lives, most likely the staff at the institution or maybe the administrator and his close associates, were abruptly and utterly destroyed by an event."

"An event?"

"I expect the closing of the institution that was in this building, or the investigation or, perhaps, the scandal."

Monty surprised them with his own translation. "Their l-lives were q-quickly and s-savagely destroyed."

Ralph added, "Well, I'd say that about sums it up."

Albert shook his head and dictated the next line, "Left by cruel vicissitudes, to languish in our lassitude."

Frank looked to Monty as he pointed to the word "Vicissitude."

Monty found it in his dictionary. "Vicissitude is a change of course."

Albert added, "And lassitude is weariness or strain. So, maybe the event was a cruel change for them and they were left devastated by it." Albert shrugged. "That's how I read it."

"Makes sense." Then Frank laughed. "I guess."

Ralph commented, "He's just repeating himself."

Frank, Albert, and Monty looked at Ralph with surprise. White Feather even opened his eyes to look.

Albert read the next line aloud. "Excluded from a proud society, like ghosts who've lost their ubiety."

Frank commented, "That's the line Lizzie quoted this morning."

Albert raked his hair back with his fingers. "This line is interesting. Ubiety means that something has a definite existence or evident existence. I read 'proud society' to be referring to the camaraderie that existed at the institution before it was exposed. It could also be referring to the wider society of the time, the eugenics movement maybe. It seems to be saying that they were shamed into nonexistence."

Frank shook his head. "Wow, deep stuff."

Ralph asked, "What's the you-genie movement?"

Albert chuckled. "Eugenics goes way back to the late 1800s. The proponents of eugenics believed that through selective breeding, the human species could manage its own evolution. The movement lasted right up through World War II, but I think that when the Nazis took it to the extreme by attempting to annihilate people that they deemed inferior, the idea became repugnant to most people."

Monty asked, "Wh-What did they mean by 'selective breeding?'"

"Well, for the 'feeble-minded' it meant birth control, but for the insane, it meant sterilization. One of the most influential proponents of eugenics was Colorado's own Dr. Richard Corwin. He was the director of the Colorado Coal and Iron Company's industrial health clinic in Pueblo for many years. Corwin lobbied for the induction of compulsory sterilization laws for the insane in the Colorado state government. But sterilization was never the law in Colorado, therefore the Colorado Institutions for the Insane were careful to not record any sterilizations . . . if they were doing them."

Frank asked, "Were they doing them?"

"Probably."

Frank wrote his translation below the line: "Banished from society like we do not exist."

Albert continued, "Okay, the next line is, 'Love's inheritance in rapturous gestation, fouled by a feckless ablation.'"

As Frank finished writing the line, Ralph began a gentle snore. Albert closed his eyes for a moment. "This line seems to be a departure from the previous lines in that it appears to be addressing a budding love affair that has also been destroyed by the event."

Frank was confused. "A budding love affair?"

Albert took a deep breath. "I have always had a theory that Dr. Stephen Weisman and Lizzie had an affair, but neither would confirm it when I interviewed them. I think this line suggests that their budding love affair was interrupted by the closing of the institution."

Monty was referencing the dictionary translation, "Our developing love affair abruptly removed." Frank wrote his translation below the line.

Albert continued, "Since Elizabeth has recited some of the lines verbatim, I suspect she has read the letter so many times she has memorized it. But, as White Feather has pointed out, I don't get the feeling that Elizabeth understands the words."

Frank nodded slowly, thoughtfully. Albert said, "here's the line that Lizzie recited at the meeting: 'Penitence wrapped in sad regalia, buried in its penetralia.'"

Frank offered his own interpretation. "Regrets wrapped in sadness, buried in the basement."

Albert smiled. "Yes, I agree that the line suggests that something might literally be buried in the basement. But it could also just be referring to the bowels of the building."

Monty looked at Albert and sighed, "Oh, dear."

Frank then asked, "Do we think that their affair sadly ended and is buried deep in the bowels of the building?"

"I seem to remember that both Elizabeth and Dr. Weisman worked at the Corwin Clinic before Weisman transferred to the institution," Albert stated.

White Feather opened his eyes and addressed Albert with folded arms, "Old clinic is museum now."

Albert's face lit up. "Records. They might have records we could look at."

"Clinic?" Frank questioned, "You mean Nujent's place?"

Albert clarified, "The original building built for the CF&I Medical Clinic is now the Steelworks Museum in Pueblo. Anyone up for a field trip?"

Ralph choked and smacked his lips as he struggled to wake up. "What?"

Albert repeated, "We're going on a field trip to Pueblo."

Ralph beamed. "Perfect! I know a great pool hall near downtown."

Albert shook his head and then asked White Feather, "Do you have some connections? Can you arrange for transportation?"

White Feather nodded and then drew a key out of his pocket, held it up and smiled ruefully. "Tonight?"

Frank declared, "Is that ...?"

Albert questioned, "Where did you get that key, White Feather?"

"Nujent's desk, second drawer on left."

Chapter 13

Steelworks Museum

THE TEN-PASSENGER WET Mountain Valley Rotary Van pulled into the parking lot of the Steelworks Museum, maneuvered around the scattered parked cars and stopped in front of the steps to the front door. White Feather handed the driver an envelope as the Five Sleuthkateers filed out. The driver handed him a card and said, "Call me when you're ready to leave."

Frank was in high spirits. This was his first excursion away from St. Jude since he had been rescued from his homeless plight and he was fascinated by the mechanics of it all. St. Jude could not afford a van to shuttle residents to doctor appointments or events. But the local Wet Mountain Valley Rotary Club provided van service for anyone in the valley. All that was required of the participants was a donation if they could afford it.

They had first taken the van into Rockcliffe with the library group. After dropping off five old ladies at the library downtown, the van had made the hour and fifteen minute drive to Pueblo. The mobility of it gave Frank a renewed feeling of freedom he had not felt since he had owned a car many years ago in better times.

"How did you know about the Rotary van service, White Feather?"

The solemn old Indian replied, "Use it all the time."

"What do they charge?"

"Accept donations."

Ralph was in his usual pessimistic mood. "They oughta take some of those donations and get a new bus."

Albert scolded him. "Looking in the mouth of a gift horse, Rudolph?"

The five old men struggled with the steep steps up to the front door of the museum and then seemed disoriented and disorganized once inside. They found themselves standing in a wide hallway. At the end of the hallway, arched openings branched left and right.

Monty was immediately drawn to the pictures lining the side walls. Frank stopped to take it all in. White Feather and Albert paused for only a moment and then walked purposefully to the arched opening on the right where a sign above the door labeled it Gift Shop/Offices.

Finally, Ralph burst in and marched down the hallway and turned left as if on a mission. Someone from the gift shop hailed him, "Sir!"

Albert took responsibility for him. "Over here Rudolph. We need to sign-in first."

Much to everyone's surprise, White Feather produced a Visa credit card and the lady behind the counter asked, "For all five?"

White Feather nodded. Frank noticed that the tall, heavy-set, no-nonsense woman could not help focusing on the spray of hair dancing above White Feather's head pulled through the hollow bone ornament and the single white feather dangling down the side of his face. Next, her eyes moved to his gaudy necklace with a band of marble-sized beads alternating with bear claws terminating into a cross-hatched pouch housing a multifaceted crystal. A white stone and a black stone hung below the pouch.

Then her eyes took in the multicolored wool poncho draped over his shoulders. Frank smiled. White Feather was, indeed, a sight to behold. The eccentric Native American waited patiently for her inspection to end and for her to return to the business of ringing up their ticket purchases.

A short and pudgy lady with a pretty round face appeared from an office behind the display counter and cash register. "Good morning, gentlemen. Come to see our little museum, I see."

Albert stepped up and glanced at her name tag. "Good morning, Mrs. Victor. We are anxious to tour your very nice facility. We've heard so many good things."

The woman's eyes twinkled behind her blushing red cheeks as she unconsciously touched her name tag. Albert continued charming the friendly woman. "I see you are a docent. Perhaps you can help us with a mystery."

Mrs. Victor raised her eyebrows and pursed her lips as she turned her head slightly to the right. "Oh, a mystery?"

Frank and Monty huddled behind White Feather and Albert. Ralph disappeared into the museum. Albert continued,

"We are hoping you can tell us something about the people who worked in the clinic in 1944."

Mrs. Victor played with her pearl necklace as she rolled her eyes in thought. "Well, I'm sure we have the roster in the archives."

The no-nonsense woman at the register interrupted with, "Sign the top copy, the second copy is yours."

White Feather took a lesson from Albert and read the lady's name tag. "Thank you, Mrs. Jones."

The crack of a smile broke across her lips as her eyes danced over White Feather once again, perhaps with a new attitude.

"Joyce," Mrs. Jones muttered as she connected with White Feather's dark brown eyes.

Mrs. Victor picked up on her suggestion immediately. "Oh, yes! Joyce worked here back then. She is our historian and I'm sure she could tell you a lot about the staff."

Both women appeared to be quite proud of their recommendation. Mrs. Victor glanced at the old grandfather clock on the wall. "She should be coming in any time now."

She smiled brightly at Albert. "Did someone in your family work here, perhaps?"

Albert tactfully answered, "We think a dear friend of ours may have."

Monty and Frank looked at each other curiously. A slight wrinkle appeared between Mrs. Victor's eyebrows. "Oh, I see."

Albert tried to reassure her. "I am, or at least I was, an investigative reporter for *The Denver Post*. My friends and I think it might be interesting to write a book about the residents at St. Jude Methodist Retirement Center. We all have such interesting backgrounds."

Albert's friends tried not to reveal their surprise. Mrs. Victor's eyes sparkled again. "Oh! That WOULD be interesting."

Then the wrinkles returned. "Where is St. Jude Methodist Retirement Center?"

Albert smiled kindly. "West of here in the Wet Mountain Valley near Rockcliffe."

As if on cue, the little bell on the front door jangled and they could hear the door handle being jiggled and the heavy old wooden door creaking. Frank sensed that someone was having difficulty getting in so he rushed to the door and forced it open. A tiny woman bundled in layers of sweaters under a heavy coat was struggling to hang on to her huge tote bag, umbrella, lunch pale, and purse. When Frank pulled open the door, he pulled the poor woman in with it and she almost lost her balance in addition to dumping all of her load on the floor.

"Heavens!" she declared as Frank grabbed her arm to steady her. The woman gave Frank a serious once over, then whispered "thank you" through tight lips. Frank released her arm quickly and stepped back. Her look had given him the impression she might have been offended by his touch.

"I'm sorry, I was just ..."

She ignored his feeble apology as she tried to straighten her sweaters and coat. Frank stooped to gather up her things splayed across the floor. When he stood to hand them to her, she was standing regally with her hands clasped in front of her waist patiently waiting for him. She appeared to him at that moment like the Queen Mom accustomed to and expecting someone to attend to her things. As he handed her the purse and umbrella, she curtly gave an unenthusiastic acknowledgment. Frank asked, "May I carry your heavy tote and pail?"

Without responding, the queenly acting woman headed for the gift shop with her attendant in tow.

"Joyce!" Mrs. Victor exclaimed as they entered the room. "These gentlemen are doing research for a book and want to know about the staff that worked in the clinic in … 1944 was it?"

Albert nodded and turned to greet the petite woman named Joyce. "Good morning, my name is Albert Stein." He reached out his hand for a handshake; Joyce extended her limp hand palm down. Albert loosely gripped her fingers between his thumb and fingers then turned to introduce his three friends. Joyce never smiled and hardly acknowledged Albert's friends, even White Feather drew only a quick once over.

After introductions, Joyce took a deep breath and suggested, "I suppose we could show you the roster for that year. We have all of the CF&I records in our archives."

Mrs. Victor blurted out, "Joyce is the archivist for the museum."

Albert glanced at her name tag which read: M Joyce O'Quin Rommel, Archivist. He then gave Mrs. Victor a warm smile. The friendly lady blushed again and then offered, "Perhaps I could show you around while Joyce finds the roster?"

"That would be grand."

Chapter 14

Joyce Remembers

As Mrs. Victor led Albert, White Feather, Monty, and Frank across the hall and through the arched entryway into another hallway passing through the center of the museum, they met Ralph returning down the hallway toward them. Monty chuckled and asked, "You th-through already?"

Ralph tossed a passing comment as he walked by. "Seen it; let's go."

Albert replied curtly, "You'll have to wait for us, Rudolph. We're just starting."

He then introduced their tour guide. "Mrs. Victor, this is Rudolph Jacobs."

Rudolph stopped and did a double-take when he saw the attractive Mrs. Victor. He turned and smiled sweetly. "Ralph, Mrs. Victor, just call me Ralph."

He walked back to extend his hand and Mrs. Victor giggled as she reached out her hand. "Nice to meet you, Ralph. It didn't take you long to go through. Would you like to join us? Maybe I can answer any questions you may have."

Ralph pushed aside his friends and offered Mrs. Victor his arm. "How delightful."

Mrs. Victor giggled again as she took his arm and led them into the first room. "This was Dr. Corwin's examining room."

Albert glanced around the room and then asked, "Perhaps you could tell us more about Dr. Corwin."

"He was an amazing man who was way beyond his time. He came here in 1881, at age twenty-nine, to become the chief surgeon for Colorado Coal and Iron Company. In the next forty-eight years, he changed the way people practiced industrial medicine. He believed that industrial medicine wasn't just taking care of workers and those injured on the job but was also inextricably linked to the health and well-being of their families and their communities."

Victor's eyes widened as she continued her story as if revealing a secret, "Dr. Corwin was a genius and a character in the truest sense of the word. He wasn't afraid to say what he thought. For instance, he was supposedly a leader in the eugenics movement."

Ralph asked, "Eugenics movement? That some kind of exercise program?"

Mrs. Victor giggled at the innocence of the man. "Not exactly."

Albert chuckled and Monty produced a fake laugh. White Feather just huffed a little, "Humph."

It seemed that only Ralph had forgotten Albert's recent description of the movement. The happy little lady walked over to a plaque on the wall and pointed. "This tells all about it."

Albert walked over to study the plaque and commented, "Must have been quite popular among the elites back in the days leading up to the war and a while afterward."

Mrs. Victor raised her eyebrows. "There is a new theory that Dr. Corwin may not have gotten involved until later in his career."

This caught Albert's attention. "What changed his mind?"

"According to the new theory, the failure of CF&I's social welfare program to influence workers may have led him to embrace principles of eugenics. He became very frustrated when the workers did not seem to appreciate the benefits they were receiving under his programs. They were getting things that other companies dared not offer. And yet, they formed unions that organized strikes that crippled the company."

She shrugged. "He was disappointed that despite the progressive programs he developed for them, they seemed unable or unwilling to want to help themselves and blindly joined the unions. He evidently came to the conclusion that they were too feeble-minded to understand how good they had it."

Frank found the discussion interesting, but was bothered by the timeline. "So, when did Corwin die?"

Mrs. Victor's eyes rolled up as she tried to remember. "I believe it was 1929."

Albert questioned, "Did his eugenics ideas linger at the clinic after his death?"

Mrs. Victor opened her mouth to answer but was interrupted by Joyce Rommel charging in with a binder containing the rosters. As she flipped through the pages, she asked, "You said 1944?"

Albert confirmed, "Yes, we believe that is when Elizabeth was employed here."

Mrs. Rommel looked up with questioning eyes. "Elizabeth?"

Albert continued, "Her name would have been Elizabeth Austin then."

The tiny woman with enormous presence pursed her lips and scanned the roster. When she stopped, she chose her words carefully, deliberately. "Elizabeth Austin. Oh, yes, I remember Lizzie."

Joyce Rommel handed the binder to White Feather standing next to her and wiped her hand across her skirt as if pressing out wrinkles. White Feather noted her name tag, M Joyce O'Quin Rommel, and then scanned the notebook. Joyce looked up to continue, "The girls resented Lizzie. Lizzie was so pretty but rough and unrefined. As I remember, she grew up in one of the coal mining camps. The families there lived in tents and conditions were crude."

Joyce raised an eyebrow. "The miners were also very crude, dirty, and raucous. It was a terrible place for a little girl."

The refined lady took a deep breath and put on a pitiful face. "Her clothes were old and ragged. Thank goodness the clinic provided uniforms ... and a shower."

Joyce snickered. "Her language reflected the language of the miners."

She threw out her arms. "So, there was that. But those were things that made some pity Elizabeth. The reason some girls resented her was her relationship with the doctors. They appeared to dote over her and some even suspected that young Dr. Weisman fancied her ... as a girlfriend."

Albert picked up on something. "But, you did not resent Elizabeth?"

Joyce smirked and sat down in the desk chair. "I knew the truth."

"The truth?"

"He didn't care anything about that little tramp."

Almost immediately, Joyce appeared regretful and put her hand over her mouth.

Albert prompted her, "What was the truth."

She shifted in the chair and her eyes darted about. "Where to begin ..."

She began as if sharing a secret. "You see, I overheard a conversation between the doctors."

She rolled her head slightly. "I've never shared this with anyone."

Her eyes looked off into the distance. "They were in the doctors' lounge and I was digging in a file cabinet for something and could hear them. They were having an argument over eugenics. Dr. Howard, the administrator of the hospital at that time, was a big proponent of eugenics, and many of the older doctors still thought it had merit. But Stephen, Dr. Weisman, found it distasteful. In fact, Dr. Weisman argued that it was baseless. He argued that people were all born with essentially the same mental potential but developed differently because of their environment."

She smiled at the thought before continuing, "Anyway, they argued back and forth with each offering examples to prove his argument."

She looked at Albert. "Elizabeth was Dr. Howard's example of 'feeble-minded.'"

She waved her hand and then continued, "Finally, Dr. Weisman bet him that he could take Elizabeth and, by working with her, he could demonstrate that she was as smart as anyone and that given the chance, she could be as refined and sophisticated as a wealthy debutante."

Joyce Rommel smiled and nodded with a raised eyebrow as if to say, "What do you think of that?"

Ralph broke the spell. "Well, that clearly didn't work."

His friends laughed at him turning to note that he had made himself comfortable in the examining chair. Albert apologized for him. "Rudolph is referring to the fact that Elizabeth is rather ..."

Mrs. Rommel finished his sentence for him, "Crazy?"

Everyone cracked up again. Mrs. Rommel quickly regained her composure and shook her head. "You are quite right, Rudolph, the experiment went terribly wrong."

Rommel's eyes closed momentarily as she continued, "For the next several months, everyone noticed the attention that Lizzie was getting from Dr. Weisman: the hours in his office behind closed doors; the special assignments working directly with him.

"Most everyone else started to believe that Weisman was attracted to her and that maybe they were carrying on an affair."

Mrs. Rommel crossed her legs and arched her back, "Of course, I knew what was really going on and was anxious to see if Dr. Weisman could pull it off."

She tilted her head and smiled. "And at first, I did see remarkable results. Lizzie's vernacular improved; she began to carry herself with more pride and confidence; she stopped cussing ..."

She sat back and shook her head. "The girls all supposed that she was putting on airs and flirting with Dr. Weisman. They began to shun her. But then, she began to change. She started to get quiet and moody. Her eyes were blank or distant, sort of dreamy. Most thought that she was just love-sick, but I was concerned. It was more than love-sickness."

Joyce's wet eyes began to glisten. "So I did some snooping around and befriended Lizzie so I could talk to her. All I learned at that point was that Stephen, uh, Dr. Weisman might be giving her some sort of medication and that Lizzie was afraid of its effects.

"She kept getting worse and worse until everyone was worried about her. Rumors were spreading that Dr. Weisman was giving her drugs."

With a low sad voice, she continued, "I worked closely with Dr. Weisman as an assistant. I noticed a letter on top of a stack of papers in his office. It attracted my attention because I recognized his handwriting and a reference to Elizabeth Austin. It was addressed to Dr. Albert Hoffman. I will never forget his name because I went to the library to research him and found some of his articles."

Rommel looked at her audience to see if they recognized the name. Albert muttered, "LSD?"

Rommel nodded and then whispered, "Yes. He's the scientist that discovered LSD. Dr. Weisman was reporting to the doctor very detailed analysis of sessions with Elizabeth after administering the drug. I don't remember the medical term they used, but I would learn that it was LSD. I wasn't able to finish reading the letter before Stephen came in, but the jest of it was that he and Hoffman were trying to determine the proper dosage for Elizabeth. Dr. Weisman detailed the effects after each dosage and expressed concern that a higher dosage had had a very adverse effect on Lizzie. He was concerned that the drug was reducing her cognitive abilities instead of enhancing them as, I suppose, they were expecting."

Ralph summed it up. "They blew her mind."

Mrs. Rommel raised her eyebrows and sadly agreed. "Yes, exactly. One day Lizzie climbed onto the roof of this building and declared that she could fly. Fortunately, we were able to at least break her fall. She was taken to the Institution for Mental Health out on 13th Street. She never returned to the clinic."

Albert was not satisfied. "Do you know anything about her stay in the institution?"

Mrs. Rommel appeared hesitant. "On 13th Street? No."

Albert asked, "Is that when Dr. Weisman left to take on the administrator job at the Wet Mountain Institution?"

Rommel appeared uncomfortable. "Yes. It was not long afterward. I think he saw it as an opportunity that opened up for him."

Albert nodded and looked down. A nasally, snorting sound interrupted the long silence following her poignant story. Ralph was snoring.

During Mrs. Rommel's compelling story, the roster had been passed around winding up with Frank. Frank nudged Albert and pointed to the name "Alvira Nujent." Albert's face lit up. "Mrs. Rommel, did you know Alvira Nujent?"

She frowned. After a moment of intense thought, her expression eased. "Oh, Ally. Yes, I remember her, but didn't know her well. She reported directly to Dr. Weisman. She was younger, I think, very shy and quiet. She appeared to be quite capable, but she left after only a short time."

Rommel's brow creased. "How do you know Elizabeth and Alvira?"

Albert explained, "Elizabeth is a resident at St. Jude Retirement center." He waved his hand around. "We all are. And Mrs. Nujent is the resident nurse."

She looked at them suspiciously. "What is St. Jude?"

Albert explained, "St. Jude Methodist Retirement Center for the Indigent. The building once housed the Wet Mountain Branch of the Colorado Institutions for the Insane."

Joyce Rommel gasped and placed her hand over her heart, unable to hide her concern. "THAT building? I thought it was abandoned after the hospital closed."

"Yes, it was. But the Methodist Church purchased it and refurbished it."

Rommel glared at Albert and appeared to be unsettled. "What are Lizzie and Ally doing there?"

"Well, as I said, Elizabeth is a resident and Mrs. Nujent ..."

Rommel waved her hand and interrupted him. "Yes, yes, so you said."

Frank found her change in mood very interesting. "You seem surprised."

Rommel did appear stunned as she took the roster from Frank and left the room abruptly.

Mrs. Victor clapped her hands and offered, "Well! Shall we continue the tour?"

As the others followed Mrs. Victor down the hallway, Frank noticed that White Feather stealthily followed Joyce back to the offices. He paused at the gift shop counter. Frank saw a light come on in the back office where Joyce had disappeared. White Feather was standing very still. Frank recognized his listening posture. The bell on the front door of the museum jingled. White Feather dashed across the hallway keeping an eye on the door, which opened slowly allowing him to get across undetected. He glanced back to make sure Joyce Rommel had not spotted him.

Frank whispered, "What's wrong with her?"

White Feather commented in passing, "Shocking news. Now making urgent phone calls."

Chapter 15

The Doppleganger

As THE ROTARY VAN pulled out of the parking lot of the museum, everyone was quiet, each Sleuthkateer processing the information learned at the museum with the exception of Ralph who had already slipped into a nap.

Frank was anxious to get Albert's opinion on his discovery that Mrs. Nujent and Lizzie were at the clinic at the same time. Frank made another connection, "Do you think that Weisman may have taken Nujent with him?"

Albert pondered the suggestion. White Feather commented from the seat behind them, "Both left about same time."

Albert turned to address White Feather, "How do you know?"

"Departure dates in roster."

Frank was impressed by White Feather's attention to detail. Nothing got past the amazing Cherokee elder. Frank was curious. "How would we go about finding out whether Weisman transferred Lizzie to his institution?"

Albert's eyes brightened and then turned stern. "That information will be difficult to get. Those records are probably sealed and stored in Denver. But I do know that they were both there."

Monty had an idea, "M-maybe w-we could ask N-Nujent."

Albert and Frank glanced at each other and then chuckled. White Feather suggested, "Or Elizabeth."

Monty's eyes grew large and he gasped as the absurdity of his suggestion registered.

White Feather added, "M. Joyce O'Quin also left the clinic a few months after Nujent."

As the van left the city limits of Pueblo and headed across the naked plains in route to the distant Wet Mountains, the conversations trailed off and naps consumed Ralph, Albert, and Monty and probably White Feather. Frank could never tell about him.

He leaned his head against the cool glass of the window and let his eyes wonder along the boring fence line beside the road. He caught a glimpse of the tall smoke stack at the cement plant near Florence. Somewhere beyond that small town was Canon City where he had lived, no survived, for the previous five years. He wondered if his home, a refrigerator crate, was still under the bridge.

His mind wandered back to that first year of homelessness. Finding the refrigerator crate behind Home Depot had been a godsend to him at the time. Before the crate, he had spent many nights freezing in different locations near the shelter. He was certain that meeting "Freddie the Freeloader," as he liked to be called, had saved his life.

Freddie had been homeless for more years than he could remember and knew all the best places to bed down at night and where to get food. Freddie had seemed quite happy to exchange his knowledge and experience with Frank in exchange for Frank's company and assistance, but he was not the easiest person to be around. Eighty-five-year-old Freddie could get very argumentative and territorial, especially when he was in need of a drink.

But getting a drink brought on different problems. When drunk, Freddie became emboldened to steal from other vagrants and often got into fights. It was an infection from a knife wound from one of those fights that finally took his life and left Frank to fend for himself.

The idea to look for a large box for shelter had come from Freddie, but the cardboard boxes that Freddie lifted from behind the Safeway store would only last until the next rain or snow storm and provided little warmth.

After Freddie's death, Frank had traveled the long journey across town to Home Depot with the hope of finding a larger cardboard box or perhaps discarded lumber. Finding the wood crate with the cardboard box enclosed was a miracle. He knew immediately that he had to have it, but also knew it would be a monumental task to drag it across town.

It would have to be done at night, of course, so he had first dragged it away from Home Depot and rolled it down into a ravine. That had kept it out of sight until nightfall, but had proven to be a Herculean task to pull it out of the ravine.

The memory caused Frank to smile. It had forced him to get creative. Needing tools, he had remembered a construc-tion site not far from Home Depot and was elated to find a hammer there. This enabled him to take the crate apart and move it pieces-at-a-time.

The roar of the van engine and the gearing down of the transmission for the climb up the Wet Mountains drew his attention away from his memories and provided plenty of curious rock formations, wild animals, and interesting log cabins to study for the remainder of the ride over the pass and down into the Wet Mountain Valley.

The van's slowing for entry into Rockcliffe worked like an alarm clock for his friends. One by one they coughed, snorted and rubbed their eyes. Only Ralph was confused. "Where are we?"

Monty was quick to provide the answer. "R-R-Rockcliffe."

Ralph tried to return to his nap. Frank turned to look at a man standing in the park staring at the van. There was something curious about the man. White Feather declared, "That's you, Frank."

His friends jerked their heads around and Ralph proclaimed, "It IS you, Frank."

Albert provided sane analysis. "It does look like a slightly older version of you, Franklin."

Frank gasped. It did look like an older version of himself. Monty declared, "Doppelganger!"

His friends laughed with delight. Frank frowned and turned his questioning eyes toward White Feather. White Feather raised an eyebrow and smiled omnisciently. Frank looked at the doppelganger again. Actually, he was not an older version. Albert was being kind. An exact duplicate of himself was staring back with eyes fixed upon him, making him shiver.

As the man disappeared behind a building, Frank whispered to White Feather, "Me?"

White Feather whispered in reply, "Back from the past . . . looking for you."

"Back?"

White Feather answered by smiling and then closing his eyes as if the mystery was solved. The van turned and headed down Highway 69 north out of Rockcliffe. Frank sat up and stared back at Main Street. "What about the bookworms?"

Albert explained, "They had another van scheduled to take them back."

As his friends returned to their naps, Frank pondered the implications of the doppelganger. Was it really him, as White Feather had suggested, returned from a trip back in time? Did it mean that sometime in the near future, there would be another time quake and he would be transported back to some point in his past? Was he locked in a continuous cycle?

Frank's imagination visualized the event. He saw White Feather dragging him to the bench beside the three junipers. The earth was shaking and a huge crevasse opened up. He could feel total fear. White Feather pushed him into the crevasse and his body bounced back and forth off the steep sides of the cavern. He began screaming, "Help me! Help me, White Feather ..."

The van rocked side-to-side, waking Frank from his dream as they pulled into the St. Jude parking lot. He felt White Feather's hand on his shoulder comforting him. Albert was staring at him. "Are you okay, Franklin?"

Chapter 16

In its Penetralia

ONLY THE CREAKING OLD building dared make a sound in the darkness of late night. Five old geezers emerged from the elevator on the first floor, checked up and down the corridor, and then followed White Feather to the locked door to the basement. Somewhere in the distance, the faint bells of an old clock struck eleven times. The crafty old Indian pulled his cell phone from his pocket and found the flashlight app. Frank held the light while White Feather tried the key he had purloined from Nurse Nujent's desk drawer.

The key unlocked the door with a little jiggling but the door itself took both White Feather and Frank to break it loose. As White Feather led the Sleuthkateers down the dark stairway, the boilers came on and belched a cloud of steam that filled the narrow stairway, startling the intruders. Monty squealed, "Gh-Ghosts!"

"Steam cloud, idiot," corrected Ralph.

Cautiously, White Feather led the anxious coterie down the sweaty stone steps to the sticky dirt floor of the basement. To the right, there was a dim flickering glow, and to the left, utter darkness. White Feather led the group to the right through an arch to a large room, dimly lit by the fire in the boilers glowing through the mist in the center of the dank, gritty smelly and oppressively hot basement room.

As the steamy cloud subsided, White Feather moved his light across the floor illuminating a distant archway where the faint image of dozens of dark rounded mounds could be seen.

"C-Creatures!" Monty declared. The four old men stumbled over each other attempting to flee back to the safety of the stairs.

They stopped when they heard White Feather call out, "Mrs. Dawson?"

"Elizabeth?" Albert questioned.

"Just checking," White Feather explained.

The boilers belched again filling the room with steamy clouds.

Albert commented from the safety of the stairwell. "Like ghosts who've regained their lost ubeity."

Ralph left a parting comment before heading back upstairs. "You're losing it, Stein."

Monty chased after his cantankerous friend leaving White Feather, Albert, and Frank to explore the foggy cavern. Albert and Frank followed the glow of White Feather's cell phone light as the fog began to clear once more.

White Feather flashed the light around the room again, revealing the empty room to the south and to the left of the boilers where they found dozens of shallow holes beside the mounds of dirt. "Lizzie has been digging?" Frank questioned. White Feather trained the light back on the floor around the holes and then proceeded forward.

"Careful of the holes," Albert cautioned.

There was a stairway on the south wall. To the west, there was another room where decaying folding doors hung ajar.

Inside they could see a concrete floor cluttered with debris surrounding a rusting and decrepit operating table in the center. The three brave sleuths explored the dark creepy room behind the folding doors. An old surgical light dangled from the ceiling. Rusting metal file cabinets lined one wall. The drawers had been forced open and old file folders were strewn across the floor. A line of metal cabinets which probably once held surgical supplies was corroding along another wall with a double sink in the center. Fat rats scurried away from the light.

White Feather backed out and searched the dirt floor around the stairway. His light stopped on foot prints. Albert speculated. "Elizabeth's footprints."

White Feather shown his light on a shovel propped against the wall next to the stairs. He bounded up the stairs and dis-appeared behind the switchback. Frank and Albert clamored after him. They found White Feather at the top of the stairs pulling open a half-door, like a Dutch door, and stooping to exit through it. It led to the south hallway where Elizabeth had mysteriously disappeared leaving her dress behind. The cooler air of the hallway prompted the hot air from the base-ment to condense, forming a thick cloud surrounding the old Indian. When it subsided, Albert explained the obvious, "The wainscoting hid the secret door."

Then Frank had an idea. "Let's go see what she dug up."

White Feather stopped him. "The holes are empty."

Albert declared. "It answers one of our questions. Elizabeth does not believe 'buried in its penetralia' is a metaphor."

Frank was not satisfied. "But, you didn't search all of the holes. How do you know that they are all empty?"

White Feather answered matter-of-factly, "She is still searching."

White Feather closed the secret door to the basement and then opened the door leading from the hallway into the corridor on the first floor. He stopped to chuckle. Albert and Frank peeked around him curiously. They saw Monty and Ralph cowering at the door to the basement beside the elevator looking down the dark stairway. White Feather tiptoed toward them with Albert and Frank stealthily following, trying desperately to keep from bursting out laughing.

White Feather managed to get right up behind them without being detected before casually asking, "See anything down there?"

"EEEEEEEEEEEEEEEEEEEIIIIIIIIIIIIIIIIIIII!!!," the two screamed as they leaped into the darkness and tumbled down the stairs.

Saturday

For you, my last incomium,
to sing my amative requiem.

Chapter 17

Feedstore Fiasco

Morrison down-shifted, turned into the parking lot of the Feedstore, parked, then revved up the Dodge Charger's big Hemi engine and shut off the ignition. As it chattered and grumbled to a stop, interestingly, he had parked in between Darla's black Firebird and Samantha's Subaru.

"I can't thank you enough, Jessie, for helping me out here. This is our first chance to have a real date."

Jessie squirmed in his seat. "No problem. I'm just really surprised with who you matched me with."

Morrison glanced over at his partner. "Really? I think you two have a lot in common."

Calhoun shrugged. "Well, you oughta know."

Darla had proposed meeting them at the Feedstore since she had been called in to work the early shift at Maggie's and might run a little late. When Samantha had heard this, she insisted on meeting them as well.

He and Calhoun rolled out of the car and walked around to the entrance of the upscale restaurant. Sam spotted Darla sitting in a booth back in the corner. And he could see the back of Samantha's head across from her.

"There they are," he whispered to Calhoun as he nudged his bashful friend in their direction. Darla smiled and waved Sam and Jessie over. As they walked up, Jessie grinned shyly. "Hi, Darla. Hello Mrs. Morrison."

Darla's eyes were on Morrison as Samantha replied, "Hi, Jessie. You may call me Sam."

The shy deputy carefully slid into the seat beside Samantha. "Long time no see."

Morrison gasped. "Jessie, uh ..."

Samantha interrupted, "I think the last time I saw you was when you wrote me that speeding ticket on Highway 69 leading out of town."

Morrison reached out to tap Jessie on the shoulder, but Darla grabbed his hand, pulled him into the seat beside her, latching onto his arm.

Morrison protested, "No! You don't understand."

Samantha continued, "The sixty-five mile-per-hour sign was just over the hill."

Jessie rocked back, crossed his arms, and stubbornly defended himself. "Well, you know, it's not a sixty-five mile-per-hour zone until you reach the sign. Technically, you were still in a fifty-five mile-per-hour zone."

Morrison tried again. "Excuse me, there's been a mistake."

Jessie glanced at Morrison and got defensive. "No, that's the law."

Samantha raised an eyebrow. "Yeah, that's what you said that day, too."

Darla giggled and pushed herself against Sam's arm. "Ooo, quarreling deputies!"

Morrison was ready to explode. "Uh, listen, uh ..."

The waitress stepped up and placed four menus in the center of the table. "What can I get you folks to drink?"

Samantha grabbed a menu and replied, "I'll have a Margarita on the rocks with salt."

Darla pressed closer and reached across Morrison for a menu. "Frozen Margarita for me."

Jessie interlocked his fingers and sat up straight. "What do you have on tap?"

The waitress rolled her eyes up. "Miller Lite and Heineken."

Jessie smirked proudly. "Miller Lite, please."

Deciding not to press the issue in front of the waitress, Morrison grabbed a menu and searched for the drinks. "Do you have milk?"

The waitress scribbled on her pad. "Miller?"

Morrison raised his voice a notch. "Milk?"

The waitress flipped her pencil over and erased vigorously. "Oh, want that with your meal?"

Morrison smiled. "No, before is fine."

The waitress bolted off. Darla snuggled and pursed her lips. "Baby needs his milk?"

Morrison blushed and glanced at Samantha. His ex-wife had fire in her eyes. He tried to unhook his arm. "I hate to be rude, but ..."

Samantha interrupted, "So how did you two meet?" She forced a tight smile as she straightened her silverware.

Darla's eyes sparkled as she declared, "We first met at the

restaurant." She rubbed Morrison's arm and smiled brightly at him. "Didn't we, Sam?"

Morrison shivered imperceptibly. "Yes. Jessie introduced me to you as I recall."

Darla giggled. "How are your feet?"

Morrison frowned. He noticed that Samantha frowned as well. Darla giggled again and pressed on. "Have they healed from all those grass burs in your backyard?"

It was Morrison's worst nightmare! Darla turned to Samantha to explain, "He was playing hard-to-get." She turned back to Morrison. "It was hilarious."

Morrison blurted out, "You were not supposed to be there ..."

Darla was undaunted. "I have to say, though, that your townhouse is SO much nicer than that stuffy little motel room."

Samantha's jaw dropped. Jessie's eyes bulged out. Morrison was infuriated. "That's enough, Darla!"

Morrison shoved Darla away from him, jumped up, grabbed Jessie's arm, dragged him over to sit beside Darla and plopped down beside Samantha. Darla folded her arms and pouted.

Samantha protested, "Sam, really!"

Morrison turned to Samantha and put up his hands defensively. "This is all a big mistake, Sam. Darla has completely misconstrued our relationship."

Samantha crossed her arms and angled away from her ex-husband. "Oh, so what IS your RELATIONSHIP?"

Morrison threw up his hands. "That's just it, Sam, we don't HAVE a relationship!"

Darla burst into tears and shoved Jessie onto the floor, stepped over him and rushed out of the dining room. As Jessie scrambled to his feet, Samantha glared at Morrison. He recognized the look that meant that everything was his fault. She pushed him aside, slid out of the booth and rushed after Darla.

Jessie was dusting off his pants. "What is going on?"

Morrison patted him on his shoulder. "I'm sorry, Jessie. Sit down and I'll try to explain."

Chapter 18

The Party

FRANK STEPPED OUT OF his room into the corridor of the third floor of St. Jude feeling very uncomfortable in the blue suit and tie that his sponsor, Judy, had brought him at the last minute. "Makes your pretty blue eyes pop." She had told him.

Frank reached up to loosen the tie and unbutton the top button of the starched shirt. He heard Ralph's door open and close. His grumpy neighbor burst into the corridor and strutted past him without acknowledging him. Frank chuckled. His contrary friend was wearing a purple shirt with multiple pleats down the front adorned with a yellow polka dot bow tie. The shirt was appropriate for a tuxedo, but Ralph had matched it up with blue nickers adorned with white flowers. For shoes, he wore his usual red Keds with black dress socks.

"Going golfing?" Frank joked.

Ralph continued down the corridor flipping a rude gesture over his shoulder. Frank heard another door open and shut, so he stopped at the next hallway feeding off the corridor to wait for White Feather. When he approached, Frank was aghast. White Feather's hair was shiny and black and the spray shooting out of the ornate dear leg bone was stiff and spiked as if coated with shoe polish and maybe Butch's Hair Wax. Stuffed into the deer bone were colorful feathers looking more like plumes. In addition to his normal gaudy necklace with bear claws alternating with large stone beads, a netted, circular pocket enclosing a crystal and two agates dangling beneath, he had added strings of beads and pearls and turquoise jeweled necklaces. A white tanned leather vest adorned with colorful beads covered a plain white shirt. His pants were of the same tanned leather but adorned with silver buttons and leather fringe down the side. High-topped moccasins sported white furry tops. Down the sides, polished bones kept the boots buttoned up. Around his waist was a leather belt with an oval silver buckle that held a large oval turquoise stone in the middle. A bulky leather pouch was attached to the belt on his side.

"Wow!" Frank uttered to compliment his regal friend. White Feather raised his chin to acknowledge Frank's tribute. As he walked by, he complimented Frank with a simple, "Nice suit."

The three men stood quietly in opposite corners of the elevator and stared blankly at the elevator doors as they rode to the second floor.

When the doors opened, Albert and Monty were waiting. Albert wore brown slacks with a beige shirt, V-neck red sweater, under a taupe wool jacket with brown patches on the elbows. A neat, red bow tie matched his sweater. Frank greeted him with, "Very dapper, Mr. Stein"

Monty smiled proudly as he waited for Frank's notice. He was wearing a camel-colored Stetson Gurnee trimmed with a small red feather. His suit was tweed with matching vest and pants, a white shirt and beige bow tie adorned with a subtle paisley design. He wore wingtips: white on top; brown on bottom. "Most debonair," Frank declared. Monty giggled as he strutted into the elevator, thumbs in his lapel.

The moment the doors to the elevator opened on the ground floor, Frank's ears were insulted by Glen Miller's Band loudly blasting out "In a Mood," echoing down the corridor from the dining room. Monty broke into a clumsy version of the Charleston, while Albert strolled out of the elevator snapping his fingers in step with the beat. In that instant, he reminded Frank of the chairman of the board, Frank Sinatra. White Feather danced out bouncing on one foot, then the other making the bells on his moccasins jingle. Once outside the elevator he spun around gracefully and then posed one foot in front of the other and then visa versa. Ralph charged past his festive friends and announced, "Oh, crap!"

The dining room was bustling with residents dressed in their finest, laughing and chattering, and dancing. Frank's heart leaped and his adrenalin kicked in. Maybe tonight he would dance for the first time in probably forty years. He scanned the room for a dancing partner. The Golden Girls, Trudy, Judy, and Moody were already cutting the rug and they looked very appealing to him. They might be fun to hang out with in this setting.

Ralph headed straight for the snack and drink carts. "Hope they have whiskey."

The dining tables had been pushed aside to allow space in the center of the room for dancing. Carts hosting a grand banquet of snacks, hors d'oeuvres, and pastries set against the north wall near the kitchen. Birdie, wearing a sparkling black dress and red patent leather flats, stood by the drink table pouring wine for the patrons.

"E-Everyone is g-gussied up," Monty observed. Frank scoured the crowd and determined that Lizzie hadn't arrived yet.

Birdie put down the wine bottle, handed Frank milk in a wine glass and winked. He asked, "I suppose Lizzie will be making a grand entry soon?"

Birdie waved her hand. "Oh, Lordy, wait 'til you see her. You won't recognize her. She looks absolutely beautiful."

Frank heard himself say, "Lizzie?"

Birdie cackled and raised her eyebrows. "You'll see."

The five old friends found their usual table crowding the tall windows along the west wall and rearranged the chairs so they could observe the room better. Ralph had loaded up a snack plate and was already digging in.

They had been people watching (or snacking) for what seemed to Frank like a long time when the music halted and Mrs. Barkley walked over to stand in front of the dining room entrance. She clicked on a microphone that caused the speakers to squeal. "Oh!" She uttered as she jumped back and moved away from the amplifier.

She smiled and tried again. "I can't say I have ever seen a more dashing group!"

She waited for laughter and applause to subside. "Last Wednesday marked the fortieth anniversary of the day when the Methodist Church purchased this building with a dream to turn it into a retirement home. It would be twenty-five years before the doors opened and the dream realized. Can you believe that St. Jude has been open now for fifteen years?"

The residents and staff applauded. "St. Jude was founded on a great promise and I feel so privileged to be a part of it. When I see the happy faces in this room, it makes everything seem worthwhile."

She was again interrupted with grateful applause.

"I would like to take this moment to thank our sponsors here tonight that have provided the beautiful dresses and suits and sound system . . . and have helped us decorate."

The residents provided lively applause and hoots for their sponsors lined up along the south wall. The embarrassed sponsors smiled, bowed, and waved. Judy looked at Frank and he waved back. As the applause subsided, the sponsors filed out waving once more. This time applause was accompanied by cheers.

"Today also marks another momentous occasion. It is the birthday of Elizabeth Dawson!"

The lights suddenly switched off and a makeshift spotlight was trained on the entrance to the dining room. Mrs. Barkley backed away to one side. It took Frank's eyes a moment to adjust and make out the woman standing in the spotlight. Long, wavy, cotton-white hair flowed down the sides of her face and lay in cascades on her shoulders and down her chest. Red lipstick on perfect lips stood out on her pale white face. A long red dress trimmed with a black lapel flowed to the floor. The woman was strikingly beautiful. Monty gasped. "G-Good G-God, wh-who is that?"

Ralph turned to look. "Holy crap!"

White Feather stood respectfully and Albert rose with him and stared in awe. Albert whispered, "Elizabeth looks stunning tonight."

"Elizabeth?" Frank, Monty, and Ralph gasped in unison. It could not be Lizzie Dawson, Frank thought to himself: *No way could that wild, scary woman transform into this raving beauty.*

Slowly, the stunned residents and staff began to stand and clap. Gracefully, regally, Elizabeth glided into the room with her head held high and her arms bent holding a large bouquet. As she drew near, Frank could see that her eyes were not focused on the room. She appeared to be mentally elsewhere, maybe reliving some distant memory. Her friends, Ruth, Kate, Mary, and Katie Mae escorted her like maids in waiting to their usual table.

Frank was enchanted by her grace and mystery. The appreciative applause lingered on as she sat, straightened her silky dress and then returned to her dreamlike stare. The applause faded as the lights slowly came on again, revealing the captivated faces of the patrons. Elizabeth appeared to be oblivious to the adoring crowd. In her mind, she was somewhere else.

Mrs. Barkley held up the microphone to her lips and began singing, "Happy birthday to you ..."

Everyone joined in as Birdie presented her with a small cake topped with red icing hosting a single white candle, "... happy birthday to you, happy birthday, dear Lizzie, happy birthday to you!"

Static crackled from large speakers. The sound of a needle dragging across a vinyl record was very familiar to the elderly residents of St. Jude. The haunting voice of Jo Stafford began to sing, "No other love ...." Frank immediately recognized the nineteen-forties adaptation of Chopin's beautiful Etude in E Major, Opus 10 Number 3. Mesmerized by the song and the mystical transformation of Elizabeth Dawson, Franklin Roberts was drawn across the room as if caught in a spell. He felt as if he were a passenger in his own body that was moving on its own toward a magical destiny.

She did not appear to notice his approach until he reached out his hand and asked, "May I have this dance, Mrs. Dawson?"

She raised her head and eyes so slowly that Frank felt time was suspended. When she looked into his eyes, he saw a perplexed, perhaps confused woman of mystery. "Stephen?" she asked.

"Stephen?" Frank awkwardly kept his hand extended, but struggled to decide what he should do. Ruth touched her shoulder and took her bouquet, "It's Franklin, Elizabeth. He wants to dance with you."

Elizabeth looked down as if profoundly disappointed. Ruth gently took her arm, "Go ahead, Lizzie, dance with the poor man."

Frank felt his face flush and his heart quake. He felt awkward and scared and embarrassed. *What am I doing?* He thought. The fog of his mesmorization began to lift and he became aware of his surroundings, painfully aware that he was making a fool of himself in front of all his friends.

Lizzie rose from her seat and took his hand. Now he had to go through with it. He placed his hand on her waist and she laid her delicate hand softly on his shoulder. One-two-three, his feet remembered and they enjoined with the subtle beat of the lovely music. Elizabeth followed him so perfectly, so gracefully as if she were a part of him; light as if an apparition, she glided with him flawlessly and they danced as a beautiful fanciful unit. *It cannot be as perfect as it feels*, he thought.

For two minutes, twenty seconds the couple captivated their audience with their floating, dreamlike dance—turning, gliding to and fro, round and round. Tears flowed down Elizabeth's cheeks streaming her mascara down her face, washing away powder and creamy makeup.

Their enchanted connection stirred Frank's heart. He was experiencing feelings not felt for decades. Feelings he had forgotten and assumed he would never feel again. Feelings he had assumed were reserved for young lovers.

Focused entirely in the moment and upon the resplendent woman in the red dress, Frank was unaware that they were breaking all hearts in the room. When the song ended, they did not stop right away. When they did stop, they did not separate right away. When they separated, they did not wake from the spell right away. Her hand remained in his. It took the slow building clatter of applause to wake them. Frank smiled at his sad partner. Elizabeth dropped her eyes modestly and curtsied. Frank bowed graciously.

Close friends quickly moved in to congratulate them with pats on the back, cheers and hugs. Although well-meaning, their friends cruelly separated them, shattering the spell.

Chapter 19

Sam's Dilemma

SAM MORRISON GLANCED AT his watch. It was only half past eight. It was not too late to call Samantha. He kicked off his shoes, wiggled his toes and sat on the side of the bed. He pulled out his cell phone and stared at it trying to focus on what he would say.

What could he say? *It was all a misunderstanding. Jessie was confused. Darla was confused. They had misinterpreted my intentions. The idea for the double date was to get Jessie and Darla together. To reunite me and you. To get Darla off my back.*

Saying the words, even in his mind, sounded absurd. What fool would arrange a double date with his ex-wife, whom he wanted to reunite with, and with his alleged girlfriend? What fool would think that that would work?

Morrison tossed the phone on the bed and stood to remove his shirt and pants. He might as well be comfortable while making this call.

Unconsciously stalling, he carefully loosened his tie and pressed out the folds before draping it over the tie rack. He slowly folded his shirt and pants and stacked them neatly in the dirty clothes hamper. He gripped the rod in the closet for balance while peeling off his socks and laying them across the shirt and pants.

He cleared his throat and decided he should have a glass of water handy for the difficult conversation. As he headed for the stairs, he remembered his cell phone. What if Samantha called?

He went back to grab the phone off the bed. Why would Samantha call? What if Darla called? Yes, it was much more likely that Darla would call. But if Darla called, he would be able to see it was she and could avoid the call.

When he reached the kitchen, his empty stomach reminded him that everything had fallen apart before they had even ordered dinner. In fact, his stomach was only full of milk and beer from his talk with Jessie. Even after going over it time and again, he was still not certain that Jessie understood what had happened. Morrison vowed right then and there to never double date with Jessie Calhoun ever again. What a moron!

He found himself bent over staring into the refrigerator. He was getting chilled. There were plenty of plastic containers full of leftovers, but nothing looked appealing. Actually, nothing looked edible. He grabbed his favorite standby, baloney and mayonnaise and set them on the counter. The bread was in the tiny pantry in the corner. He washed out a glass and poured some milk.

He was too nervous to sit, so he slapped mayo on the bread and peeled the plastic ring off the baloney with his teeth. He smashed the baloney between the bread slices and picked up the sandwich in one hand and the milk in the other and headed for the living room to pace.

He imagined making the call: *Hello, Sam, please don't hang up. Let me explain ...*

His rehearsal was interrupted by the sound of the low rumble of a big engine with glasspack mufflers. He rushed to the front window and pushed aside the drapes with his milk glass. Through the sheer curtains, he saw disaster in the form of Darla's black 1968 Firebird stopping in front of his house. "No!" he grumbled. "It can't be."

As Darla strode across the yard to the front door, Sam frantically tried to decide what to do. He was placing the sandwich and milk on the kitchen table when the front door opened and Darla stepped in, "Sam?"

He dashed across the room. "What are you doing here?" he exclaimed.

Darla looked up at him with sad, puppy dog eyes. "I came to apologize."

Morrison was stunned by her reply. Then she noticed his attire, or his lack of attire, and giggled as she snapped the elastic band of his boxer shorts and pushed past him into the living room to sit on the edge of the couch. Morrison was dumbfounded as he closed the door. Darla looked at the floor and continued as if he were not there. "Samantha is so nice. We had a great talk."

Just the thought sent chills up his spine. "Talk? What did you ..."

Darla ignored him as she continued, "You were a fool to let her go, you know."

She looked up at him and stared for a moment before returning her attention to the floor. "I came by to tell you that I won't be bothering you anymore."

She headed for the front door, apparently not expecting him to reply. He did not. He just watched her walk to the door, open it, turn and add, "I can see that she still loves you. Don't let her get away again, Sam."

Chapter 20

The Fight

FRANK WAS FORCED TO endure the jokes and the praise of his friends who had pulled him away from Elizabeth. He caught glimpses of her at her table enduring the same treatment from her friends. Friends who meant well; friends who presumed they were encouraging them. Friends who presumed they were sharing in the joy and tragedy of the event.

But that is not how Frank saw it. To Frank it was: a cruel intrusion; an interruption to a most wonderful and enchanting moment; destroying what might have been; what might have developed; what may have been stifled forever.

And even though he had felt that he had connected with Elizabeth in an almost spiritual way, he felt as if Elizabeth had been dancing with some memory or some unrequited dream. Perhaps the dance had not connected her to him as it had him to her, but the longer they danced the more connected he felt they had become. Maybe given time and opportunity, she could have transferred her affection to him and shifted that connection. Instead, friends had come between them and

ended it leaving him to sit from afar and wonder what might
have been.

It was approaching nine o'clock and the party was losing its
luster. Very few residents of St. Jude had the stamina or the
desire to stay up late for any occasion. Frank longed to
summons the courage to dance with Elizabeth just once
more. She had captured his heart like no one had since his
late wife. He had forgotten what it felt like to find someone
so tantalizing and overwhelming.

For now, their friends had left them and coupled up
spending the rest of the night dancing to the music of the big
bands—the aged becoming ageless. The music and atmosphere
had transformed the residents of St. Jude from indigent outcasts
into companions and colleagues of another time, a time in
their lives when the promise of the future was unlimited and
bright. Now they were huddled at tables, sharing stories, tired
and sleepy.

Even the old Cherokee wizard, White Feather, was
surrounded by three old ladies clumsily trying to follow his
practiced dance moves. He seemed completely absorbed as
he stomped, spun around, chanted and shook the gourd
rattle, singing some Cherokee dance song. These were the
ladies that had confessed to White Feather when they learned
he was Cherokee that their mothers had told them about a
long lost Cherokee relative among their ancestors. White
Feather had been tolerant having heard it a million times.

Frank wondered what age his mystical friend might have been transferred back to. What age, what culture, what point in his life was he reliving now?

Frank realized that it was his chance to return to Elizabeth and try to rekindle the enchanted moment he had experienced dancing with her. All he needed was the right song—another slow, enchanting melody full of meaning and hope. Unfortunately, the old dance songs and big band razzmatazz was what the others were enjoying and demanding.

He stole another glimpse of her still sitting alone and trancelike at her table. The beauty she had worn into the room had faded or been blotted away with attempts to correct the damage done by her streaming tears. Now her lips sagged at the edges and looked sad and pathetic. The semblance of scary Lizzie was beginning to peek through the melting makeup no longer enhancing her beauty or disguising her frightful side.

Not once had he caught her looking his way. No doubt, she had not been struck by him as he had been by her. More and more he came to understand that she had just mistaken him for someone else. She had called him "Stephen" when she first looked into his eyes. To her, he had been that long lost love named Stephen Weisman.

Startled by the old grandfather clock striking nine bells, he jumped to his feet. Staring at Elizabeth and taking a deep breath, he mustered the courage for the first step toward her. No one was watching. It was his last chance to salvage something. As if on cue, Glen Miller's "Fools Rush In" began playing.

But, just as the vocals began, he saw her! Nurse Nujent appeared at the entrance to the room with a younger stranger by her side. The stranger was tall, a bit over-weight, refined in her dress, stern in her appearance and yet, apprehensive. Had she been crying? Her face carried the sadness of a person who was straining to keep up appearances. Frank stopped.

Nujent appeared even more apprehensive, almost frightened, if that were possible for such a bold woman. The two women paused at the entry and scanned the room. When Nujent discovered Elizabeth, she seemed to take a deep breath before pointing out the scary woman to her guest. The newcomer appeared to be startled by Elizabeth and started protesting to Nujent. After a short discussion, Nujent led the woman over to Elizabeth and appeared to be introducing them to each other.

Elizabeth seemed disinterested as the two women joined her. Frank returned to his chair to watch. He wondered if something had happened to Elizabeth that warranted a visit from the nurse. He glanced around but no one seemed at all concerned about Elizabeth. No one else seemed to notice the nurse's visit.

Then Frank saw that White Feather had noticed and was covertly watching them while continuing to dance and shake his gourd rattle. Perhaps he was now summoning the spirits to bless the meeting of Lizzie, Alvira, and her mysterious guest.

Nujent and Elizabeth looked more like old friends reminiscing at first. By their body language, he presumed an intimate conversation. As he continued to watch, the conversation became more intense. Elizabeth appeared to be getting upset and started raising her voice and waving her hands, pointing at Nujent and the stranger. Her anger appeared to be escalating and she began yelling at them, "I tell you it cannot be! Stephen told me ... I saw her ..."

Nujent appeared to be trying to defend herself while trying to calm Elizabeth and plead with her. Elizabeth's words were clearly hurtful for Nujent and especially the other woman.

Then the once pretty woman in the red dress and the nurse stood to yell into each other's faces. Lizzie screamed, "She's buried down there!"

The scary Lizzie persona had returned and appeared to be getting the better of her friend, or enemy, or whatever their relationship at this point. Lizzie turned and stomped off toward the exit with Nujent hot on her heels snapping and shouting, gesturing and pleading. The other lady remained at the table, dropped her head onto her arms resting on the table and began quietly sobbing.

Chapter 21

Remorse

Exiting the dining room, the quarreling ladies turned left into the corridor and headed toward the elevators. Then Frank slipped out of the dining room and glanced down the wide corridor. He was too late; it was empty. He rushed to the elevators and, remembering Ralph's trick, checked the lights. The light came on for the second floor and then for the third floor where it stopped and remained lit waiting for the next rider.

Frank felt sad and alone as if his connection to the dreamy myth of Elizabeth had now been taken away. It felt like Nurse Nujent had once again burst his bubble and trampled on him.

As the forlorn paramour stood at the elevator, he found himself pausing. His conscious mind began to question his unconscious action searching for purpose or reason. His eyes had wandered away from the elevator light and were now fixed on the door to the basement.

"Door to penetralia." The comment was coming from White Feather standing beside him.

Frank frowned and looked at the door to the stairwell. "You think she went to the basement?"

White Feather shook his head. "No." He pointed at the elevator light stuck on the third floor.

He pushed the button to call the elevator. When they reached the third floor and stepped into the corridor, they could tell that the light was on in Lizzie's room by the shaft of light across the floor. But there was no sign of Nujent. They slipped up to listen at Lizzie's door and could hear shuffling noises and perhaps muffled sobs. Frank started to knock but White Feather grabbed his wrist. He gave one more glance at her door. What was she feeling? Was she angry? Was she crying? What new tragedy had Nurse Nujent introduced to her?

Frank turned to trudge to his room. Yet for some reason, he did not want to enter his room. He did not want to end the night . . . not this way. "What do you think happened, White Feather?"

The old Indian folded his arms and closed his eyes in thought. "Hurtful past; painful memories."

White Feather was always careful with his choice of words. Frank knew that there were deeper meanings in his deceptively simple explanation. "Her past . . . from the steelworks?"

White Feather answered without expression, "Perhaps afterward."

"When she was in the institution?"

White Feather did not answer. Frank wondered if that meant he agreed, or that he was so far off it did not merit an answer. "Do you think they knew each other after the steelworks?"

White Feather opened his eyes. "They must have."

"Who was the strange woman with Nujent?"

White Feather stared deep into Frank's eyes. "Someone Dawson does not want to know."

With that, the old Indian turned away. Frank opened the door to his room and paused to look again at Lizzie's door. "Good night, Elizabeth," he whispered as he stepped inside. A door behind him closed softly. Frank looked back, then decided it must have been White Feather and closed his door.

As he pulled off the uncomfortable suit loaned to him for the occasion, it was like a metaphor. The night, the affair, had just been lent to him for the night. What happened between him and Elizabeth was just for that night and their relationship would now return to what it was before. Now, as he folded the clothes and put them on the chest of drawers, he was in affect folding up the night; folding up his tryst; placing his feelings, hopes and desires neatly away.

Sam watched the digital numbers on his phone's clock click over to 10:00 PM. Samantha would be herding the kids off to bed now. He had missed his chance to call her. Perhaps he did not need to call her now with Darla out of the picture. *What did they talk about?*

His stomach tightened as the possibilities marched through his mind. *Would Darla reminisce, or perhaps brag about their encounters? No doubt, she would unintentionally put the worst possible slant on them. If she portrayed me as a willing participant, or, more like, a flirt or tease, will it permanently ruin my relationship with Samantha? Will she ever forgive me?*

To be fair, from Darla's point of view, how could she tell it any other way? It was what she had said at the time; what she had fussed at me about; what she, no doubt, believed.

He crawled into bed, covered up and tried to relax and let sleep take him away from his dilemma. His overactive brain would not have it. Now it wanted to imagine what Samantha's side of the conversation would have been. What did Samantha say that made Darla respect her so much? What words were spoken that made her set him free?

He remembered what Darla had said. "I can see that she still loves you. Don't let her get away again, Sam."

Did Samantha say that? Did she say to Darla that she still loves me? No. Darla said, "I can SEE ...," not the same thing. But she must have said something that led Darla to think she still loves me.

A tear sprouted in the corner of his eye. Samantha always knew what to say. She was always grounded and never let her heart misguide her. She was a rock. Darla was right about one thing, he was a fool to have ever let her get away.

So many times he had replayed the conversations and events leading up to her leaving him. She had been so clear. He had been so confused, so blind, so stupid. She had plainly explained to him what her concern was. She had plainly explained what she needed from him. It was his obsession with his work. It was putting his work first and his wife and kids in second place. It was simple neglect.

Why hadn't he seen that reality? What had prevented him from looking beyond his career to see the importance of his family? And then, when she hit him over the head with a two-by-four, the ultimatum that she was leaving, why hadn't he fought for her? Why had he just curled up like a wimp and let her move out?

Am I more mature now? Have I learned my lesson? Are my eyes open now? Am I ready to get my priorities straight?

In his mind, the answer was yes, but his thoughts raged on through another sleepless night.

Sunday

Vast the distance between our hearts,
once interstitially apart.

Chapter 22

Frank in the Box

A DISTANT SHRIEK! IT was so distant that it might not be heard without the backdrop of total silence, yet undeniable. An urgent scream loaded with fear and desperation; a woman's scream.

Frank Roberts felt compelled to act but the darkness was so thick that nothing was visible or even discernible. So thick, in fact, he felt unable to even move. Paralyzed by fear and uncertainty, Frank squeezed his eyes closed. What vile predator had she encountered? Would it come for him next?

The wooden crate and thick cardboard of the refrigerator container that was Frank's humble, or perhaps humiliating, home could not keep out the cold winter chill let alone a nocturnal predator. Frank tried to pull his tattered old covers more tightly around him but they were gone. He searched up and down his body with his hands but could not find the ragged quilts. Outside the wind howled. No, wait ... it sounded more like the ocean. But, how could the box that he called home and had placed under the bridge near a park in Canon City, Colorado, have relocated itself to a beach? Could it be the stream running under the bridge?

Tentatively, he pushed open the improvised flap he used as a door for his tiny domicile and peered outside. He was not on a beach; he was not under a bridge. He was in a large poorly lit room where an old television was displaying "snow" and broadcasting static. The station had gone off the air.

He could see that he was sitting in a soft, old Victorian-style high-backed chair, not a cramped refrigerator crate. He had been dreaming about the wooden crate he had called home for five years as a homeless vagabond. That was before he had been rescued and accepted by the St. Jude Methodist Retirement Center for Indigents. This was his home now.

The sequence of the night's events were becoming clear to him now. He remembered being unable to sleep and getting up, leaving his room and coming into the TV room to watch television. He had quickly fallen asleep. The feelings of fear from the dream lingered in his heart and he searched his memories for remnants of the dream.

A scream? Was the scream real or just in the dream? Frank had a theory about dreams. *Dreams are when the brain takes a dump.* Frank had always thought that dreams were how the brain relieved itself of random, unaddressed events that were put back to be resolved at a later date. He believed that the reason dreams were sometimes illogical or weird was because in sleep the main resources for interpreting our world are shut down and the interpreter that is left cannot always resolve things correctly.

Frank had determined that images and events occurring in a dream could be traced to a curious event that the conscious mind had, for whatever reason, put off interpreting. These items are kicked down to the subconscious to be dealt with later. When later never comes, it is left up to the subconscious to try to interpret them and then discharge them in the alternate reality of a dream.

In addition to these stored events, a dream could be the product of some outside stimuli occurring during the dream. Without the complete toolbox full of senses, the subconscious is inept at interpreting these stimuli in dream form.

But, because of recurring dreams in which he was back in "the box" instead of at St. Jude's led him to wonder if maybe the interpreter working in his mind with dreams was different than the one interpreting and working with all of the senses during the day. Perhaps the "dream weaver" was not connected to the "day weaver". If they were the same interpreter, the dream weaver should be informed of current events.

So, was the scream a latent event awaiting interpretation, or had someone actually screamed during the dreaming process and the subconscious had done its best to interpret it and create a story around it?

Frank searched his memory for latent events involving a scream. The only one that came to mind happened several months before. Lizzie Dawson had screamed maniacally at now deceased Benny Cook. Frank replayed the scream from memory. No, it was not a match. And it was not normal for events in Frank's experience to wait that long to come out in a dream. So, perhaps it could have actually occurred while he was dreaming.

He found the clock on the wall. It was 3:13 AM. He attempted to go back to sleep. Not because he was tired or sleepy, but because he wanted to return to the dream, find the woman, learn what was happening to her, and rescue her.

But sleep eluded him. He shifted and forced his eyes shut, but his pulse had quickened from the excitement of the woman in distress and now he was rejuvenated. He clicked off the TV, pushed himself out of the chair, and forced his stiff body to return to his room.

As he followed the hallway to the corridor, he trained his senses on the late night quiet of the old building. He ignored the creaking sounds of the building and hushed snoring of residents, instead listening for sounds of something that would confirm that someone had been in distress.

He reached the corridor and turned to his left toward his room, noticing a shaft of light reaching out from under a door. That would be Lizzie's room. The crazy old woman's light was still on. Maybe he was wrong. Maybe it was Lizzie who had screamed. Maybe the sound had been altered by the corridor and hallway between them. He wondered what horrible thing could scare a scary woman.

A pocket of damp, chilling air passed through him. He shivered and rubbed his shoulders. The ancient building was drafty and poorly insulated. All the stone, wood, and brick in the walls treated heat unequally and the outmoded boiler-style furnace system was indeed inadequate. He hoped that would change with the new system.

He reached for the doorknob to his room and then paused to look down the corridor at the shaft of light again. He decided to go listen outside her door. He could faintly hear what must be Lizzie weeping softly. It made his heart ache. She had lived a tragic life according to his friend, Albert.

He started to knock but then thought better of it. He wondered what haunting memories might be keeping her up so late at night. Was she still lamenting the fight with Nujent?

Sadly, he turned toward his room . . . almost expecting the woman to yell at him. The adrenalin from the dream had worn off. He was starting to feel tired again. Perhaps he could sleep now.

Chapter 23

Creepy Woman

"FRANK, WAKE UP. FRANK."

The soft melodic voice surrounded him from the lush forest so green it appeared to be dripping with moisture. The flowers appeared so bright that they must be fresh from an artist's pallet. The voice so appealing that it had to be from an angel.

He felt the angel's soft touch on his shoulder and started blinking his eyes and searching for her face. The silhouette of a woman stood before him and for one brief moment her face materialized. It was a strong face with deep lines creasing the once lovely features. She was glaring at him. "Elizabeth?" he questioned.

He opened his eyes and the drab, colorless walls and ceiling of his room greeted his eyes replacing the beautiful forest in his dream. It was so unpleasant he wanted to return to the dream. Then his eyes found her face and her beauty lit him up like an artist throwing brilliant colors on the pallet of his retina.

"Stacie?"

The jaunty resident's aide of St. Jude Methodist Retirement Center giggled. She was standing beside his bed holding a food tray. She explained her reason for interrupting the slumbering octogenarian. "You're going to miss lunch if you don't get moving, sleepy head."

Frank woke up in a panic. He had fallen back to sleep and now he would be late for lunch. "Oh! Stacie. Thanks. I-I don't know why ..."

He glanced at the tray. "Oh, Stacie, you didn't need to ..."

Stacie looked at the tray. "Oh, this is for Maire, Frank, but I would be glad to bring you one."

Frank was embarrassed. "No, no, I need to get up; I have slept too long."

Stacie brushed his hair out of his eyes and turned to leave. "What time is it?"

Stacie glanced at the clock beside his bed. "It's eleven-twenty."

"PM?"

Stacie laughed. "No, it's AM."

"What are you doing here? You work the night shift."

"I have a big test tomorrow. I traded with T.J. so I could have the evening to study."

Stacie smiled and left the room. Frank threw off the covers and hurriedly pulled on his clothes. He rushed out of his room into the corridor. The elevator was almost across from his room and the doors were opening. In his rush to the elevator he almost collided with Stacie stepping up to the elevator empty handed.

"Oh! I'm sorry, Stacie."

The ebullient young girl beamed a broad smile and reassured him. "No problem, Frank."

Frank followed her into the elevator and pushed the button for the ground floor. As the doors closed, it dawned on him for the first time the fact that Stacie had taken a tray to someone on his floor. She had said My-ra?

He went through a mental checklist of residents on the north end of the residence. He had heard his neighbor, Ralph, gargling in the shared bathroom so it probably was not for him. Lizzie and Ruth resided in the corner rooms and Mary and Kate were down the hall.

Frank smiled and asked, "Who did you say the tray was for?"

"Her name is Maire; she is a new resident. She likes to stay in her room."

The bell on the elevator dinged; the elevator shuddered and then came to a stop. After a pause, the doors opened and Stacie rushed down the corridor to the dining room. Frank followed at a more moderate pace. When he entered, he spotted Mary, Ruth, and Kate sitting at their usual table. His brow wrinkled as he searched the table where he and his four friends sat. Ralph was busy shoveling eggs into his mouth. The others were busy discussing something. Frank was anxious to share the news of a new resident with his colleagues.

As he set down his tray and pulled out a chair, across the table his friend, Monty, interrupted his futile attempt to share his news by offering a mystery of his own. "Wh-Who is that?"

Frank followed Monty's eyes to a woman sitting alone at a table across the room. In his peripheral vision, he saw the heads of his three other friends at the table swivel and focus on Monty's diversion. She seemed alone in her thoughts . . . in her own world . . . not a part of this place. Her stringy graying hair was disheveled and unkempt, but hinted of being a recent development. The sagging skin and wrinkles on her face did not hide the hint of a once handsome face. The way she held her fork, the way her other arm draped across her lap, the way she leaned over her plate sitting on the edge of her chair all hinted she had once been privileged. She was a lady vanquished to a den of tramps.

Only his jaded, grumpy old friend, Ralph Jacobs, could not feel the power of her distress. With but only a glance, he turned away and labeled her "creepy." Then his interest returned to his food tray.

Across from him, Monty continued to stare at the "creepy" woman. He was a robust man whose grand frame barely contained his voluminous heart. A tear dropped from wet eyes onto Monty's cheek. Frank was touched by the depth of his empathy. He had, until this moment, characterized Monty as a bit of a simpleton.

Sitting next to Frank, his aloof Native American friend stared at the woman with empathetic eyes. Frank sensed that White Feather understood the woman's pain as only a spiritual priest could. In White Feather's eyes, Frank saw an omniscient understanding that read the woman like a twin reads his sibling.

Frank looked at the woman and when their eyes met, he felt a connection so powerful, for an instant he felt as though he knew her. Yes. Her sad face and bearing was the image that matched his deep feelings of foreboding and sadness from his dream. The dream came streaming back to him. It was a dark night, so dark not even stars or the moon were present. He could hear the powerful roar of the ocean broiling within itself, pulled and stirred by conflicting gravitational forces. He could feel the gritty sand against his buttocks and the heels of his feet as he hugged his knees and fought the heavy feeling of loneliness and dread.

A woman's distant wails sent a stinging surge of fright through his heart. He could hear in her sobs and feel in his heart her pain and distress. Suddenly, her cries were silenced by the echoing opening of a door that jolted his senses. And abruptly, he had been yanked from the chilling, dark, dreary seaside to a verdant, warm, bright forest. Some mystical force had separated him from the woman in distress to prevent him from rushing to her rescue. He vowed to ignore the lure of this Utopian temptation and search for a way back to her.

That was when Stacie had awakened him.

The "creepy" woman must be the woman in his dream. He was sure of it. Her arrival had no doubt reached into his subconscious and then emerged in his dream. His lip twitched and he quickly discounted such a supernatural notion. Frank was a practical man, not accepting of mystical explanations. Still he could not ignore what he felt when the mysterious woman looked at him.

Her look was but a glance and now she was thoughtfully picking at her food. Ralph interrupted his trance. "You still tryin' to figure out that creepy woman?"

Without waiting for an answer, the bold man rose and strode across the room toward the lady's table. Frank chuckled at the crooked old man who saw himself as a lady's man, with huge feet plop, plop, plopping across the wood floor. He watched the man who obviously pictured himself as suave, address the lady and then help himself to a chair at her table. Frank could see that the refined woman was not impressed and her reply resulted in Ralph holding up his hands as if apologizing, rising and returning apparently undeterred.

Ignoring his friends' focused attentions, Ralph sat down and resumed eating. Monty could not hold back. "Wh-What's the story?"

Ralph looked up, raised his eyebrows and sarcastically pronounced, "She prefers to be left alone."

Monty chuckled, "It would appear so."

White Feather put it together. "Nujent's guest at party."

Frank was reminded. "Of course, she was the younger woman that Nujent tried to introduce to Lizzie."

Chapter 24

Missing Person

Gabby smacked her gum as her eyes raced across the lines
of the suspenseful words in her Agatha Christopher murder
mystery. She jumped and shrieked when the phone rang on
her desk. Breathing heavily, she pressed the open paperback
against her chest and punched the lighted button on the
switchboard. "Sheriff's Office, how may I help you?"

The caller did not respond for a moment. The part-time
dispatcher of the Wet Mountain County Sheriff's Office
could hear heavy, labored breathing. Finally, a man reported
urgently, "My wife is missing!"

Gabby put down her novel and positioned her fingers on
the keyboard to log the call into her dispatch journal. "What
is your name, please?"

There was a long pause. She was not sure, but suspected
the man was sobbing or perhaps in shock. He took a deep
breath and continued, "She wasn't home when I woke up and
the bedroom is in shambles."

Gabby persisted, "Your name, sir?"

"Agatha, her name is Agatha Phillips."

Gabby typed in the name, "Yes, sir, and what is YOUR name?"

"She wouldn't just leave like this."

Checking the caller ID on her program, Gabby asked, "Is this John Phillips?"

The caller hung up.

Gabby typed in the phone number of the caller listed on her screen and then ran a reverse search that turned up the name of John Phillips and his address. She made a note and logged the call.

She picked up her novel, glanced at the cover and smiled curiously. *What a coincidence, the author of this book is named Agatha.* That triggered Gabby's memory of the encounter just a few days prior with the author Agatha Christopher. She searched the log and found the entry noting that Phillips was the author's real surname. She had come to the office distressed and had spoken to Deputy Morrison.

John Phillips must be her husband. She decided to call Deputy Morrison on his cell phone and reached his voice mail. "Hi, Sam, Gabby here. I got a curious call about a missing wife named Agatha from a number belonging to John Phillips. Remember . . . she's the woman who came in recently. ... Okay, bye."

Deputy Morrison was stopped at the intersection where Highway 69 turns right to avoid downtown Rockcliffe, listening to a voice mail from Gabby, the dispatcher. Phillips was, as Gabby had remembered, the distressed woman who had come in to complain about her drug addicted son. Her son had changed and she was frightened of him. At the time, something in his gut had told Morrison that he had not heard the last from her. He had felt sorry for her and told her he would try to find her son to talk to him. He had placed a request with the Tulsa PD to look for him and had searched the database but had found nothing so far. The next step would be to find his friends to see what they might know.

He pressed his cell phone to the side of his face. "Sam Morrison."

An excited man's voice asked, "Deputy Morrison?"

Morrison insisted, "This IS Deputy Morrison. Who is this?"

The man was not listening or perhaps hard of hearing. "She's gone! I've looked everywhere. She just disappeared!"

Morrison pulled away from the stop sign and idled down Main Street. "Please calm down, sir. Who is gone?"

"Agatha. She's just vanished. I found your card by her bedside table."

Morrison tried again. "Who is this?"

The man seemed to have calmed down slightly, "Oh. This is John, John Phillips. I'm Agatha's husband."

Morrison pulled his Dodge Durango into a parking spot in front of the county library. As he shifted into park, he resumed his conversation with Phillips. "Okay, Mr. Phillips, let's start at the beginning. When did you first realize that Agatha was missing?"

"Well, she wasn't in bed this morning at around 7:30 AM, and she usually sleeps 'til around 8:00 or so. I just thought that maybe she had come up with an idea for her novel. It happens from time to time."

Morrison sighed and turned off the engine. "You searched the house?"

"I went into the kitchen and the coffee maker wasn't on. When she gets up, she always turns on the coffee. So, I went to look for her in her study and when she wasn't there, I began to worry."

Morrison prompted him. "You look outside?"

"Yeah, so, I went to look outside next. Sometimes she likes to take a walk. I looked in all the places where she usually goes, but nothing."

Phillips paused and Morrison asked, "Her car gone?"

Phillips resumed, "I didn't know what to do, so I just kept looking around until finally I thought to check the garage. Sure enough, her car is missing."

Morrison offered a suggestion. "Maybe she just went into town."

Phillips got excited. "Yeah! That's what I thought, so I went ahead and fixed me some breakfast, figurin' she'd be back soon. That's when I found her purse in the living room beside the couch. Then I went into the bedroom and that's when I noticed the lamp laying on the floor, and a picture frame and some other things broken and scattered around."

"Like there was a struggle? You didn't hear anything last night?"

There was a long pause. "Well, actually, I wasn't here most of the night. I came in around four and slept on the couch so as not to wake Agatha."

"So, you didn't check on her until this morning?"

"I think she might have been kidnapped!"

"Why would they take her car? Is there another car there?"

"Well, no other car here. It just don't make no sense."

"Okay, Mr. Phillips. What kind of car does she drive?"

Phillips paused before answering, "Dang. I nearly drew a blank. It's an Outback, a 2000 Subaru Outback."

Morrison pulled out his notepad and asked, "What color is it?"

"Green."

"License number?"

Phillips was quiet again. "Let me think. Is that on the registration?"

Morrison answered, "Yes, it should be."

Phillips responded, "Okay. Let me get my billfold. I carry that in my billfold."

After several moments, Phillips returned to the phone with the license number. Morrison told him that he would look around town and at the grocery store and then drive out to their house.

Morrison reported in and told Gabby his intention to search for Mrs. Phillips in town and then drive out to their residence. He looked at his phone as he hung up. At that moment, he felt strong and had the courage to call Samantha. But as he pressed his thumb on "contacts," his brain seized control. *Samantha is at church. No place to talk.*

He checked the time again. The call would have to wait until after his visit to the Phillips' place. He shifted into reverse, checked for traffic and backed out. As he shifted into drive, he glanced at the tag number he had written in his notebook, memorized it and then proceeded down the almost empty Main Street searching for a green Outback.

He drove past the Jones Theater and turned into the grocery store parking lot. There were two Outbacks but neither was green. He checked the tags anyway. As he turned back to drive through the next lane, he spotted Samantha entering the grocery store. He jammed on the brakes and then searched for an empty parking spot. *What luck!* He thought.

Pulling into the first available parking spot, he started to get out when his rational side took control again. It was a public place. What could they say in the grocery aisle with other shoppers around? What if she was angry with him?

Morrison rubbed his face with his palms; he wanted to talk to her now, not later. Maybe he could just wait and follow her home. He pictured following her into her driveway. What if the kids saw him pull in?

No. He needed to call her first. If she wanted to talk, she could slip into her bedroom for privacy. He threw the gear shift into reverse.

Chapter 25

Creepy Women

LAWANDA BEAUDREAU, THE HEAVY-SET St. Jude head cook fondly known as Birdie, approached their table with a question. "Well, what are the Five Sleuthkateers doing with themselves without a crime to solve?"

Albert chuckled and addressed the question, "Maybe we ARE working on a mystery, Mrs. Beaudreau."

Birdie slapped her hip and chortled. "I don't doubt that!"

She aimed her pointing finger at the old Jewish resident and wiggled it at him. "So, what mystery have you found in this place?"

Ralph corrected. "It's a mysterious woman."

Birdie's eyes lit up. "Oh, of course, you're investigating the new gal."

Continuing to stuff food into his mouth, Ralph scoffed, "She got a name?"

Birdie threw up her hands in self-defense. "All I know's her name is Meyer, Mrs. Meyer."

"Meyer," Frank repeated as if searching for a reference in his memories. It sounded familiar.

"Good luck, sleuths," Birdie cackled and waddled over to the next table.

"Has an accent," Ralph added.

This piqued Albert's interest. "What kind of an accent?"

"Foreign, maybe Boston."

His friends chuckled. Monty interjected, "W-Would you l-look at that."

His friends turned to look at that. Mrs. Meyer had been joined by Nurse Nujent. Albert found their interaction interesting. "They seem to be cordial. It is as if they know each other."

Monty added, "L-Like friends."

Ralph put it in perspective. "Nujent and friends is an oxymoron."

Albert asked, "Did you say they were at the party together?"

Frank reiterated, "They came in together. It appeared that Nujent wanted to introduce her to Lizzie, but Lizzie got angry for some reason and stormed out. Nujent left with her but Meyer stayed at the table with her head down as if crying."

Now the nosy sleuths were watching the uncharacteristically happy chatter coming from Nurse Nujent. The two women were laughing at times and clearly enjoyed each other's company.

Albert observed, "Nujent is old enough to be her mother."

Frank added, "After they fought, White Feather and I followed Lizzie and Nujent but they beat us to the elevator and by the time we got up to the third floor, Nujent was gone and Lizzie had locked herself in her room."

Albert frowned. "All this happened last night?"

Frank smiled proudly. "Yes. I think you were distracted at the time."

Ralph remembered. "The Bobbsey triplets had us cornered."

The Sleuthkateers hushed to watch Nujent and Meyer leave the dining room and turn toward the elevators in the corridor. Frank glanced at White Feather who pushed back his chair. They rushed out of the dining room to the elevators in time to see that the ladies had taken the red elevator to the administration offices on the top floor.

White Feather turned and headed toward the dining room. Frank asked, "You goin' to finish your lunch?"

White Feather answered over his shoulder, "Gonna take a walk."

Frank replied, "I think I'll go upstairs."

White Feather shrugged as if to say, "Who cares."

On the way to his room, Frank ran into Stacie. Seeing her reminded him of her earlier comment. "I thought you said Meyer likes to stay in her room."

Stacie stopped and looked at Frank with a puzzled look on her face. Then, she almost immediately changed into her happy, bright smile, "Oh! Hi, Frank. I guess my mind was on school. Sorry."

Frank smiled and repeated, "The tray you had for Mrs. Meyer, did she change her mind?"

"Oh! Maire . . . across from your room?" Stacie pointed, then leaned forward as if she was about to share a secret with

Frank and whispered, "She is our new resident. She stays in her room."

Now Frank was intrigued. "Stays in her room?"

"Agoraphobia."

Frank had heard the word, but was not sure what it meant. "Fear of farming?"

Stacie giggled and then explained, "Fear of leaving her room."

"Oh." Frank thought about it and quipped, "I don't blame her. There are some scary old geezers out here."

Stacie giggled again and slapped Frank on the chest, "Oh, silly."

Frank was confused. "But I just saw Meyer in the dining room."

Stacie's face screwed up. "You did? Are you sure?"

"That's what Birdie called her."

"Hmm, that's curious. I'll have to check on that." Stacie looked over to her room and commented, "She picked up her tray."

Stacie smiled warmly and cocked her head to one side. "Couldn't be in two places at once," and then headed for the elevator.

Frank decided to check out the room that the new resident was afraid to leave. Maire's room was the first room in the hallway off the main corridor across from his room. It was an inside room with no windows. Maybe someone with agoraphobia would want it that way. Frank tiptoed up to the door and placed his ear against it. It was quiet, but just as he turned to leave he heard a cough. He listened and heard the cough again, confirming someone was in the room.

Frank knocked on the door . . . silence. He waited then knocked again. A high-pitched voice declared, "There's no one home. Go away."

Frank shook his head. *Not another Lizzie*, he thought. "Sorry, I'll come back when someone's home."

There was no reply. Frank turned to go to his room, then paused to think. *She couldn't have beat me up here from the dining room. White Feather and I saw her heading for administration.*

He touched his chin, *Unless Nujent and Meyer took the regular elevator, or separate elevators. But I think I would have noticed that.*

He turned back and noticed Lizzie's room. Frank decided to check on her. He crouched and peeked through the keyhole. It was blocked. Lizzie must have left the key in it.

"Get away from that door, Peeping Tom."

The voice was deep and authoritative. Frank fell back on his back side. He heard chuckling. *How can she see me?* he wondered since the keyhole was plugged. *Maybe through the door's peephole?* He pushed up for another look.

Someone whacked him across the head from behind. Frank's head slammed into the door. He dropped down on his hands and knees and then managed to push himself up and turned to find Mary standing with her fists on her hips and her arms akimbo glaring at him.

He felt a little dizzy as he rubbed his brow. "What was that for?"

"Peeping Tom!" she scowled. "You leave that lady alone."

Frank raised his hands as if surrendering. "Yes, ma'am, I just thought she might need help."

"Not your kind of help, Freak."

"No. It's not like that, Mary."

Mary doubled up her fist and shook it in front of his face. "It's gonna be like THIS, if you don't get out of here."

Keeping his hands raised, Frank backed up and slipped into his room.

Safe behind his closed door, he dropped into the old, worn recliner and sighed. He had never seen this side of timid little Mary. He supposed that being Lizzie's best friend, some of Lizzie's grit must have rubbed off.

Chapter 26

Phillips' Investigation

DEPUTY MORRISON PULLED UP to the Phillips' house on their seven-acre plot in the sprawling Bull Domingo development and before getting out, called his boss, Chief Buster Crab. "Buster, this is Sam. We've got a missing person."

"Yeah, Gabby told me."

"I checked around town for her and now I'm at their place to nose around."

Crab asked, "You suspect foul play?"

Morrison confided, "Not at this point, but Agatha came in several days ago reporting she was afraid of her druggie son. He had called her and upset her, probably stoned. Now she's missing. Left her purse at home, her car is gone, and Mr. Phillips woke up to find her missing."

The Chief responded, "Husband is usually the prime suspect."

"I know. I'll keep you posted."

As Morrison ended the call and replaced his phone in his pocket, he noticed the door to the Phillips' house open and

John Phillips stepping out on the porch. It was obvious that he was waiting for the deputy to walk up to the porch. Morrison reached out his hand, "I'm Deputy Morrison. Are you John Phillips?"

Phillips nodded and shook the deputy's hand. Morrison could smell alcohol on his sweat beneath the strong stench of cigarette smoke. "Hear anything from Agatha yet?"

John Phillips shook his head then asked, "Find anything in town?"

"No, sir."

Phillips invited him inside. Morrison asked to examine the bedroom. He noticed as they walked through the living room that the house was cluttered and looked "lived in."

The bedroom smelled of perfume, leather, and dusty linens. The bed was in shambles with some articles of clothing scattered about on the floor. Morrison pointed at a feminine bathrobe draped with pajamas on top of the bed, "That Agatha's?"

Phillips nodded. Morrison commented rhetorically, "Got dressed before she left."

Glancing around the room, he also noticed a broken wedding picture of the couple on the floor. There was a hook on the wall where the picture had apparently hung, and he found a lamp in pieces in the corner by the closet. He looked at Phillips who had an opinion. "She must have thrown the lamp at somebody."

Morrison thought to himself, *looks more like an act of anger.*

The folding doors to the closet were open. "Any clothes missing?"

Phillips shrugged. Morrison sympathized. Most men paid little attention to their wife's wardrobe. Morrison looked at the nervous husband. "You think she was gone when you got home?"

"Yeah."

Morrison pulled out his notebook and scribbled some notes. As he wrote, he asked, "What time did you discover she was missing?"

Phillips took a deep breath and hesitated. "Well, I discovered her gone around seven o'clock."

Morrison looked up from his notebook. Something about Phillips' answer seemed odd. "So, where were you so late?"

Phillips fidgeted and answered reluctantly, "I was at the Dome with some friends."

That explained the stench of alcohol on him. The Dome was a local bar inside a domed structure in the center of Rockcliffe.

"When is the last time you saw her?"

"I had a job in Rockcliffe and called her around five to tell her I was going to stop off at the Dome. She was home then."

He made another note and moved into the living room. "That where you found her purse?" He pointed at the purse sitting beside the couch. A blanket was crumpled on the couch where Phillips had slept.

"No, sir, it was in the bedroom."

Morrison made a note. "She have more than one purse?"

Phillips scratched his head. "Well, yes, now that you mention it."

Morrison set the large purse on the couch and searched for a smaller billfold-type purse inside. "I don't see any credit cards."

Phillips looked over his shoulder. "I think she carried a small red wallet with her cash and credit cards in it."

They gave the bedroom one more search and then searched the rest of the house without finding the wallet. Morrison stated, "So, she must have taken her wallet."

Phillips was still confused. "Why would she leave her purse?"

"Let's look outside."

Off the left side of the porch, a crumbling sidewalk connected to the detached garage. Phillips led the deputy through the side door of the garage where Morrison grabbed his arm and asked him to stay put while he searched for foot prints on the dirt floor. Unfortunately, the patch along the side of the garage where the car would have been parked was well-worn and produced nothing of distinction.

Morrison glanced around at the disarray of tools and odd items hanging on the walls. "How long have you lived here?"

Phillips rubbed his chin. "Oh, let's see, moved here about fifteen years ago."

Morrison nodded and thought, *Long enough to junk up the place.*

"John, did you know that Agatha came by the sheriff's office a few days ago to file a report on her son?"

"Seth? What's he done now?"

"She said he called her. He was probably stoned on something and scared her."

Phillips became agitated and shook his head. "That damned kid has really gone to the dogs."

"When's the last time you saw him?"

"It's been a while. We heard he was in Oklahoma working for an oil company. Don't know which one or where specifically."

Morrison pulled out his notebook again. "Did he have any friends here in Rockcliffe?"

Phillips rubbed his chin. "Let's see. He used to run around with Willy Madden and Josh Hagen. But I think he had a fallin' out with them."

"Know where I can find them?"

"Willy works over at Triple D Automotive, I think."

Morrison promised to keep Phillips informed and then drove to the office.

As he stepped into the open area of the office, Gabby waved Morrison over and reported, "Sam, someone has reported a crash on Highway 96 down on Hardscrabble at mile marker eighteen. A car skidded through the guardrail. The car is a green Subaru Outback."

Morrison inquired, "Melton out on call?"

Gabby answered, "Went home to check on Peggy."

"Any injuries reported?"

"Person said there was nobody in the car. Probably happened last night."

"Is this the first report you've gotten?"

"Yeah. Crazy, huh?"

He stepped into the open area and Calhoun looked up from his computer. Morrison asked, "You in the middle of something?"

"Shoot no."

"let's roll."

Chapter 27

Crash Site

Deputy Melton set the TV tray aside and tucked the lap quilt around his wife and kissed her on the forehead. She smoothed the wrinkles out of the quilt lovingly. Her friends in the local "Comfort Quilt" group had given it to her after she had received the bad medical report. She attempted a smile that looked more like a smirk. He commented, "You've got your water, and here's the remote. Don't forget to take your medication."

Peggy waved him off. "Get out of here; I'll be fine."

Bill grabbed the TV tray and backed away. "If you need anything ..."

"I'll call Megan."

Bill felt slighted. Megan was the young mother that lived next door. She had a new baby and a three year old named Dash that hung around Peggy as if she were his grandmother. Peggy loved it and kept the spoiled little monster filled with cookies and cake.

"You know Dash tires you out."

Peggy huffed. "No, he doesn't. He's adorable."

"You know you can call me."

Peggy smiled kindly. "Go keep us safe, deputy, and stop worrying about me."

Reluctantly, the senior deputy left his wife and headed for the Sheriff's office. Dispatch squawked on his radio, "Bill, you out there?"

"Yeah, what's up, Gabby?"

"Morrison and Calhoun are on a 10-37 on 96 at mile marker eighteen. Sheriff wants you to help with traffic."

"I'm on my way."

As Melton eased around the switchback that precedes the sharp curve at mile marker 18 on Highway 96, he spotted skid marks in the right lane ending well before the curve and another set starting further down in the left lane and ending at the mangled guardrail.

He drove down and parked next to the gaping hole in the railing. He got out and looked back at the skid marks suggesting to him that someone was coming around the previous curve going too fast, pulled into the other lane, lost control and skidded through the guard rail. The other skid marks were short and suggested the driver had control before entering the curve. *They may not be related,* he thought, *that curve is unforgiving.*

He walked up to the rail and looked into the deep canyon carved out by eons of erosion. The tops of the trees were snapped off forming a path where the car had sailed to the bottom of the canyon. It had landed nose down and was sticking up like a monolith in the middle of the rushing waters below.

He focused on the wreck. It was a green Subaru Outback. The license plate was obscured by mud. He could see Morrison's SUV parked near the crash.

Melton returned to his car, drove down the highway to where a gravel road fed off and led to a parking area near the stream. Morrison met him at the graveled turnaround and greeted him with, "No sign of the driver."

Calhoun walked up to provide his theory. "Went through the windshield and the stream broke his fall. Probably wandering around out here somewhere in a daze."

Morrison rolled his eyes. Melton looked up at the broken guardrail three hundred feet above the crashed car. He shook his head. "It would take a miracle to survive that."

Calhoun persisted, "He was probably drunk, real loose. The water broke his fall."

Morrison confided with Melton as he got out of his car, "Description matches the missing Phillips' car."

Calhoun was confused. "The Phillips' car?"

Morrison ignored Calhoun and led Melton to the wreckage. Melton examined the driver's side. "Air bag deployed. Seat belt is unfastened."

Morrison added, "Wasn't cut."

They stood by the stream racing past the nose of the car. It was too shallow to break anyone's fall, but they did not state that fact. Morrison glanced up at the road. "Might have bailed out before it crashed."

Melton glanced up. "Or got out and let it go through on its own."

Morrison shook his head. "Tire tracks indicate they stayed on the brakes all the way through the rail."

"There are two sets."

Morrison added, "Tried to pass and lost control? Person being passed stopped, maybe?"

"Yeah, that would make sense."

Calhoun added, "Probably wandering around out here in a daze."

Morrison gritted his teeth. Melton suggested, "Calhoun, why don't you climb up on the car and see if you can get the tag number."

Morrison burst out laughing. Calhoun looked up at the shaky car leaning precariously against a tree. "You serious?"

Melton ignored Calhoun and proposed, "If the driver lost control trying to pass on the curve, and the person being passed stopped, he or she might have driven down and helped extricate the driver."

Morrison glanced up at the broken rail and then searched the gravel parking area with his eyes. He pointed at a spot on the road. "Those could be fresh tracks."

The two men strolled over to investigate. Melton commented, "Yeah, I think you're on to something." He pulled out his cell phone.

A Colorado State Patrol car pulled into the parking lot followed by Sheriff Bailey's pickup. Morrison approached the two patrolmen and the sheriff. Sheriff Bailey asked, "Who's Melton calling?"

"Parkview Hospital in Pueblo. We think the driver of the crash vehicle lost control while passing someone. That someone may have come down to help the crash victim and then drove him to the hospital."

Sheriff Bailey nodded and then turned to greet the patrolmen. "Afternoon Bill, Dan. Thanks for coming out."

Bill Replied, "Afternoon, Sheriff, what've we got?"

Morrison updated them. "Green Subaru Outback skidded through the guardrail and crashed into the stream. Driver is missing. Car matches description of our missing person, Agatha Phillips, but the tags are covered with dirt."

He pointed at tracks in the gravel. "We think someone may have stopped to help. Maybe took the driver to the hospital."

Dan rubbed his chin. "Yeah, these tracks could be fresh."

The sound of breaking tree branches, squeaking metal, and a screaming deputy startled the five men. Melton dropped his phone and shouted, "Calhoun!"

The men rushed to the crash site to find the car lying on its side, still rocking in a cloud of dust with Deputy Calhoun entangled in the thicket past the rear end of the car.

Morrison managed to push through to his partner. "Calhoun! You okay?"

Calhoun smiled and proudly answered, "Colorado 3-7-1, India, India, Victor."

Chapter 28

The Doppelganger Returns

FRANK WAS ASLEEP IN his recliner when a knock on the door startled him. He rubbed his eyes and tried to focus. Another knock. "Yes?"

Albert stepped in. "You okay, Franklin?"

"Oh, come in, Albert. I was just sleeping. Had a little nightmare."

"We were worried about you when you came by the pool room."

"The pool room? I wasn't ..."

"You just looked in and then rushed off like you were afraid to come in. We thought you might be avoiding us."

"No. It wasn't me; I've been up here."

Albert shook his head. "Sure did look like you."

Frank felt uneasy. Albert crossed the room to sit on the bed. "Are you sure you're okay, Franklin? You've been acting strangely today. It is not like you to sleep so much."

Albert was right. He was normally up early and seldom took naps. In fact, he more often had trouble sleeping at night. Oddly, he still felt groggy. "I think I'm fine. I guess the party tired me out more than I realized."

Albert raised an eyebrow. "You didn't hook up with Elizabeth after the party did you?"

Frank laughed. "No! Lizzie locked herself in her room after the fight with Nujent."

"What was that about?"

"It appeared to have something to do with Mrs. Meyer as White Feather said, but I don't know over what."

Albert stood to leave. "Well, just wanted to check on you. I'm glad you are all right."

Frank laid his head back and exhaled again. He had not been honest with Albert. He did not feel right. He was experiencing weird dreams and grogginess. Something was wrong but he could not put a finger on it. He took a deep breath and gripped the arm rests to pull himself up when he heard his door open. Albert again? "Who's there?" Frank challenged.

A man peeked around the door. Frank was startled by the man's appearance. "Who are you?"

The figure did not respond. But as Frank's eyes adjusted, he could see that the man was tall and thin, older maybe by a few years, and very familiar. Then he recognized the figure; it was the doppelganger.

"How did you get in here?"

The man who was his double smiled, closed the door and walked over to sit on the bed. He glanced around the room as if searching for something. "I've been looking everywhere for you. What day is this?"

Frank was dubious. The man did not even know what day it was? The man was squinting at the circle Frank had drawn on the back of a calendar hanging on the wall. Frank pictured the year as a circle with the months listed counter-clockwise around it. Normal calendars were confusing for him. He liked to put hash marks below each month on his circular version to keep track of time.

When White Feather had seen his drawing, he had proclaimed that Frank was one of those rare people who could "see time." When he had told Stacie about it, she had recognized the condition as a form of synesthesia.

Frank was uneasy. "What do you want?"

The man looked at him and gave him an eery knowing smile. "Don't you recognize me?"

Frank was irritated. "Should I?"

The man chuckled. "I'm you."

"Me?" Frank could see the striking resemblance but could not accept that this stranger could be him.

The man explained, "I'm back. White Feather was right. The time warp is real."

Frank challenged him. "No, it didn't work. We sat there for over an hour and nothing happened. It's all in White Feather's imagination. It's not real."

The man countered, "No. It didn't work that time. It really was an earthquake, not a time quake. The real one happened later."

"What do you mean?"

The doppelganger took a deep breath and looked at the circle again. "It has been so long. I can't be sure what year for sure, but I think it happened a year or so after I ..." he turned to look at Frank, "... we moved here. White Feather woke me one night and dragged me out to the bench. He had me pick a point in my life where the path changed direction. I picked our third year in college. Do you remember that pretty girl we met at the dance whose father was a big rancher? She was dancing with a nerd and we could tell she wanted to get away from him. So we cut in and she was so grateful. And it turned out to be one magical night."

Frank remembered but was agitated. How did this fellow know about that? He had never told anyone about it. The stranger continued, "I have always wondered what would have happened if I had married her instead of ..."

The man's eyes saddened and he stared into space as if remembering some tragic part of his life. He looked back at Frank. "Don't do it. It doesn't work out."

He shook his head and then looked down. "It's not good to change things."

Frank was beginning to feel afraid. The man was too believable. How could this be happening? He did not really believe that time travel was possible or that he was special because he visualized time differently than most people.

The man must have sensed his feelings. He stood up and addressed Frank, "I know it is a lot to absorb. I'm sorry if I have upset you. You don't have to do anything. I intend to get White Feather to help me go back and fix everything. But if White Feather convinces you to go back instead, just remember that anything you change will have profound consequences."

The doppelganger slipped off the bed and left. Frank was stunned and sat there trying to understand what had just happened. He was startled by a door slamming shut. He rubbed his face with his sleeve and exhaled with relief. *A dream! I think I was dreaming!*

He pushed himself out of the recliner and headed for the second floor.

Chapter 29

Hello Again, Sad Journal

INVESTIGATING THE CRASH ON 96 had taken all afternoon. The tags did not match Agatha Phillips' missing car. Melton had located the owner of the vehicle and had driven over to interview him at Parkview Hospital. Morrison had waited for the wrecker to arrive to extract the vehicle. The Colorado State Patrol had finished their investigation and concluded that the driver had lost control driving too fast coming down the switchbacks trying to pass a car. The tread pattern on the second set of skid marks matched the tread pattern of the tracks down in the turnaround near the crashed Subaru. They agreed with Morrison that the person he passed had gone down to rescue him.

Morrison's stomach was in knots. She had been in the back of his mind all day. It did not make sense that making a simple phone call could upset him so much since he was on the phone all the time at work and was accustomed to making difficult calls, but this one did. On the drive home, he had made a commitment to call her as soon as he walked in the door of his townhouse.

Pulling into the garage, he noticed the hammer and drill on the work bench so he put them away. On the way into the house, the pangs of hunger began to gnaw at him so he stopped at the refrigerator. A long investigation concluded with the realization that there was nothing of interest in it.

He paused to decide whether to go somewhere to eat or go pick up something. Haunted by the need to call Samantha, he decided to call first. He pulled out his phone and as he turned it on, his stomach began to grumble. He clicked off the phone and headed for his car.

He found the burger joint closed. As he struggled to decide upon an alternative, Maggie's restaurant appeared ahead. He almost turned in when he realized that Darla might be working there tonight. The gas station caught his eye. He checked the gas gauge and turned in to refill his tank. The station had a small convenience store. So after filling the tank, he went in and strolled down the aisles looking for something to eat. After revisiting the shelves three times, he finally grabbed a can of Dinty Moore beef stew.

He checked his watch as he entered the townhouse. It was 8:15. He had plenty of time to eat before calling.

At 9:45 Sam was staring at his phone, trying to decide whether he could wait another day to call her. He huffed and clicked on the call button. His stomach began to swirl as the phone rang and rang and rang. Realizing that he might have to leave a message, he began to panic. What would he say?

"Hello, Sam." Samantha's calm voice startled him. He fumbled for what to say.

"Hi, Sam," he managed. He reached into his memory for the speech he had been rehearsing all day. Samantha was quietly waiting.

"I wanted to talk to you about ... the Feedstore thing."

He heard her huff. "Okay."

"It was all a mistake ... a misunderstanding."

"It was definitely that."

"I ..."

"Look, Sam, I know you've been seeing Darla. That's okay with me. We are not married anymore. You are free ..."

"No! You don't understand. She keeps coming over and I keep trying to tell her that I am not interested in her, but she doesn't ..."

"Oh, good grief, Sam."

"It's true, I swear."

"So you expect me to believe that setting me up with Jessie and asking her to double date with us was somehow going to straighten things out?"

"She was supposed to be Jessie's date. You were supposed to be my date."

Samantha laughed and replied sarcastically, "Oh, well that makes more sense."

Sam could see that it made no sense whatsoever. "I know, I know, it was a really dumb idea, really dumb."

Morrison exhaled. "I can't believe that it ever sounded good to me, but, crazy as it may seem, when it first came to me, it sounded like a way to kill two birds with one stone, you know?"

"Get rid of both of us at once?"

Sam fell against the back of the couch and slapped the side of his face. "No. Palm her off on Calhoun and set up a date with you."

He shook his head. "I don't know how on earth I ever thought that would work."

Samantha was quiet now. Her silence was more unnerving than if she were yelling at him. She should be yelling at him. He would prefer she yell at him.

He leaned forward. "Sam, all I can say is I'm sorry. For some reason I can't ever seem to think straight around you . . . I mean anything concerning you. Damn, I don't know what I mean. I love you, Sam. I always have and I've made such a mess of it."

He stood and began pacing. "I don't blame you for leaving me. I was so stupid. And I don't blame you not wanting to get back together. It just drives me crazy, though. I want things to be like they were."

Samantha remained silent.

"No, I don't mean like we were, I mean together again ... a new start."

Sam felt like he had said too much. That he had not said it correctly. That maybe he had made matters worse. He paced in front of the couch waiting for a response. Samantha continued to remain quiet. He had a sinking feeling; the feeling that it was over; that his inadequate plea was pathetic.

He stopped and tried to summon the courage to try again but the phone went dead. Samantha had hung up.

He threw the phone across the room in a rage. It ricocheted off the chair in the corner into the curtain and slid across the floor. He gripped his hair and cursed loudly. Then he took a deep breath and picked up the phone to see if it still worked. It did. He paced back and forth in the living room reliving every word of the conversation: reconstructing what he should have said; what he said wrong; what her reaction might be. Was it over? Could things ever be patched up now?

Sam Morrison would not sleep that night.

Samantha wiped her eyes and then sobbed again. She could not help herself. It was too much. Sam had said all of the right things but still it was too much. She thought that she had gotten over him. When she had threatened to leave him in Denver and he had just shrugged it off, she had hoped that it was because he just did not know what to say. Maybe she had caught him by surprise.

When the days passed and he continued to act as though nothing was wrong, she had made the critical decision to call his bluff and leave. Then, when he did not come after her, her world caved in. She could not back down at that point and made one last desperate attempt to force sense into him: She filed for divorce.

When she received the signed papers back, she swallowed her pride and tried to put her life together again and move on. Then, he showed up in Rockcliffe.

Samantha snatched several tissues from the holder, wiped her eyes again and blew her nose. She dragged herself down the hall from her bedroom to the den. "Okay, kids, time for bed."

She expected Tammy to protest. But when her perceptive daughter looked at her, she could see that her mother was upset. She jumped up and took control, fussing at her lazy brother and pushing him to cooperate. Samantha was grateful. Sometimes Tammy showed great maturity.

While Tammy handled getting herself and Jerry to bed, Samantha numbly went through the motions of setting the timer for the coffee pot and then winding the old German clock. The kids were quiet now. She turned out the lights and made that long journey down the dark hallway to her bedroom, cradling a cup of warm tea in her hands.

She set the tea down on the nightstand and switched on the lamp. After getting ready for bed, she crawled under the covers and sipped the tea. She debated skipping writing tonight, but decided she needed to vent in order to get to sleep. Monday could be rough after a sleepless night. She opened her journal ....

Hello again, Sad Journal. Sam called. I don't know what to think anymore. He claims the double date was supposed to be me and him, Darla and Calhoun. I swear, Journal, he is either the dumbest man in the world or the most conniving. Why do I hope it is the former? What do I have then? What does that make me?

Samantha reached for her tea and sipped the warm liquid for a moment before continuing.

I don't know if I have the strength to deal with Sam again. I had things under control until he showed up here. He is such a little boy sometimes and I just want to mother him.

She paused for another gulp of tea. It was getting tepid now.

Maybe I am being selfish. Maybe for the kids' sake ...

I don't know, Journal, I just don't have the answers tonight. Maybe tomorrow ....

Monday

Lives destroyed with deft celerity,
ravaged by such harsh severity.

Chapter 30

Where's Lizzie?

T HE ARRIVAL OF THE huge flatbed truck shocked everyone including Mrs. Barkley. No one had expected the new heating system to arrive so soon. Within minutes of its arrival, the entire residency and staff of St. Jude had assembled on the front lawn and gathered around Mrs. Barkley and the truck drivers to listen in on their conversation.

The two men explained to Mrs. Barkley that they had taken turns driving the truck across country and that they had driven straight through, only stopping for food, bathroom, and gas. They explained that they needed to call their boss to let him know they had arrived since he would coordinate with the crew who would come in to unload the equipment.

This news was a great disappointment to the residents and stirred them to noisy bickering with each other around Mrs. Barkley and the drivers, making it difficult for her to hear the truckers' intentions. They tried to explain that they intended to unhook from the trailer and asked for a recommendation for a place to stay.

Mrs. Barkley led the men into the building and up to her office for privacy. She booked them cottages in the tiny town of Hillside just down the road from St. Jude. A trucker placed a call to their boss and was told that the site would have to be inspected before any crew could be scheduled to unload the equipment. Unfortunately, they could not give her any more information about the equipment installation.

As the drivers unhooked and pulled away leaving the flatbed trailer, the residents and staff were entertained for a while by Ralph's animated explanation of the capabilities and purposes of the furnace and all of the parts and accessories that he speculated were beneath the tarps. As a retired construction engineer, this activity put Ralph in an unusually good mood. His resident friends seemed to be tolerating his technical jargon and confusing descriptions spurred by their curiosity and desire to explore and understand the lumps and shapes hidden on the trailer.

Frank, Albert, Monty, and White Feather sat together on benches shaded by the shadows of a giant cottonwood tree watching their friend but Frank found his attention wandering from the engineering seminar being given by Ralph to search for the mysterious woman who had captured his heart, Lizzie Dawson. "Where's Lizzie?"

His friends looked up and began searching the crowd. "Th-that's curious!" Monty exclaimed.

Albert appeared concerned. "Has anyone seen Elizabeth today?"

"I haven't seen her since the party," Frank admitted.

White Feather suggested, "Ruth would know."

Frank took it upon himself to approach the no-nonsense friend of Lizzie. "Hi, Ruth."

"Good morning, Frank."

"We were wondering about Lizzie. We haven't seen her since the party. Is she ..."

Normally calm and collected, Ruth appeared edgy with Frank's inquiry. "We haven't seen her either. She's locked herself in her room and won't respond to us."

Ruth produced a crumpled tissue from her purse and dabbed her nose. "She has done this before . . . locked herself in her room, I mean. But we are starting to worry since it has been over twenty-four hours."

Mary and Kate appeared next to Ruth and stared at Frank as if waiting for orders to attack him. Ruth explained, "Frank was asking about Elizabeth. Did she answer the door this morning?"

Mary broke down into tears and Kate answered, "No! She refuses to answer us."

Frank asked, "Are you sure she is in there?"

Mary and Kate answered excitedly. "Yes! We can hear her in there stirring around."

Frank suggested, "Maybe we should inform Mrs. Barkley."

Mary blurted out, "Oh! No!"

Ruth explained, "Elizabeth would be furious with us. She hasn't stopped fussing since the last time when we, as she puts it, 'ratted on her.'"

Frank was concerned. "She has to eat."

"She keeps a stash of snacks in her room. You've probably smelled them. She could last for months!"

Frank was not satisfied with the ladies' reluctance to update Mrs. Barkley, but he did understand their reluctance to roil Lizzie.

The residents and staff were filing into the building as Frank tried to link up with his friends.

Albert asked, "Did the ladies know anything about Elizabeth?"

"Yeah, Lizzie has locked herself in her room and won't talk to them."

Albert followed up. "What is she upset about this time?"

"They didn't say."

Ralph had a suggestion. "Let's eat."

Chapter 31

Madden and Hagen

Deputy Morrison walked into the offices of Triple D Automotive. Jack Davis, one of the owners, was in his office.

Davis looked up from his paperwork. "Come in, deputy." He motioned toward a chair. "Have a seat. What brings you out here?"

Morrison removed his hat and sat down. "Lookin' for Willy Madden. Heard he's working for you."

Davis sat back in disgust. "Not anymore. Didn't show up today. I've warned him too many times."

Morrison followed up. "He misses work a lot?"

Davis crossed his arms and nodded. "Drugs."

Morrison had to ask, "Why'd you hire him?"

Davis took a deep breath. "Favor to Ben Madden, his old man. Ben's an old friend of mine. Promised me the kid had cleaned up his act but evidently not."

"Any idea where he might be?"

Davis reached over and spun the Rolodex and handed Morrison a card. "Here's his address."

Morrison jotted down the information and returned the card. "How long has he been missing?"

Davis replaced the card. "Called in sick yesterday; haven't heard from him today."

Morrison asked the obvious, "Sure he isn't sick?"

Davis huffed. "Could be, I guess."

Morrison put on his hat. "I'll let you know."

Willy Madden's house was located in the older area of Rockcliffe. It was small, dilapidated, and unmaintained. Morrison had asked Deputy Melton to join him as backup. It was his experience working for homicide in Denver that house calls could get violent quickly.

They waded through the weeds to the front door where the screened door hung ajar. "Obviously, no one ever uses the front door."

Not expecting an answer, the deputy knocked, waited and looked at his partner. Bill Melton was a soft-spoken, no-nonsense, down-to-earth, conservative Christian. At least that is how he would be described by friends and acquaintances. Morrison had learned that he was, underneath, a sensitive, caring man who held his feelings inside and preferred to speak with his actions, not his words. One of those actions had been sponsoring White Feather for residency at St. Jude Methodist Retirement Center.

Morrison noticed that Melton turned and let his eyes feast on the majesty of the Sangre de Cristo mountain range. He appeared to appreciate the cool, crisp breeze stinging his face and was pausing to appreciate the moment. Morrison could hear the sincere man whisper a short prayer for Willy Madden.

Melton blinked as if waking from a daydream. "I have never understood why people complicate their lives. Why are young people self-destructive and always searching for new and more deadly activities to destroy their futures? I don't understand why folks can't find happiness in simplicity and unselfish living."

Morrison smiled and shrugged. Melton added, "God gives us the gift of happiness, but some manage to turn it into hell somehow."

After a respectable amount of time, they waded through the weeds and clutter of discarded junk around to the side of the house. A gravel driveway led to an old dilapidated garage set off from the house. Morrison knocked on the side door and it felt loose against the impact of his knuckles. He tried the door and found it was sticky but unlocked.

He pushed it open about four inches and yelled, "Hello? Sheriff's office. Anyone home?"

There was no answer so they considered their options. "Davis told me that Willy called in sick. Maybe he's too sick to respond. Maybe he needs help. What if he overdosed?"

"We better check."

The house was trashed and stunk from cigarettes, marijuana and other offensive smells the deputy did not recognize. In the studio-style kitchen, food was molding on the small dinette table.

The living room was cluttered and in need of serious cleaning. There were no pictures on the walls. The furniture was sparse and well-worn, no doubt from a used furniture store. The large coffee table was littered with paraphernalia common for ingesting drugs and circles where beer bottles had been. A motorcycle magazine was carelessly discarded and ashtrays were only half-heartedly used for flicked ashes.

Melton remarked, "Madden can afford cigarettes, drugs, stereos, booze, big screen TV, and pizza, but I'll bet he considers himself down on his luck and broke."

They ventured into the bedroom that was a wreck like the rest of the house. Although the bed was unmade, it still did not appear to have been slept in. Melton came to a plausible scenario. "He more likely crashes on the couch in a drunken stupor every night."

The life of the pitiful youngster who had rejected the good sense and lifestyle of his parents was on display, but he had left no clues of his current whereabouts. Morrison kicked a tennis ball out of his path and suggested, "Let's go check out Hagen."

The slobbering Rottweiler barked viciously from behind the aging slat fence that lined the border of Josh Hagen's backyard. Morrison squeezed the handle of his pistol cradled in its holster. He hated the unpredictable breed that was outlawed in so many communities. He was ready if the rotting fence could not hold the vicious animal.

Hagen's house was almost a repeat of Willy Madden's crumbling abode. As the deputies moved closer to the house, the dog's intensity increased with each step they took.

Morrison prided himself on his self-control, but this dog was grating on his patience. Melton was clicking his tongue as if trying to calm the big dog.

Shadows crossed the curtains of the front window. "I count three people at least," Morrison whispered.

Someone peeked out from the side of the window curtain and then jerked the curtain closed. As the deputies mounted the stairs to the porch, even over the deafening barks of the Rottweiler, they could hear voices and scrambling from inside the house.

As Morrison reached up to knock, the front door was pushed open a few inches. Josh Hagen allowed one eye to peer out at the deputy. "Yeah?" he asked.

Deputy Melton recognized the boy, but still asked, "Josh Hagen?"

"Yeah."

"May we come in? We need to ask you some questions."

"What?" Hagen cupped his ear with his hand to indicate the dog was too loud for him to hear what had been said.

Melton repeated himself but Hagen angrily interrupted him by stepping out onto the porch and yelling, "Shut up! Shut up, Daisy! Shut up!"

Reluctantly the mean dog shut down to a whimpering protest. Josh pulled the front door closed behind him. "Sorry, deputy. What is it?"

Josh stunk of marijuana, cigarettes, and alcohol. He wore only a tee shirt and boxer underwear. Melton looked down at his dirty bare feet, "Have you seen Willy Madden?"

The tall, lanky young man tugged at his scraggly beard. "Willy? What's he done?"

Melton looked the boy in the eye. "He called in sick yesterday and no one's heard from him today. We went by his house and he wasn't home."

Hagen relaxed. "Oh. No, I ain't seen him."

Morrison got to the point. "How about Seth Brogdon? When was the last time you saw him?"

Josh seemed confused. "Seth? Hell, I ain't seen Seth in months. He ain't even in Colorado no more."

Melton asked, "You know where he is?"

Josh shifted his weight to his other foot. "I heard Oklahoma. But I don't know where."

Morrison explained, "He came home recently and got into a fight with his mother. Know anything about that?"

Hagen pinched the bridge of his nose and rubbed it between his fingers as if massaging a headache, then looked away. "Nah, didn't see him."

Morrison studied the kid as he shared, "Mrs. Phillips is missing. You know anything about that?"

Hagen seemed shocked at first and then angry. "Why would I know about that?"

Morrison stared him down. Josh shifted around nervously. "I don't know nothin' about the Phillips woman. I hardly even know her. I haven't seen Seth in months, man, honest."

Morrison studied him a moment longer and then said, "If you see Seth or Willy, you call us, all right?" He handed him his card.

Josh shrugged. "Sure. But, I tell ya, we don't hang out with Seth no more."

Melton looked into his eyes again. "Why's that?"

Josh shifted again. "No reason, man, just don't see him no more, you know? He moved off. He does his own thing now."

Melton added, "If you see him, you call."

Josh saluted with Morrison's card. "Sure. No problem."

As the deputies walked back to their cars and the Rottweiler resumed his protestations, Morrison considered calling in a raid, but decided that Hagen and his friends already had enough time to clean up the evidence.

Chapter 32

Nujent Connection

THE SLEUTHKATEERS ATE QUIETLY, lost in individual thoughts until Monty spotted the new resident entering the dining room. "L-Look."

The well-dressed sixtyish woman carried her tray to an empty table, removed the plates, glass, and silverware from the tray and placed them on the table. She set the empty tray in a chair and sat down. She shook out the napkin and placed it neatly in her lap and picked up her fork to begin eating. Nurse Nujent appeared and joined her.

"S-See that?" Monty whispered.

Ralph glanced over at the two ladies. "Eatin' together again?"

Albert remarked, "They appear to be acquainted with each other . . . as if they have known each other for a long time."

Frank's eyes widened as he remembered the party. "They better hope Lizzie doesn't decide to come down."

Ralph smiled broadly. "That would be good."

Monty offered, "M-Maybe th-that's why L-Lizzie locked herself up."

Frank answered, "You may be on to something, Monty."

Albert challenged White Feather. "What do you think, White Feather?"

The solemn old Indian nodded ominously.

Albert mused, "It would be nice to know what Alvira and Elizabeth were fighting about. It must have something to do with Mrs. Meyer."

Frank agreed, "Has to be. Mrs. Meyer was clearly hurt by whatever they were fighting about."

Ralph wiped his mouth with his napkin, placed it beside his plate and pushed his chair back. "Let's ask 'em."

His friends gasped. "You can't do that!" Frank protested.

It was too late. Ralph had already sauntered over to their table. Nujent's expression was a glaring stare to begin with. But as Ralph spoke, her mood turned to outrage. She stood wagging her finger in Ralph's face and spitting her words at him. Ralph raised his hands and backed up slowly, finally turning and slinking back to join his friends. As he sat down, he directed his comment to White Feather, "You'll have to ask her. It's none of my business."

Frank had begged off joining his friends for a game of pool. He was in the mood for some good literature. As he searched the dusty old books in the third floor parlor, he heard the elevator ding and watched the doors open to reveal TJ with a food tray.

"TJ!" he called to the happy young aid.

TJ stepped out of the elevator and searched for the source of the voice calling her. Spotting Frank in the parlor, she beamed a bright smile and answered, "Hidee."

Frank rushed out with his hand held up signaling for her to stay put. "TJ, what do you know about Mrs. Meyer?"

TJ's eyes rolled up in thought. "Well, she just moved in last Saturday, I think it was. She is our first paying resident."

Frank was surprised. "St. Jude is taking paying customers now?"

TJ shrugged. "No, I don't think so. Mrs. Nujent set it up somehow."

"Why would she do that?"

TJ glanced around and then whispered, "I think they are related."

"Related?"

TJ shrugged again timidly. "She is listed as Diana Elizabeth NUJENT Meyer."

Frank's eyes bulged. "Really?"

TJ got nervous. "You can't tell anyone I told you that, Frank. It may be confidential."

Frank assured her, "Oh, no, TJ. Don't worry."

He looked at the tray. "That for Maire?"

TJ smiled. "Yes."

Frank cozied up to the teenager. "What do you know about her?"

"I've told you too much already." TJ bolted away.

Frank's pulse was galloping now with this amazing information. He pushed the down button on the elevator. He could not wait to share with the Sleuthkateers.

When he rushed into the pool room, Ralph was leaning over the table stretching to reach the cue ball sitting only a few inches behind the eight ball lined up on the corner pocket. When Frank exclaimed, "Guys!" Ralph lurched, stabbing the cue stick tip into the table top spiking the cue ball over the eight ball and into the corner pocket.

Ralph flew into a rampage, swinging the cue stick and threatening Frank with decapitation. Frank ducked and dodged as he apologized. "Sorry, Ralph, I'm sorry! Please don't kill me. Please, please ..."

But just as Ralph was about to let up, Frank burst out laughing, infuriating the angry old man again. White Feather stepped up and grasped the pool cue, stopping it inches from Frank's head. Ralph glared angrily into the calm eyes of the Indian and then calmed down and backed away.

Monty offered, "C-Calm d-down, Ralph. L-Let's just s-set it up and sh-shoot again."

Monty placed the cue ball on the table where it had been and then folded his arms, giving Ralph an accommodating smile. Ralph took a deep breath, straightened up as much as his crooked spine would allow and plodded over to snatch the pool cue out of White Feather's hand and stepped up to the table to try again. The room fell deathly quiet as the crooked old man stretched across the table again and drew back the cue stick slowly. After a couple of practice strokes to get the feel of the cue, he lunged forward stabbing the cue stick tip into the table again, launching the cue ball over the eight ball, bouncing off the side of the pool table and into the quick hand of White Feather.

The room roared with laughter. Ralph spun around, hurled the cue stick at Frank and marched out of the room shouting expletives.

It was too much to ask for anyone to sympathize with Ralph. The laughter and jubilation carried on and on until Frank finally managed to calm down his friends and get their attention. "I've got some news, guys."

He motioned for them to crowd around him. "You're not going to believe what I found out just now."

He flashed his beaming smile around to each of his curious buddies. "Mrs. Meyer and Nurse Nujent are related!"

His friends gasped. Albert asked, "How did you find this out, Franklin?"

Frank glanced around and then whispered, "I can't tell you my source. Mrs. Meyer's full name is Diana Elizabeth NUJENT Meyer."

Again, his friends gasped. Of course, the exception to this sort of emotion is always White Feather. But even the austere Indian opened his eyes and registered a microscopic twitch in the corner of his mouth.

Albert rubbed his chin and speculated, "Her daughter, perhaps?"

White Feather countered, "Not married."

Albert showed concern. "How do you know that, White Feather?"

"Last name was Nujent on steelworks roster."

Frank nodded. "That's right."

Monty offered, "S-Sister m-maybe?"

Albert nodded thoughtfully. "A much younger sister, perhaps."

White Feather gave Albert an ominous look. "Diana Elizabeth?"

Chapter 33

Agoraphobiac

SHERIFF BAILEY WAS LEAVING his office when he spotted Morrison and stopped to inquire, "Anything on the Phillips case?" Morrison updated him. "Melton ran the tags on that crashed car at mile marker 18. Belongs to Frederick Geisendorff; he lives over in Wetmore."

Bailey shook his head. "So, now we have two missing persons?"

Melton strolled up, cradling a cup of coffee, "Geisendorff was admitted to Parkview Hospital by an unknown good Samaritan. Suffered cracked ribs, gash on head, bruises from air bag. He was legally drunk when checked in. He claims he doesn't remember any of it."

Morrison asked, "Does he remember who brought him in?"

"He said it might have been a woman but the hospital staff said they never saw who brought him in."

Chief Crab strolled out of his office. "Melton, can you follow up on the Geisendorff case? Check with the Dome. My guess is Freddie was heading home after partying there."

Morrison added, "Ask them if they saw John Phillips there that night."

Melton's brow furrowed. "At Parkview?"

"No, at the Dome."

Melton gave him a two finger salute. "Right."

Crab updated Bailey. "State Patrol determined that there were probably two cars involved in the crash. Geisendorff was passing someone who managed to stop but then he skidded through the guardrail. Prints from the other car match the tread of the tracks in the road near the crash site."

Bailey turned to leave. "I'm late for a meeting. Keep me posted."

Crab turned to Morrison. "You hear back on the warrant?"

"Judge approved it. Sent it off but haven't gotten the ping back from the phone company yet."

Morrison's radio squawked. It was Gabby in dispatch. "Sam, got that information you've been waiting on."

Morrison and Crab rushed into dispatch, asking in unison, "Whatcha got?"

Gabby pointed to the screen. "Got a ping on Phillips' cell."

Crab asked, "Where is that?"

"Up north on Highway 69."

Morrison studied the picture. "A friend's house, maybe?"

Crab added, "Gotta be near St. Jude."

"I'm goin' out there today. Want me to check?" Morrison and Crab were startled by the sudden appearance of Deputy Sydney Jacobs. Sydney was about five-foot-eight, stocky, with a well-tanned face. Her broad nose and puffy lips gave her a distinctive appearance. She was sort of attractive in a quirky way.

Crab questioned, "Going north?"

Sydney bowed up defensively. "St. Jude. Time to visit grumpy Grampa."

"Oh, yeah, I forgot that Ralph Jacobs is your grandfather."

Sydney plunged her hands into her pockets. "Wish I could forget it."

Morrison butted in, saying, "Let me give you Phillips' description."

Frank stood in front of the door of Maire, the agoraphobiac, listening from a safe distance. There was silence. "Anyone home today?"

There was still silence. He knocked softly and waited. He heard shuffling noises and then the floor creak. The peep hole went dark. She was looking at him. "Anyone home today?" he repeated.

"Go away, pervert!"

Frank smiled brightly hoping his friendly face would change her mind.

"If you're not gone in two seconds, I'm calling Edith ... Mrs. Barkley."

Frank frowned. "Just trying to be neighborly."

"I'm dialing."

"Okay, okay." He turned and headed toward his room. Her rejection made him even more determined to learn more about Maire. White Feather's room was close, so he went there and knocked. There was no answer so he headed to the second floor.

He found Ralph and Monty still playing pool with Albert sitting in his favorite chair against the wall reading a newspaper. Frank took the chair next to Albert. Albert greeted him through the paper, "Good afternoon, Franklin."

Searching for White Feather, Frank did not answer. Albert closed the paper and studied his friend for a moment before asking, "What is troubling you?"

"Maire," was his short answer.

"The new resident . . . the agoraphobiac?"

"Yeah, that's the one. When I knocked on her door, she called me a pervert and threatened to call Mrs. Barkley."

Albert folded the paper and set it aside. "It would stand to reason, Franklin, that an agoraphobiac would want to be left alone."

"There's something not right with that woman, Albert."

Albert held out his hands, "Of course, she is agoraphobic."

TJ peeked into the room. "Oh, there you are!"

She raced across the room to Frank and whispered into his ear, "Mrs. Barkley wants to see you."

Frank gasped. "What for?"

TJ smiled and shook her head. "I don't know, but it sounded urgent."

TJ wiggled her finger. "Follow me."

Even Ralph stopped to watch TJ lead Frank out of the room.

As they stood in front of the red-doored elevator, Frank remembered the time Nurse Nujent had caught him trying to use it. She had scolded him and reminded him that the residents were not allowed to use the red elevator.

The doors opened and Frank waved in TJ first. As they rode up, Frank asked, "It's about Maire, isn't it?"

TJ frowned. "I really don't know, Frank. Did you do something to Maire?"

"Was just trying to be friendly."

TJ laughed. "She's not a friendly person. I hate delivering her tray."

"What does she look like?"

"Distinguished, I guess. She's about my height, petite, uppity, always wears a sweat suit."

The elevator lurched and the doors opened. TJ led him out into the wide corridor. As on all of the floors, a wide corridor ran the length of the building north-south. From the elevator, they turned left and TJ led him to the last office in the northeast corner. Frank was surprised to find the fourth floor in worse shape than the other floors. Since it held the administration offices, he expected this floor to have received the most attention.

Mrs. Barkley had a huge office. It was about the size of Lizzie's and Ruth's rooms combined, he guessed, and was positioned directly above them.

Mrs. Barkley looked up. "Have a seat, Frank. Thank you, TJ."

TJ quickly exited, closing the door behind her. Frank feared he was about to be banished from the Retirement Center. Nervously he offered, "Nice office."

Then he realized that it was not a nice office actually. It was old and decaying. Mrs. Barkley smiled and replied, "Thank you. Rather quaint wouldn't you say?"

She got to the point. "I got a call from Mrs. Rommel. She has accused you of harassing her."

"Is that Maire?"

Mrs. Barkley nodded and gave Frank a stern look. Frank answered meekly, "I was just trying to be friendly."

Barkley smiled. "I am sure you were, Frank. That is just the way you are and we all love you for it."

"I will leave her alone. I didn't know she was so ...."

"I think that would be best, Frank. Mrs. Rommel is very sensitive and is going through a difficult time right now."

Mrs. Rommel? The name sounded familiar to him, but he could not place it. He repeated the name in his mind several times hoping not to forget it.

"Maybe she needs a friend," Frank offered.

Barkley laughed out loud and then caught herself. "No." She looked out the window. "No, Frank. I don't think that is what she needs right now." She looked back into Frank's eyes. "I think we best respect her privacy. Okay?"

Frank held out his hands. "Sure, if you think that is best. Sure."

Mrs. Barkley raised an eyebrow. "Will you pass that on to your friends? I know how curious the Sleuthkateers can be.

They shared a short chuckle and then Mrs. Barkley got serious. "So, how is everything with you, Frank? I'm so proud of the way you seem to have adjusted."

Frank tilted his head. "Well, good, I guess."

Mrs. Barkley smiled and waited. Frank felt pressured to say something more. "I am worried about Lizzie, though. No one has seen her since the party."

"Yes, Ruth thinks she is angry about something and locked herself in her room. I stopped by and knocked but she did not respond. I thought I could hear her moving around, but she wouldn't talk to me."

"Kind of curious isn't it?"

"Yes, I suppose, but it is not the first time. Lizzie gets her feelings hurt and likes to pout sometimes."

"Maybe you should check on her."

"I tried that once before and it made matters ten times worse. I thought she would never speak to me. I think I would like to give her a little more time before I try that again. Like I said, I could hear her moving around so I think she is probably okay."

"Yeah, I can understand your reasoning."

Barkley smiled. After a moment of awkward silence, Frank raised his hands as if to say, "That's all I have."

Barkley stood. "Well, okay, Frank. Thank you for stopping by."

Frank replied, "My pleasure," regretting his choice of words immediately. Barkley chuckled as he slinked out.

Chapter 34

Grumpy Grampa

Sᴛ. Jᴜᴅᴇ's ғʀɪᴇɴᴅʟʏ ʀᴇᴄᴇᴘᴛɪᴏɴɪsᴛ, Naomi Johnson, looked up from her desk and smiled. "Good evening, Sydney."

"Hi, Naomi. Is my grumpy Grampa behaving?"

Naomi laughed. "Of course not."

Sydney cracked a rare smile. "You're working late."

"Had some paperwork I had to get done before a deadline."

Sydney pointed up with her thumb and Naomi waved her by. "Sure, go on up." She looked at the old grandfather clock. "He's probably in the pool room on the second floor."

The first floor was dark and quiet, almost spooky. Sydney strolled over to the elevator, pushed the button and hooked her thumbs in her heavy gun belt. The mic attached to her collar squawked. Bobby Joe was reporting in from Highway 69 South requesting a 10-27. He probably had another Texan pulled over for speeding.

She found her grandfather alone in the pool room slumped down in a chair with the pool cue leaning against his shoulder. He was asleep. He looked so pathetic that

Sydney almost let a tear loose. On the surface, Ralph was grouchy and cantankerous, but she knew that he had a big heart deep down and seeing him sitting there all alone was heart-wrenching for her. Her grandfather had suffered a lot of misery in his life, mostly thanks to Grammy Maggie.

Ralph's marriage had not been good. All she remembered of her Grammy Maggie was an overbearing woman, always drunk and demanding the center of attention. They had divorced when Sydney was eight years old, so most of what she knew about the marriage was from eavesdropping on her father and mother discussing it privately.

Ralph had lost his lucrative construction company in the divorce settlement. According to her father, Maggie had not wanted the firm but just wanted to spite Ralph. After the divorce, She immediately returned to Australia where her sister lived. The construction firm soon went into bankruptcy. Ralph was left a broken man who spent the rest of his working life doing odd jobs in construction and home repair.

Sydney had never liked either Maggie or Ralph growing up. Around Maggie, Ralph's life had been miserable. Then after the divorce, he had become sullen and irritable. He and her father argued constantly so over time they had stopped visiting him.

Her mother had taken so much abuse from Maggie that she hated her. And she had seemed to transfer her hatred to Ralph after Maggie had left the scene.

But through the infrequent visits, Sydney had learned a new side of her grampa. He treated her tenderly and for some reason was always patient and kind to her. She could never understand why he could not be that way with her father. They had become very close as she became older and got out on her own. After Ralph's brother died, she became the only family member Ralph had that seemed to care about him. But California was too far from Colorado so when his health finally prevented him from doing the only thing he knew, construction, Sydney had helped get him admitted into St. Jude.

Sydney sat down next to her slumbering grandfather and patted his knee. Her touch startled him and he glared at her at first and then smiled and then cleared his throat and restored his grumpy facade.

"What're you doin' here?"

Sydney smiled. She knew he was glad to see her. She saw that little smile and twinkle in his eye when he first saw her. "Looks like you're eating well, Grampa."

Ralph grumbled and then added, "Food's edible, barely. Birdie tries."

"Where's all of your friends?"

"They got tired of gettin' beat and went to bed."

"Maybe you should let'em win occasionally."

"Humph."

There followed a span of silence. Sydney felt badly that they didn't have much to talk about. Now she really wanted to bring up the Phillips case but Ralph surprised her by saying, "You look like you're eating well."

At least he was trying to keep the conversation going.

"I snack too much." She pushed her unruly hair out of her eyes.

Ralph sniped, "Shoot anybody lately?"

Sydney smirked. "It's been tempting at times. Need anybody shot?"

Ralph chuckled. "Too many to list."

Sydney saw it as an opportunity to segue. "Any new residents?"

Ralph seemed to perk up. "Yeah, actually, we got two new hags."

"Two?"

"Yeah, Meyer and Maire."

"That's odd. Do your names have to rhyme to get in at the same time?"

"Evidently."

Sydney was stuck. So, she tried a joke. "I guess you've got a new girlfriend now."

"Pshaw."

"Too ugly for you?"

Ralph rolled his head. "Meyer's okay, but stuck up."

Sydney chuckled. "Sounds like you've approached her."

"Told me she prefers to be left alone."

"Interesting. What does she look like?"

"Queen Mum."

"Of England?"

"Overdressed. Stiff posture. Eats like a bird."

"Tall, short, skinny, fat?"

"Plump, medium height. Kinda reminds me of your mother."

Sydney compared his description to Morrison's description of Agatha Phillips. They sounded pretty close. But her own mother would fit the description, too. Sydney glanced into the TV room behind the rec room. "She wouldn't happen to be in there, would she?"

Ralph glanced into the TV room. "Why? You want to meet her?"

Sydney said, "Sure."

Ralph shook his head. "What for? I ain't interested in her no more."

Now it was awkward so Sydney spilled the beans. "She sounds like a missing person we've been looking for."

"Her name Meyer?"

"No, Phillips . . . Agatha Phillips. She's also an author. Pen name's Agatha Christopher."

"Figures."

Sydney studied her grandfather. "What do you mean?"

"Them authors are all stuck on themselves." Ralph stood and ambled to the TV room. Sydney followed him, drawing the attention of the half dozen ladies sitting around the TV. Sydney smiled and gave a reserved wave. The ladies continued to glare at her. Ralph turned around and ambled out. "Ain't in here. Too high fallutin' for these hags."

The hags gasped and began whispering. Sydney was embarrassed and scolded her grandfather. "That wasn't very nice, Grampa."

"They know what they are," he retorted.

"What else do you know about Meyer?"

"She's apparently related to Nurse Nujent. Checked in Saturday."

"When Saturday?"

"Must have been late. We first saw her at the party that night with Nujent."

"Nujent's daughter?"

"Probably. Two peas in a pod. Albert could tell you more. He knows everything."

Sydney was intrigued. "Could we speak to him?"

Ralph led her down the corridor to the south hallway. Albert's room was at the end of the hallway on the left. Ralph banged on the door. "Open up, it's me."

"Grampa!" Sydney scolded. She listened closely and thought she could hear someone moving around. Ralph banged loudly on the door again, "Open up!"

"Shhh. Maybe he is asleep."

"Good."

The door cracked open and a puffy-eyed old gentleman with wild hair in a black robe peeked out. "What is it, Rudolph."

"Sydney wants to ask you some questions."

Albert looked at Sydney and then backed away opening the door wider for them to enter. "Please have a seat, Sydney. Nice to see you again." He switched on the light. The bed covers were pulled back.

"Nice to see you, too, Mr. Stein. Didn't mean to disturb you."

"Where do I sit?" Ralph whined.

"There's a spot on the floor over there, Rudolph."

Ralph pushed Sydney aside and plopped down in the recliner. Albert shook his head. "Perhaps we could share the foot of the bed, Deputy Jacobs?"

Sydney nodded and waited for Albert to straighten the covers before sitting on the bed. "Could I offer you something to drink? I have a nice wine opened." He looked at the uniformed deputy. "Unless you are on duty or something."

"No, a glass of wine would be nice."

"How about you, Rudolph?"

"I don't drink wine no more. Ex-wife did all the drinking for both of us."

Sydney frowned. She had seen Ralph drunk many times after he and Maggie divorced. Albert opened a small apartment refrigerator and peered in. "I have a Dr. Pepper."

"Oh, wonderful, wine'll have to do. Sydney is looking for an author that's gone missing. Thinks it might be Meyer."

Albert poured three wine glasses one-quarter full of red wine. "Oh? What makes you think it is Mrs. Meyer?"

Sydney shifted on the bed. "Oh, I don't know if there is any connection, but Grampa says she showed up here about the time Mrs. Phillips disappeared and the description matches."

Albert handed a wine glass to Sydney and then one to Ralph before sitting next to Sydney. "Interesting. We have learned that her name is Diana Elizabeth Nujent Meyer. We are just assuming that she is related to Alvira because of the Nujent part of her name. Although no one but Rudolph has actually spoken to her that I know of. Well, except, of course, she and Nurse Nujent spend a lot of time together. What do you know about Mrs. Phillips?"

"Agatha Phillips, alias Agatha Christopher, has lived in the valley for many years with her second husband, John Phillips. She dropped by the office several days ago and talked to Deputy Morrison about her son. Then we got a call Sunday from her husband that she was missing."

"Why would she come here?" Albert asked.

"Don't know that she did, but we have reason to believe that she has been hiding out in this area."

Albert nodded. "Interesting, but not likely she is our Mrs. Meyer."

"Grampa said there is another new resident."

Ralph answered, "She's worse than Meyer. No body's seen her."

Albert clarified, "All we know about her is that her name is Maire and that she is agoraphobic. She stays in her room so we have not seen her."

"Do you know when she checked in?"

"It must have been sometime Saturday night. No one that I know of saw her come in. I am sure Mrs. Barkley could fill you in."

Sydney glanced at her watch. "I'll bet she has already gone home."

Albert agreed. "Oh, yes, she would have gone by now. Maybe you could call her tomorrow."

Sydney felt that Mr. Stein was speaking to her like a child, but he was such a kind old man, she did not mind. He felt more like a father talking to her.

Ralph had downed the wine and was fiddling with the empty wine glass. "You're a cop. You could just go over and make Maire talk to you."

"Maybe I should talk to Mrs. Barkley first, Grampa."

Tuesday

Left by cruel vicissitudes,
to languish in our lassitude.

Chapter 35

Checking on Lizzie

FRANK WAS UP BEFORE daylight. As he finished shaving, his mind was on Lizzie. It had been more than two days since anyone had seen her. He heard a door shut. It sounded like it might be Lizzie's. Could it be? He rushed over, cracked open the door and peeked into the corridor, but it was empty. He stepped out to double-check only to find Lizzie's door was closed.

He decided to get dressed and check on her himself.

When he stepped out again, the corridor was still quiet. In the darkness, he could see that the light was still on in Lizzie's room. He found it curious that every time he had looked, the light had been on day and night since she locked herself inside.

He stopped at the east hallway that intersected with the corridor. To the right were the rooms of his neighbor, Ralph, and across the hallway, one of Lizzie's friends, the stern but responsible friend, Ruth.

He and Ralph shared a bathroom like Ruth and Lizzie. Frank chuckled to himself remembering his first day at St.

Jude when he had locked the door to Ralph's room when he used the bathroom to get cleaned up and forgot to unlock it afterward. Ralph had come charging through his room grumbling and scolding him for locking him out of his own bathroom. It was his first encounter with the grumpy old man.

A light came on in Frank's brain. Ruth and Lizzie had the same arrangement! Ruth could go into Lizzie's room from the bathroom at any time. She could lock Lizzie out of the bathroom, but he did not think that Lizzie could lock Ruth out of her room. Why had Ruth not thought of that?

Frank took a few more steps down the corridor to the north. He looked to his left down the west hallway where the doors to the rooms of Lizzie's friends Mary and Kate were on the north side of the hallway. He was now standing in front of Lizzie's door.

He placed his ear to the door and listened. Just as Mrs. Barkley and others had said, he could hear occasional ruffling sounds. Lizzie was either shifting in her bed or perhaps moving around in the room. He decided to knock gently on the door. The ruffling sound stopped. He listened. The ruffling started up again.

"Lizzie? Open up; it's Frank."

He listened. The ruffling sound stopped. "Lizzie, I know you're in there."

The room was quiet.

He was startled by a voice from behind him. "What are you doing, Frank!"

He spun around, his heart pounding. "Oh! Ruth, you startled me."

Ruth remained stoic. Frank tried to make an excuse. "I saw the light on in Lizzie's room and thought I would check on her." Ruth appeared to be unimpressed. He tried again. "I could hear her stirring, so I thought she must be awake."

"She won't come out, you know."

Frank was filled with anxiety. "No, I guess not."

He took a deep breath and summoned his courage to ask, "Have you gone into her room to check on her?"

Ruth glared at him, but he challenged her. "You share a bathroom with her, right? You could just peek in and check on her."

Ruth's confidence appeared to be slightly shaken by his suggestion. She looked away and thought for a moment. "You don't understand. Elizabeth appears to be so strong, but she is really very fragile."

Frank thought he might be beginning to understand. "You are afraid that she would be offended. That she might explode if you invaded her privacy?"

Ruth looked him in the eye. "Yes, exactly. Besides, she locks the door to her room from the bathroom."

Frank was puzzled. "You can't lock that door."

Ruth huffed, "Of course you can."

Frank was ready to argue, but Ruth turned and crooked her finger beckoning him to follow her into her room. The bathroom was immediately to the left.

Frank was impressed. Ruth's room was as neat as a pin and tastefully appointed. She pointed to the latch below the door knob. She demonstrated as she spoke, "See. Just turn the latch."

Frank was about to say that his door did not have a latch, but then decided to check first. "I guess I just never noticed."

"Most of us keep it locked for security as well as privacy."

"Excellent idea. But that means we have no way of secretly checking on Lizzie. Do you think it has been long enough that we should go to Mrs. Barkley?"

Ruth looked down and shook her head. "We had better have a very good reason before we go to Mrs. Barkley with this."

Frank was sympathetic. Knowing what little he knew about Lizzie, he could see that Ruth was right. He shrugged and asked, "It's been two days. How long do we wait?"

Ruth sighed. "Good question. I had hoped she would have reached out to me by now."

Frank was feeling a closeness to Ruth that he had never thought possible. Inside her stolid facade, maybe there was a big heart capable of compassion. Maybe, just maybe he was touching her compassionate side now. "Do you think that her run-in with Nujent and Mrs. Meyer is behind this?"

Ruth's vulnerability evaporated instantly. "What do you know about that?"

Frank's vulnerability flew to the forefront. "I-I just saw Lizzie arguing with Nujent and Mrs. Meyer at the party. Mrs. Meyer was upset. That's all I know."

Ruth backed off slightly. "I missed that. I heard about it later. Must be what this is about. Lizzie hasn't come out of her room since then."

Frank confessed, "I know it is none of my business, but I am just worried about her."

Ruth looked him over critically. "Why would you be worried about her?" Ruth raised an eyebrow and then matter-of-factly asked, "You danced with her at the party, didn't you? You got a thing for Miss Lizzie?"

Frank blushed and looked down. Ruth rubbed his shoulder. "It's okay, Frank. Few people see that side of Elizabeth. She is really a beautiful person inside. But her life has been a nightmare."

Frank looked at the door to Lizzie's room. "I know about some of it."

Ruth looked at Lizzie's bathroom door, then walked over and carefully turned the door knob. The deadbolt prevented her from pushing it open. She shrugged and led Frank back into her room and closed the door to the bathroom. "Would you like something to drink, Frank? I have a pot of tea on."

Frank muttered, "That would be nice. Thank you."

Ruth waved her hand over the recliner. "Please have a seat and I'll pour tea for us. Do you like sugar in yours?"

Frank sat down. "Yes, thank you."

Ruth fetched a couple of tea cups and saucers from a small cupboard next to the mirror above the lavatory in her room. The pot was sitting on a single electric burner on the counter. She poured sugar into the cups and then poured the steaming tea. As she washed a teaspoon and stirred each cup, Frank admired her spectacular view. She had double windows over her bed and double windows on the east wall.

"How did you manage such a great view?"

"I was one of the first residents. I sort of got my pick of rooms."

She glanced at Frank. "You are on the inside, aren't you? Bummer."

She handed him a cup and then pulled out a small chair from beside the lavatory for herself. She looked toward the shared bathroom. "I have known Elizabeth for some . . .," she stopped to add up the years, "sixty years, maybe."

Frank was surprised. Ruth took in a deep breath then sipped her tea. "It doesn't seem possible. Anyway, she was my very first case when I became a case worker for the Pueblo County Department of Social Services. She was a terrible wreck then. She had been a patient in the institution . . . this very building."

"Yes, I heard about that."

Ruth's brow wrinkled. "What did you hear?"

"Just that this building was originally an institution and later a hospital before it was a retirement center."

"Oh. Anyway, Elizabeth had overdosed on a drug and had been admitted to the institution for rehabilitation. When the institution closed, she was released and moved back home with her family. I was assigned to do periodic wellness checks."

Frank sipped his tea and then inquired, "How did she do after leaving the institution?"

"Well, she was very moody and depressed. Her parents didn't understand. They had supported admitting her because they thought she was possessed by the devil." Ruth chuckled. "So, when she came home, they were not convinced she had been ...."

Ruth looked at Frank and raised her eyebrows. "Exercised, if you know what I mean. It was not a happy homecoming.

Then a fire mysteriously started in the house and only Lizzie escaped alive. There was a big investigation and the papers blew it all out of proportion. I really don't know how she survived that period in her life. She moved in with an aunt who I think did an amazing job of comforting and under-standing poor Lizzie."

Ruth stopped to sip her tea and then resumed. "I spent a lot of time out there talking to Lizzie and her aunt. I was determined to save Lizzie."

Ruth stopped to stare into space as if remembering. "Eventually, we managed to get Lizzie a job working as a waitress, of all things, at a cousin's diner. To our surprise, she was amazingly good with the customers. They loved her crude, uncultured personality. She gave 'em heck and they loved it. And it was good for her as well."

Ruth had a little twinkle in her eye that told Frank she was having a good memory. "Then she met a boy. He was ... well, uncultured like her and they hit it off. After they got married, the case was closed. So I lost track of Lizzie."

Frank was curious. "When did you see her again?"

"We didn't get reacquainted until she moved in here!"

Ruth grew more serious. "What about you, Frank? What attracted you to her?"

Frank squirmed in the chair. The question caught him completely by surprise. "Wow! I don't know, Ruth."

Frank paused to come up with valid reasons. "Actually, I was afraid of Lizzie until the party. I guess it was when she walked into the dining room looking so poised and ... well, frankly, pretty. Maybe it was the contrast. Maybe it was seeing such a different side to her. It just tugged at my heart, you know? Here was a woman clearly battling demons who suddenly seemed to pull it together and triumph over it."

Ruth smiled and put her slant on it. "She was, if but for a moment, vulnerable."

"Yeah. She was so ... vulnerable and sad."

They both paused and sipped on their teas. Suddenly, Frank looked at the bathroom door and exclaimed, "Bathroom! Has she gone to the bathroom? You would notice that, wouldn't you?"

Ruth's face lit up and then her brow furrowed. "You know, I haven't heard her in there. That's a good point, Frank. I guess she could have, I mean, I haven't been here every minute."

"I don't know, Ruth, maybe we should ..."

Ruth looked into the distance and whispered, "Maybe we should."

Chapter 36

What's That Smell?

NAOMI JOHNSON HAD SPENT the morning working on her routine duties as the receptionist for St. Jude Methodist Retirement Center. She had put on the coffee, dusted the reception area, vacuumed the worn, aged carpet, and sorted the mail. She had taken the mail up to the fourth floor and distributed it to the desks of the staff. Now she was enjoying a quiet moment at her desk with her coffee.

She glanced at the old grandfather clock sitting in the southwest corner of the room and remembered that it needed to be wound. It was as she was twisting the last turn with the clock key that she heard the noisy men barging in.

She concluded immediately that the four men dressed in Khaki shirts and Levi pants were blue collar executives. "Yes? May I help you?"

The men started to answer in unison, but then deferred to the taller heftier man. "Good morning, ma'am, I'm Joe Conti, Lead Project Manager for CMI, Inc. This is Nelson, David, and Kirk. We're here to take a look at where the furnace is going and get the installation scheduled."

Naomi smiled at the men. "Hello. We weren't expecting you so soon! The furnace only arrived yesterday. I'm Naomi Johnson, the receptionist. Please have a seat and I will notify our administrator, Mrs. Barkley."

Joe put up his hands and declared, "Thanks, but I've been on my butt for three hours and it feels pretty good to stand."

The other three nodded agreement. Naomi picked up the phone, punched a button and pointed. "There is coffee on the table over there. ... Mrs. Barkley, there are four gentlemen here to talk to you about the furnace. ... Okay, I'll tell them."

Naomi hung up the phone. "She'll be right down. Make yourselves at home."

Chief Crab was appalled by Morrison's story. "What part of your brain thought that would work?"

Morrison leaned over, put his face in his hands and propped up his head with his elbows perched on his knees. "I know, I know. I think I've really blown it this time."

"She just hung up?"

"Yeah. What should I do, Buster?"

"You haven't tried to call her?"

"I can't. I just can't get up the nerve."

Crab shook his head. "Well, she ain't gonna call you back, you know."

"There's gotta be another way."

Crab reminded him, "You can't let this get in the way of seeing your kids."

"The kids! Oh, crap, Buster."

There was a soft rap on the door before Sheriff Bailey peeked in. "Working on the case?"

Morrison sat up and rubbed his eyes. Crab motioned for Bailey to come in. Bailey assessed the situation and replied, "Oh! I didn't mean to interrupt something personal."

Morrison insisted, "No, no, come in."

Sheriff Bailey walked in and sat in a chair next to Morrison. "Where do we stand?"

Morrison replied, "I've called Agatha's cell a dozen times. Just goes to voice mail. I keep asking her to call me back."

Bailey suggested, "Why don't you call John Phillips and ask him if he's heard from his wife?"

"Great idea." Morrison pulled out his cell phone. He had the Phillips' number in his contacts and dialed him. It rang and rang and finally went to voice mail. Morrison left a message to call back then directed his question to Undersheriff Crab. "Any idea what John Phillips does for a living?"

Crab sat back and raked his hand through his curly white hair. "I just assumed he and Agatha are retired, why?"

"Because he didn't answer my call just now"

Bailey asked, "Heard from Sydney?"

"No, not yet."

"I saw her coming out of the break room." He opened the door and hailed her to come in.

Sydney strolled up to the door clutching a steaming cup of coffee. Crab prompted her, "How's your Grampa, Sydney?"

"Grumpy as ever. I asked him and Mr. Stein about the new residents at St. Jude last night."

"Learn anything?"

Bailey suggested she sit so she slipped out to bring in another chair. "Two new residents checked in Saturday night . . . a Mrs. Meyer and a recluse named Maire."

"They have the same name?"

"No. One's last name is M-E-Y-E-R. The other's first name is M-A-I-R-E."

"One is a recluse?"

"She has one of those crazy phobias and stays in her room."

"Both checked in Saturday night? That sounds curious," Crab remarked.

Jacobs agreed. "That's what I thought."

Morrison asked, "Either one fit the description?"

"Meyer, M-E-Y-E-R does, actually, but according to Mr. Stein, she is related to Nurse Nujent." Sydney pulled out her notepad. "Her full name is Diana Elizabeth Nujent Meyer."

Crab repeated, "NUJENT Meyer?"

Morrison made a note, and then asked, "Your grandfather know anything about the recluse?"

"No one in Grampa's circle has seen her. All they know is that her first name is Maire. I'm going to call Mrs. Barkley later and see what she knows."

Bailey commended her. "Good work, Jacobs. They both sound interesting."

Morrison added, "Phillips could be hiding out there ... changed her name."

Crab added, "When you talk to Edith, ask her what she knows about the recluse's background."

And Morrison added, "See if she can give you a description of the woman."

As she pulled out her cell phone, Jacobs headed out of the office.

The three men had just finished pouring and prepping their coffee when Mrs. Barkley entered the room. After introductions, Mrs. Barkley clasped her hands and asked, "How may I help you?"

The phone rang and everyone looked at Naomi as she picked it up. Joe Conti glanced at his colleagues and then asked, "Could we start by looking at the area where the furnace is to be installed?"

"Of course, follow me."

As she passed by Naomi Johnson's desk, Naomi put her hand over the receiver. "It's Deputy Jacobs for you."

Mrs. Barkley paused. "Is it urgent? Can I call her back?"

Naomi asked and then nodded. Mrs. Barkley instructed her to get the cell phone number and then led the men into the wide corridor and to the stairwell next to the elevator. She explained, "The basement is off limits to the residents, so we keep it locked."

She produced a keyring with assorted keys, rifled through them to find the basement door key, inserted the key and then tugged on the door. The very old door was stuck, so one of the men grabbed the knob and jerked it open.

A whoosh of hot air rushed over them and delivered a horrible stench that made even the tough construction engineers gag, cough, and back away. "What the ..."

Mrs. Barkley covered her nose and mouth and exclaimed, "Oh, dear, what is that smell?"

Joe declared, "Smells like something died in your basement!" He slammed the door shut. But it was not soon enough to save the corridor from filling with the malodor. Barkley waved her hand in front of her face and declared, "Peeyoooweee."

Birdie and several residents rushed out of the dining room holding their noses. When Birdie saw Mrs. Barkley, she questioned, "You smell that?"

Barkley declined to remove her hand from her nose and nodded. Then she pointed toward the basement door and explained, "Something died in the basement."

Birdie shook her head and waved her hands around her head as if shooing off flies. "Lordy! We better get some fans set up and open the doors."

While Birdie took charge of this task, Mrs. Barkley turned to Joe. "You sure you want to see the basement?"

Joe rolled his head, "No ma'am," and then laughed heartily. He turned to David. "Go out to the truck. I've got some masks in the toolbox."

While David was retrieving the masks, the other men helped Birdie set up fans and open doors. When David returned, he passed out the masks. After they donned them, Joe turned on his heavy duty spotlight and they proceeded down to the putrid-smelling basement.

At the base of the stairs, he found a switch that turned on a single dim light mounted over the boiler across the room. Joe flashed his spotlight around to get his bearings. "Looks like you've got prairie dogs down here."

Barkley questioned through her mask, "Prairie dogs?"

Conti focused his light across the room and through a wide arch into another dark room where dozens of mounds could be seen. "Good grief!" Barkley declared as she waved her hands around her face. "Where did all these flies come from?"

Dave said, "They're attracted to the spotlight."

Barkley replied, "But I haven't seen a fly in months."

"What's that?" Kirk shouted, pointing at something red on the floor near the center of the antechamber.

Joe aimed his light on it. "Looks like a body!"

They rushed over to the bloated body in an evening gown. Barkley screamed, "Lizzie!"

Chapter 37

Surprise Discovery

CRAB'S PHONE BUZZED. "CRAB here. ... When? ... Oh, my god! Thanks, Gabby."

Crab looked up. "We have a homicide at the retirement center."

Morrison responded, "Who?"

"Elizabeth Dawson. Melton, you've got the Phillips case. I'm putting Morrison on the homicide out at St. Jude."

Melton put down his coffee and gave his trademark two-fingered salute, and then requested, "I want Sydney."

Crab frowned and pointed a thumb discretely at Calhoun. Melton shook his head as he picked up his coffee. Calhoun was glaring at the chief like a deer caught in headlights. He whined, "I'm already on the case."

Crab grabbed his coat. "You still are." Then he turned to Morrison. "Follow me out there; I want to see the crime scene."

Sheriff Bailey offered, "I'll call the coroner and ask CBI for a team. I'll come out later. Let me know what you find."

Morrison had grabbed his coat and was already rushing out the back door. "Roger that."

Frank and Ruth had tried to call Mrs. Barkley to request a meeting to discuss checking on Elizabeth, but she was not answering her phone.

"I don't have her cell phone, do you?"

"I don't have a cell phone," Frank admitted.

"Oh, well, let's get dressed and go look for her."

It was a quiet ride down in the elevator to the ground floor. They would start by checking with Naomi in reception. When the doors opened the smell overwhelmed them and they began coughing and gagging. All of the doors on the first floor were flung open and fans were set up to try to push the stink out, but it was too strong.

Frank and Ruth found a growing crowd of lookie-loos gathering in the corridor.

A dozen or so had had enough and tried to flee into the elevator to escape, forcing Frank and Ruth to have to fight their way out. They found Mrs. Barkley standing with four men. Ruth charged up to her. "What's going on?"

"Oh, Ruth, I am so sorry. It's Lizzie."

"Lizzie? That's what we've come to talk to you about."

Barkley placed her hand on Ruth's shoulder. "She's dead, Ruth. We found her in the basement. She's been stabbed."

Ruth gasped and put her hands over her mouth, tears began streaming. "Stabbed?"

Frank was in shock. "Murdered?"

Barkley broke down. "Yes, she's been murdered!"

"When did it happen?"

Barkley shook her head. "That's all I know."

Undersheriff Buster Crab and Deputy Morrison burst through the doors from reception, stopped and grabbed their handkerchiefs to cover their nose and mouth and pushed their way to the basement stairway where Mrs. Barkley and four unfamiliar tough-looking men were waiting. They looked like bandits with their masks covering half of their faces.

Frank and Ruth were joined by White Feather. They had a front row seat by the elevator doors. Buster got to the point. "What've we got?"

Mrs. Barkley answered, "We found Lizzie dead in the basement! Oh, Chief Crab, these men are with CMI. They came to get the furnace installation started."

Joe reached out his hand. "I'm Joe Conti, Lead Project Manager for CMI, Inc. This is Nelson, David, and Kirk."

Buster shook their hands. "I'm Undersheriff Buster Crab of the Wet Mountain Valley Sheriff's Office and this is investigating Deputy Sam Morrison."

Mrs. Barkley continued, "When we opened the door to the basement, the smell was overwhelming. We knew something had ... anyway, we found Elizabeth down there."

Joe Conti butted in. "Looks like she's been dead for several days . . . stabbed."

Mrs. Barkley was defensive. "We last saw her Saturday night at our party. We also celebrated her birthday that night." Then Mrs. Barkley broke down sobbing.

Crab put his hand on her shoulder. "I'm sorry, Edith."

A tall man approached. County Coroner Al Vanderberg was not a young man, but was trim and physically fit. Crab hailed him over, "Al, over here!"

Al waved and hurried over. Crab handled introductions. "Al, you know Sam, and this is Edith Barkley, St. Jude's administrator."

Barkley reached out her hand. "Oh, yes, I remember you from the poisoning."

Al shook her hand and frowned. "Poisoning? Oh, yes, yes, Benjamin Cook as I recall."

He addressed Crab, "What do we have this time, Buster?"

"We haven't seen the body yet. Edith found Elizabeth Dawson dead in the basement, apparently stabbed to death."

"In the basement? Oh, okay, well can you show me?"

"We need to see the body, Edith."

Barkley handed Crab the key. "I'm not going down there again, Buster."

"That's okay. Joe, can you show us the body? We'll need for everyone else to remain up here."

Conti nodded. "Sure."

"Al, this is Joe Conti. He is here to install a new furnace and was with Edith when they found the body."

Conti shook hands with Vanderberg and then helped Crab force open the sticky door. The malodor of death and hot air blasted them, offending their senses and driving away the lookie-loo residents. One of the men handed masks to Buster and Morrison, but Al waved off his. Instead, Vanderberg pulled out a small green jar and swabbed Vicks under his nose. Joe switched on his spotlight and led the two law officers and coroner to the basement.

As they entered the large room housing the boiler, Joe shined his spotlight into the next chamber. "The body's over there in that room."

Al touched Joe's arm. "Thank you. We can take it from here."

Joe nodded gratefully, passed over his spotlight, and returned back upstairs.

The basement was almost unbearably hot and sultry. Al cautioned, "We'll have to be careful of the crime scene, Buster. We don't want to disturb any of the tracks around the body. Give me a minute and I'll mark off an area where we can walk."

After a few moments, Al waved them over. "We're okay up to this line. I've marked off a space east of the body that has no tracks. You can examine the body from there. There is a jeweled handle, maybe a knife, lodged in her chest. I don't see any other wounds. It is hard to tell how long she's been dead. With this heat, the body would decompose quickly. I'd say she's been dead only a couple of days."

Buster looked over the body with the narrow beam of light, quickly spotting the jeweled handle standing upright in the middle of her chest. Morrison questioned, "Ever seen a knife like that?"

Crab was old enough to remember. "Looks like a fancy letter opener."

Her swollen hands were gripping the handle of what was either a knife or perhaps a letter opener. Morrison knelt down to get a closer look, waving his hands to shoo away the flies. "Where did all these flies come from? We don't have flies like this up here."

Al answered, "They come out of nowhere when there is a dead body. There'll be maggots."

Morrison leaned over to examine the weapon. "Man, this thing is really old. It's rusty."

Buster suggested, "Let's get out of here. The CBI team should be here soon."

When they turned to leave, they were startled by the presence of the old Indian resident. "Good, Lord, White Feather, you scared the bejesus out of me!"

"There are two."

Crab frowned. "Two?"

White Feather pointed to a shallow grave nearby. "Long time dead."

Al challenged. "Who are you? This is a crime scene. You shouldn't be down here."

Crab raised his hands. I'm sorry, White Feather, you'll have to ...."

White Feather turned and strolled off toward the stairway. Al advised, "This one's been dead for years."

He cautiously marked off an area for them to walk near the second body. Crab and Morrison were shocked by the shriveled remains in a flowery dress, only partially visible from the waist up.

Morrison kicked into detective mode. He pointed beside the grave. "Note the shovel and broom. Someone's been digging, possibly searching for this."

Crab looked at the dirt floor. "Footprints by the body."

Morrison expanded, "Small . . . looks like a woman's footprint."

Al motioned for them to take a wide path to bypass the bodies and prints. Morrison swept the area with his flashlight. "They should be able to lift some prints."

Crab was curious. "What do you think happened here?"

Morrison shook his head. "Hard to say. Looks like maybe Elizabeth surprised someone digging up an old grave."

Crab questioned, "Wonder what she was doing down here, especially in that party dress?"

"Barkley mentioned a party. Her birthday party, wasn't it?"

Crab sighed. "Yeah, happy birthday . . . ."

Morrison pulled out his phone and started snapping pictures. Al pulled out a camera and joined him. Crab turned. "I'll be out front. I want to talk to Edith."

Morrison answered as he continued to shoot pictures, "I'll be right up."

Al added, "Tell her I'll need next of kin and all that."

Chapter 38

Leads

CRAB FOUND WHITE FEATHER and Joe Conti waiting in the corridor. He shoved the basement door closed and pointed to reception and led them out front for fresh air.

Joe questioned, "I guess the basement is a crime scene now?"

"Oh, yes, probably for several days at least."

Conti reached into his shirt pocket. "I guess we'll get out of your way." He handed Crab his card. "Can you call me when it's okay for us to check out the basement? We're staying at Hillside."

Crab nodded. Conti joined his colleagues waiting by their rented pickup. They loaded up and left.

Crab remarked to White Feather, "Edith says that Lizzie was last seen at a party Saturday night."

"Had fight with Nujent. Went to room. Presumed she locked herself in. Could hear noises inside."

"So, she wasn't thought to be missing?"

Crab took White Feather's silence to be an affirmative answer. White Feather was prone to avoid answering or stating the obvious. Buster's phone buzzed. It was Sheriff Bailey. "Sean. ... Yeah, we found Elizabeth Dawson stabbed in the chest. Her body is in the basement. She's been dead several days. ... Yes sir, they thought she had locked herself in her room. Thought they could hear her in there. ... I haven't talked to Edith yet, just White Feather. ... Roger. There's more, Sean. There's another body down there. . . . Yeah, and it looks like someone tried to dig it up. Been dead for years looks like. ... Okay, I'll keep you posted."

Edith Barkley and Deputy Morrison came out the door and joined White Feather and Crab. Her eyes were puffy and red and she was pale.

"Edith, White Feather tells me you thought Elizabeth was holed up in her room."

"Yes. I went by to check on her several times, but she wouldn't talk to me. I thought I could hear her inside so I let her be."

Buster was seeking clarification. "But you didn't go in to actually check on her?"

Edith dropped her head. "No. Looking back, I should have, but it wasn't the first time Elizabeth has locked herself in her room for several days. Last time she was furious when I used my master key to enter uninvited. She stayed angry for weeks."

"So, you didn't want to make matters worse. Knowing Lizzie, I understand.

Morrison asked, "Did you know about her fight with Nujent Saturday night?"

Edith's eyes expressed surprise. "Fight?"

White Feather stepped in, "Nujent introduced Meyer to

Dawson. Dawson got upset, started yelling, left dining room. Nujent followed."

Barkley was clearly agitated. "Alvira didn't tell me about that."

Morrison made a note. "I think we should talk to Nujent. And I would like to look at Lizzie's room."

Morrison, reading from his notebook, added, "Maybe I could talk to Mrs. Meyer? And I would also like to talk to the new resident, Maire."

Barkley pushed her hair back and sighed. "That won't be easy. Maire won't let strangers into her room. She has agoraphobia."

"I assume you have seen her?"

"Yes."

"Can you describe her?"

Barkley put a finger beside her mouth and looked into the distance. "Well, she's in her eighties, refined, petite ..."

Morrison looked up from his notepad. "Petite?"

"Tiny little lady about this high." Barkley held her hand up about shoulder high. Morrison judged it to be about five foot even, maybe. He put a star next to her name.

Crab asked, "Not her?"

Morrison shook his head. "Nope. Age is wrong and Agatha is a hefty woman and much taller."

Barkley's brow wrinkled. "Who is Agatha?"

Crab smiled. "Missing person."

Morrison looked at Barkley. "What can you tell me about Meyer?"

Barkley cocked her head to one side. "Well, she IS hefty. She is reserved and attractive for her age—sixties, I would say, and stylish in a subdued way. She's about my height, five-foot-eight."

"Do you know where she came from?"

"Oh. She is Alvira's daughter. Her name is Diana. She is recently divorced and moved back from somewhere in Africa. She was with Doctors Without Borders, I believe."

Crab asked, "Does she qualify to live here?"

Barkley smirked. "Well, not really. She actually pays for her room and board. We granted her the privilege because of Alvira. It's just temporary. As you know, Buster, housing is difficult in the Wet Mountain Valley."

Crab and Morrison nodded in agreement. They knew. Morrison suggested, "Can we start with Nujent?"

The stench on the first floor prompted Birdie to set up sandwiches for residents in the parlor on the second floor. Frank found Albert, Monty, and Ralph and they took their trays to the pool room. Frank glanced around. "Where's White Feather?"

Albert answered, "We haven't seen him for a while. We left after Undersheriff Crab arrived. The smell was unbearable. White Feather stayed."

Ralph commented, "Injuns are used to stinky dead people."

Albert rolled his eyes. Monty protested, "Th-That's r-ridiculous."

Frank needed confirmation. "Was it really Lizzie?"

"That's what we heard."

"So who's been stirring in her room all this time?"

Albert stated the obvious, "It clearly was not Elizabeth."

Chief Crab, Deputy Morrison, Mrs. Barkley, and White Feather found Nurse Nujent at her desk in the St. Jude clinic. Mrs. Barkley began the conversation, "Alvira, Chief Crab and Deputy Morrison want to talk to you about Lizzie."

Nujent's jaw flexed. "What did she die of?"

Chief Crab sat in one of the guest chairs. "It looks like she died from a stab wound."

Mrs. Barkley took the other chair leaving White Feather and Morrison to stand. Nujent looked at White Feather. "What's he doing here?"

Chief Crab chuckled. "Is there a problem?"

Nujent shifted in her chair. "There's another chair in the examining room."

White Feather folded his arms and closed his eyes. "I'm fine."

Morrison found the chair and dragged it in, pulling out his notebook as he sat. "When was the last time you saw Mrs. Dawson?"

Nujent glared at the deputy. "Saturday night at the party."

"I understand you and Mrs. Dawson had an argument."

Nujent glared at White Feather. "That is correct."

Morrison crossed his legs. "Want to tell us about it?"

Nujent shifted her glare back to Morrison. "No."

Buster squinted at her. "If you don't want to talk about it here, Alvira, we can go down to the Sheriff's office."

Nujent folded her arms and pursed her lips stubbornly.

Mrs. Barkley asked, "Alvira, would you be more comfortable if White Feather and I left you three alone?"

Nujent squirmed in her chair avoiding an answer. Mrs. Barkley stood. "Come on, White Feather, let's give them some privacy."

She and White Feather strolled out to the hallway. Barkley put her mask back over her nose and mouth. "Oowee!"

White Feather produced a small canister from a pouch attached to his belt and handed it to her. "Smear a little in your nostrils."

Mrs. Barkley opened the small jar, swiped some of the salve on her finger and rubbed it around the edges and under her nose. She sniffed, raised her eyebrows and handed back the jar. "Old Indian recipe?"

"Vicks VapoRub."

Barkley laughed. "Shall we go sit in the parlor to wait?"

White Feather closed his eyes. "I'll wait here."

"Oh, Okay. Then I think I'll go up to my office."

White Feather backed up to the wall, closed his eyes and listened.

Chapter 39

Nujent's Story

In Nujent's office, Morrison tried his question again. "Tell me what you and Mrs. Dawson argued about."

Nujent huffed. "That's between me and Elizabeth."

Crab stepped in. "Alvira, Elizabeth has been murdered."

Nujent squirmed in her chair. "I don't want this to get out. Others are involved."

Crab leaned forward. "This is a murder investigation. We can't promise that we can keep your secret."

"You have to promise me you'll try."

Crab's curiosity was really piqued now. "If at all possible."

Nujent took a deep breath, snatched a couple of tissues off her desk, sniffed and complained, "I don't know where to begin."

Morrison's trite answer reflected his impatience. "Just start at the beginning."

Nujent rolled her eyes. "Lizzie and I go way back. We met at the Steelworks Clinic. I was just a teenager, maybe seventeen. We were living in Pueblo. Father worked for the Steel Mill as a smelter. Mother worked in the admin office.

It was a good place to work back then. They were good to the employees and the company paid well. The company even had its own clinic."

Nujent looked at Crab for reassurance. He asked, "You met Elizabeth at the clinic?"

"Well, when a job opened up at the clinic for a nurse's aide, my mother pulled some strings to get me hired. It was a low-level starting position, but I was very excited and grateful for the opportunity. That's where I met Elizabeth."

Morrison was surprised. "In Pueblo?"

Nujent blew her nose again and explained, "Elizabeth was already working at the clinic. She had been there probably six months when I started."

Nujent paused to stare into space. "She was so pretty back then. She had long blonde hair, a perfect figure, and a bright, happy personality. Everyone loved her."

Nujent looked into Buster's eyes. "Including me. She was sort of assigned to be my mentor and we hit it off right away. She was so much fun. We laughed and cried and worked hard and felt like we were making a difference by helping people . . . making the world better for others."

Nujent was smiling now, a twinkle in her eye from the memories. "At that time Dr. Howard was in charge but there was also a handsome, young, brilliant doctor named Stephen Weisman."

Morrison was getting impatient. "This is all very interesting, but is it pertinent to your argument with Mrs. Dawson?"

Crab recognized the name. "Stephen Weisman wrote Elizabeth a letter, I think. We found it when we were looking for her before."

Nujent stared at Crab as he pulled out his phone and searched for the picture of the letter. Crab showed it to Morrison.

Morrison asked Nujent, "Did you know about this?"

"Oh, yes, I gave it to her."

Morrison read the letter again and then returned the phone to Crab. "Does he have anything to do with your altercation with Mrs. Dawson?"

"He has everything to do with it."

Buster encouraged her. "Tell us about Dr. Weisman."

Her face expressed a strange mixture of sadness and fondness. "All the girls swooned over Dr. Weisman. We all flirted with him; he flirted back. After I finished my initial training, I was assigned to be his assistant. All the girls were jealous of me."

Her eyes sparkled for a moment. "I loved it. He was great to work for. He let me call him Dr. Steve."

Morrison noticed her glance back at a picture on her credenza. It was a handsome young man dressed in a white smock. "Is that Dr. Weisman?"

Nujent looked back again and paused. "Yes, that's Steve, Dr. Weisman. It was taken at the clinic."

Crab concluded, "So, you had a thing for each other?"

"Well, I had a crush on him, but it was Elizabeth that really caught his eye. She was clearly his favorite. Pretty soon they were looking at each other in that way lovers steal glances of each other; touching each other as if accidental; meeting privately in his office. It didn't take a rocket scientist to see that they were having an affair."

Morrison goaded her. "How did you feel about that?"

Nujent looked down and rubbed her hands together. "I was happy for her. But then Elizabeth began to change. At first I thought she was just in love. Her eyes would be watery and her face flushed. She started having trouble concentrating and became forgetful."

Nujent looked across at Buster. "He was giving her drugs. I don't know what, but she got worse and then started hallucinating and suffering dizzy spells and disorientation."

She paused to reflect. Morrison prompted her. "What happened?"

Alvira shook her head. "One day she snapped. I was coming back from a patient's room when I saw the staff racing down the hall toward the front door. Out of curiosity, I followed them."

Nujent closed her eyes. "Elizabeth was standing on one of the projections on the roof, like a fancy drainage spout. It was barely wide enough for her feet, but she was balanced out on the end of it with her hands raised to the sky, like she was spreading her wings. Her eyes were closed and she was smiling with her head tilted back. The breeze was blowing her hair and her dress back as if she were flying."

Nujent opened her eyes. "Dr. Steve, I mean Dr. Weisman, ordered us to grip a blanket and hold it up just as Elizabeth leaned forward and sailed off the roof, rotating and landing on her back in the blanket."

Nujent started fiddling with her nurse's apron. "Elizabeth was checked out in the clinic and then transferred to Thirteenth Street."

Morrison interrupted, "Thirteenth Street?"

Nujent glanced up. "The Mental Health Complex on Thirteenth Street there in Pueblo. Dr. Steve was devastated by the incident. He visited Elizabeth regularly."

Nujent shrugged and pursed her lips. "Not long afterward, he was given the position of director for the Wet Mountain Branch of the Colorado Institution for the Insane." Nujent raised an eyebrow. "This building was originally the Wet Mountain Institution for the Insane."

Morrison looked up. "This building?"

Crab nodded his head. "I had heard that." He turned to Morrison. "This building was originally a branch institution. Later it was repurposed as a hospital.

Morrison questioned Nujent, "So, what happened next?"

"The previous director was forced to resign under pressure. He had created quite a mess and there was a terrible scandal. Steve was so excited, though. He had all these lofty ideas for how to run the institution and help the mentally ill."

Nujent looked up and stated with pride, "He took me with him. I was so starry eyed and so in love with him, I didn't even notice that he kept me in the position of a lowly nurse's aide. I just wanted to be with him, to work beside him. I worshiped him. I would have done anything for him."

She took a deep breath. "Almost immediately, he transferred Elizabeth over. He told me that she was being mistreated at Thirteenth Street and he wanted to try to help her. When she arrived at Wet Mountain, I hardly recognized her. She looked terrible. Her beautiful hair was natty, her eyes puffy and red, her lips chapped and bleeding, and she smelled. She was drugged heavily and listless.

"Dr. Steve tried to act as if she was just another patient, but I could see it in his eyes. She became an obsession for him. He was determined to restore her to her former self. She became his little experiment."

Nujent paused to reflect. Then she shivered and resumed the story. "It didn't take long before Steve realized he was in over his head at the Wet Mountain Institution. All his lofty ideas ...." She teared up. "Things were so bad; he was so overwhelmed. There was little chance to enact his great plans. There were too many patients and too little staff and too little money. He had to resort to what the previous director had done, manage them with drugs.

"Elizabeth became his number one priority. And he assigned her to be my number one priority, too."

Tears welled up in her eyes and her lower lip trembled. "I don't think he even realized how much he hurt me. I don't think he meant to be cruel. He couldn't help it. He was still in love with Elizabeth. I thought he loved me, too. Seeing him pay so much attention to Elizabeth was hurtful. But I loved him so much; I couldn't stop loving him. I just sucked it up and put up with it.

Alvira continued, "Elizabeth did start to improve. She had good days and bad. I really thought that she might recover. The hardest part was yet to come, though. Elizabeth turned up pregnant."

Nujent began to tremble all over. "I was furious! How could a brilliant man be so stupid? How could the director of a huge institution be so incompetent? How could he be so insensitive? How could he do that to me?"

Nujent broke down. Her pain penetrated Buster's heart and left him wishing he could wring the doctor's neck. He wished there was something he could do to wipe away her broken heart. He stood, "How about some coffee?"

She nodded. Morrison raised a finger to include himself.

Chapter 40

It All Came Crashing Down

THE CHIEF HANDED MRS. Nujent and Morrison coffee and reclaimed his seat opposite the nurse. She had calmed down and was no longer shaking. She enjoyed several gulps of coffee before Morrison encouraged her to continue.

"We had been there about a year when it all came crashing down. When Elizabeth began to show, Steve had moved her to the fourth floor and assigned me to look after her. By then, Elizabeth had made good progress. She was off the drugs, had gotten her color back, and was becoming more rational, more normal. She wasn't her old self, you understand. She wasn't the bubbly, happy, confident girl that she was when I first met her. But she seemed to be reconciling with her situation and resigned to her fate."

Morrison asked, "How did she feel about being pregnant?"

"Most of the time she seemed happy about having a baby, although anxious at the same time. I don't think Steve was very excited about being a father. Of course, it was a dagger in my heart watching him with her.

"Then it happened. I had just been with her and was about to make my rounds when I saw Steve coming down the hall. I could tell immediately that something was terribly wrong. As he got closer, I could see that his eyes were crazed, his face red, his shoulders hunched. He grabbed me by the arm and dragged me to a corner to whisper one word, 'Inspectors!'"

Buster repeated, "Inspectors?"

"I didn't get it at first. He just kept repeating urgently 'Inspectors, inspectors.' Then he said, 'You've got to hide her.' 'Where?' I asked. He was panicked. 'The basement,' he said."

Buster shifted in his chair and glanced at Morrison for his reaction. He encouraged Nujent. "Please continue."

"I asked him when they would arrive and he told me they were in the lobby waiting for him. He instructed me to use the south stairway and to steer clear of hallways and elevators.

"I raced back into Elizabeth's room, grabbed her and threw a blanket over her shoulders. Strangely, she didn't ask questions, just followed me to the stairwell. She was probably close to eight months pregnant. Descending five stories down stairs was a risky feat for her. We had to stop often and by the time we reached the basement, she was in great pain and exhausted.

"As we descended the last flight, I realized how stupid I had been. The basement was hot, stinky, and dark. I had only brought the one blanket and no flashlight or food or anything. I left Elizabeth sitting on the steps and rushed back up to the first floor. Steve was standing in the corridor talking to four men in cheap suits. When he saw me, he excused himself and rushed over to me.

"He whispered that he had stuffed Elizabeth's file in a drawer behind the reception desk. He wanted me to get it and hide it. I told him that Elizabeth was in bad shape and that I needed to take some things to her. He was perturbed and insisted I 'first hide the file.' Then he rushed back to the men.

"I found the file and decided to hide it under the driver's seat of my car. When I came back inside, one of the inspectors was waiting for me. My stomach flew up into my chest. He said that Steve had told him I would help him go through the files. I couldn't believe it! Hadn't he heard me tell him I needed to get back to Elizabeth?

"I tried to beg off by telling the grim man that I could get him started but then I needed to get back to my rounds. I led him into the file room and quickly explained the filing system. But when I tried to leave, he demanded I help him find the file for Diana Elizabeth Austin."

Nujent took a deep breath and shook her head. "I went through the motions and acted surprised when the file was missing. I told him I would go get one of the file clerks to search for it. But it was as if he couldn't hear me or my words were in another language. He insisted that I find it.

"Pretending to look through the files and then checking a couple other files, I mumbled something about misfiling. Then I insisted we get a file clerk. He followed me to Joyce's office. I felt badly dumping him on her, but I was desperate to get back to Elizabeth.

"I used the south stairs to avoid running into anyone. I got some warm clothes from her room, some more blankets and found a flashlight in the hall maintenance closet. When

I got back to Elizabeth, she was slumped over and leaning against the wall beside the stairs. I switched on the flashlight and scanned the floor. Big rats scampered out of the light beam everywhere I flashed it. Poor Elizabeth, how could I leave her down there on a dirt floor in a dark room full of rats?

"She was in terrific pain and having contractions but bravely soldiered on with me into the cavernous rooms. It was steamy hot down there. There was this one room behind the boilers where the previous administrator had performed secret sterilizations. It had a concrete floor, an operating table, and cabinets and files along the back walls. Surgical lamps hung from the ceiling. I switched on the lamps and helped Elizabeth on to the operating table where I hoped the mice would not bother her. I covered her with the blankets and she curled up into a fetal position.

"I told her that I would be back to check on her and handed her the flashlight. I turned out the light and, fortunately, the boiler provided enough light for me to find my way out.

"I slipped back up to the first floor break room, which was next to the stair well, I snuck into the kitchen, raided a sack of sandwiches from the refrigerator and filled a thermos with coffee. Luckily, I found another flashlight in the cabinet and raced back to the basement.

"Elizabeth was drawn up with pain. When I showed her the food and thermos, she simply nodded. I realized later that she had gone into labor. But at the time, my mind was cluttered with a million other things.

"I found Joyce and the inspector exchanging heated words in the file room so I tried to calm them down, telling the inspector that obviously the file had been misplaced. That Joyce and I would need to go search the other offices. I suggested we start in Dr. Weisman's office but the inspector protested. He argued that if the file was in the doctor's office, why would Dr. Weisman have sent him to the file room?

"I was persistent and managed to convince him there was merit to checking Steve's office. Steve came in while we were searching and explained that Elizabeth was not in her room so he had organized a search party to look for her. He suggested Joyce and the inspector go check the other offices for the file. With them out of the way, he directed me to go get the file, take out any paperwork that pertained to her pregnancy, and present it to the inspector. I told him that Elizabeth was suffering great pain and needed attention. So, he promised me that while I was getting the file, he was going to slip down to the basement. He wanted me to join him after I gave up the file."

Nujent placed her hand on her forehead and pushed her hair back. "I was shocked when I joined Steve and Elizabeth in the basement. There were towels, bottles of alcohol, and surgical equipment scattered on the bloody blanket around Elizabeth. She was unconscious and Steve was wiping his hands on a towel. He told me that Elizabeth had given birth but the baby was still born and ordered me to get rid of the fetus. That's when I realized that he had performed a C-section on poor Elizabeth on a dirty blanket in that filthy room without adequate antiseptic. I was appalled. He had dumped the fetus in a metal box. He told me that I should get a shovel and bury it.

"He picked Elizabeth up and we headed for the center stairs that came out next to the elevator. We managed to sneak into the elevator and get Elizabeth to the third floor. Steve explained that a room below Elizabeth's was vacant. We got her safely into that room and into bed. He sent me to find the search party and tell them that apparently Elizabeth had gotten confused and thought she was in her room on the fourth floor."

Nujent exhaled and stood, smoothed her dress and excused herself. She walked right past the coat stand, but did not notice White Feather hiding behind it.

Buster refilled everyone's coffee cup and sipped thoughtfully for a moment thinking, *What an incredible story.*

As Morrison finished up his notes, a shadow moved across his shoulder and covered his notepad.

A deep voice spoke softly, "Don't forget the argument."

Morrison whirled around to find White Feather standing next to him. "Huh? Uh-uh, the argument?"

"Argument with Dawson."

Morrison appeared irritated. "I think she is leading up to that."

White Feather folded his arms. "Humph. Perhaps leading away."

Morrison made a note and circled it. When he looked back, White Feather had disappeared.

Chapter 41

Final Episode

FRANK KNOCKED ON RUTH's door and waited. It took the stoic woman several minutes to answer. When she opened the door, Frank could see that she had been crying. She blotted her nose with a tissue and glared at Frank. "What do you want?"

Frank was struck by her cold retort. "I'm sorry about Lizzie, Ruth."

Ruth appeared to soften slightly. "Thank you."

Frank could not think of a smooth segue. "I ... well, I was wondering what we've been hearing in Lizzie's room?"

Ruth looked in the direction of Lizzie's room with concern. She looked back at Frank, and then pushed the door open to let him follow her into the bathroom. She tried Lizzie's door. "It's still locked."

She placed her ear to the door and listened. "There it is, the shuffling noise."

"You think someone is in there?"

Ruth turned to Frank with concern. "It certainly sounds like it."

Frank sidled by her and listened for himself. It definitely sounded like someone shuffling around in the room. "Let's go find the chief."

Ruth frowned and snapped, "White Feather? What for?"

Frank chuckled. "No, Chief Crab."

Ruth managed to laugh at herself. "Oh! Of course. Give me a moment."

Frank stepped into the hallway as Ruth closed the door behind him. He heard someone knocking on a door in the corridor. It sounded like it might be his door. He heard Albert's voice. "Franklin?"

Ralph plodded around the corner into the hallway heading toward him. "Where are you going, Rudolph?" Albert asked.

The grumpy man answered, "To take a crap."

Ralph disappeared into his room without looking up. Frank strolled down the hallway to find Albert and Monty standing in front of his door. "Looking for me?"

Albert smiled. "Hello, Franklin. We wondered where you slipped off to."

"I wanted to see if Ruth could still hear stirring in Lizzie's room."

Monty was curious. "C-Could she?"

"Oh, yes, I can hear it, too. We are going to find Chief Crab."

Albert strolled down the corridor and put his ear to Lizzie's door. After a moment, he raised his eyebrows. "Yes. I hear something as well."

When Nujent returned, Chief Crab and Morrison allowed her to drink her coffee in silence. They both felt overwhelmed by her amazing tale. Morrison played with his empty cup for a moment and then looked at his notes. He circled the word argument again. Crab asked, "Did it fool the inspectors?"

Nujent picked up her coffee cup and shook her head. "No. We knew it was over when the inspector, the doctor in the bunch, asked to examine Lizzie."

Nujent leaned back and reached up to run her fingers through her hair. "What followed was a nightmare. The Institution was soon flooded with auditors and doctors. Every file was examined and every patient examined and interviewed. By the time I left, Steve was looking like a zombie. His eyes were red and swollen, his hair a mess, his face pasty and blotchy. I'm sure he was over medicating himself to get through the stress.

"I have to hand it to him, though, he took responsibility for everything. He even called his old alma mater and got me a scholarship. By then, the rest of the staff had gone. He insisted I leave but I protested, of course. I confessed that I loved him and would stay by his side. He just snorted and told me it was over. He was certain that he would be going to jail."

Crab was curious, "Did he?"

Nujent teared up. "No. By the time the press got a hold of the story and the state finished their investigation, Steve was a vegetable. It turned out that he was doing some very shady things; criminal things; things I had no idea he was doing. They found that he had systematically euthanized at least twenty-eight patients to reduce the population. He had used drugs to manage others—that part I knew.

"Ironically, by the time they went to trial, Steve was declared unfit and, ironically, sentenced to life in an institution for the insane."

Morrison questioned, "Is that when you left for college?"

"Yes. But before I left, I visited him one last time at Thirteenth Street."

"The Institution in Pueblo?"

"Yes. He was completely insane. He just talked in riddles that made no sense."

Crab interrupted, "Like in Lizzie's letter?"

Nujent glared at him. "Yes. He gave me that letter. But it was meant for Joyce."

"Joyce?" Crab and Morrison said in unison.

"Joyce O'Quin, the pregnant file clerk that I tried to foist the inspector on."

Crab and Morrison looked at each other quizzically.

"She was another aid that Steve brought over from the clinic. It wasn't until he asked me to deliver the letter to Joyce that I even realized that they were probably having an affair. I suspect she was pregnant with his baby, too."

Crab was confused. "Then why did you give the letter to Elizabeth?"

She explained, "I had no idea how to get ahold of Joyce and I needed to get to school so I kept it. Over the years, I forgot I had it. When I came to work here again, it was the first time I had seen Elizabeth since the investigation and closing of the institution. I often wondered if Elizabeth made it, but didn't know how to find out. Really, a part of me didn't want to find out, I guess.

"Meeting again under these circumstances was ... poignant. I didn't know what to expect, you know? I figured she hated my guts, but it turns out that she considered me her only friend. She told me that I was the only person who really cared about her back then. She never knew about my feelings for Steve or our affair. I chose to leave that skeleton in the closet.

"So when I was unpacking, I found the letter and decided that Lizzie deserved it more than Joyce anyway. It was a mistake, though. It was filled with big words Elizabeth had no chance of understanding."

Crab quizzed, "Did he give you a letter?"

Nujent snickered, "No. I never heard a word from him after I left the institution. I don't think I ever meant anything to him. I was just a convenience: someone who would faithfully do his bidding, no questions asked; someone to provide sex; someone to sooth his ego.

"Oddly, though, I did run into him years later. In a weird twist, I became a mental health inspector. I was transferred to Colorado and was inspecting the main facility when I ran across his name on the roster. I went to visit him out of curiosity. He was old and withered. He didn't recognize me ... or anyone at that point. I took Diana to see him. She was old enough to understand that he was her father and I wanted her to at least meet him before he died."

Morrison leaned forward. "Who is Diana?"

"Diana? Oh, my daughter. But, of course, she isn't MY daughter."

"Oh?"

"Diana is Elizabeth's daughter. I named her Diana Elizabeth."

Buster gasped. "Lizzie's daughter?"

Nujent took a deep breath. "You see, the day that Elizabeth gave birth, after we took her up to her room, Steve sent me back down to the basement to bury the box with her baby. When I got there and started to close the lid on the metal box, the baby started squirming!"

Nujent smiled warmly with a tear in her eye. "She wasn't dead as Steve had told me. She was alive! I cut and tied off the umbilical cord and sneaked her into an empty room to clean her and wrap her up. Then I went back to the basement to bury the metal box with the umbilical cord and birth skin. I slipped out of the building, drove to Rockcliffe to get formula and diapers and took her home with me. No one ever knew."

Buster was in shock. "So, where is she now?"

Nujent gave him a slanted smile. "Here at St. Jude." She looked him in the eye. "Diana Meyer."

"Mrs. Meyer is Diana?"

Nujent nodded. "Diana Elizabeth Nujent Meyer."

"Were you going to tell Lizzie?"

"Oh, yes! That was why Diana came here. I had told Diana the truth when she came back from Africa after her divorce about five years ago."

Morrison circled argument in his notebook again. Buster was obviously confused. Nujent tried to explain. "While in college, she had gotten all rosey-eyed about the Doctors Without Borders program and ran off to Africa. I was furious and we had a falling out. I only heard from her occasionally

over the next forty years. I knew she had married a doctor
named Meyer, but not much else. When they got a divorce,
she flew home and we managed to patch things up. That's
when I told her about her birth mom."

Nujent rubbed her forehead as if pausing to remember
and then continued, "At first, Diana was angry, then confused.
And she adamantly refused to meet Elizabeth."

Nujent looked at Crab. "It was too much. She had just
gotten up the nerve to reconcile with me only to learn that I
wasn't her real mother.

"Recently, she called and told me that she was ready. That
she wanted to meet Elizabeth. So, I suggested she move in
here and get to know her."

Morrison put it together. "Is that what the argument was
about?"

Nujent nodded her head sadly and admitted, "We went
about it all wrong. We should have let things happen gradually.
But, on an impulse, we, well I decided that it might make a
great birthday gift for Elizabeth. We sprung it on her at the
party. I never dreamed it would affect Elizabeth the way it
did. She had always believed that her daughter died in
childbirth and was buried in the basement."

Nujent raised her eyebrows. "Of course, that's what Steve
told her. When she learned about the new furnace, understandably she got terribly upset. I'm sure she envisioned the
possibility that they might dig up her daughter. It would be
like disturbing her grave. I can see now that after reconciling
herself to her daughter being buried here and being near her
by living here, to learn suddenly that her daughter was alive
was ...."

Nujent seemed unable to find the words to finish her thought.

Morrison summed it up. "That is what you fought about at the party."

Nujent looked up sadly and nodded. Morrison had been very patient. He knew that Nujent was a friend of Buster's. But, he was there to do a job and finally the conversation had come around to the night of the murder. "So Elizabeth went to the basement to produce proof that her daughter was buried down there and you followed her to the basement and ..."

Nujent's teary eyes shifted into rage. "No! I followed her to the elevator trying to reason with her. We argued all the way up to her room and then she slammed the door in my face."

Nujent looked down. "That was the last time I saw her."

"Where did you go after that?"

"I started back down to the party and met Diana leaving. We went to her room and stayed up until around 3 AM talking. I went home after that."

"Did anyone see you leave? Can anyone confirm you went home?"

Nujent teared up and shook her head.

Morrison decided it was time to drop a bomb on her. "What can you tell me about the other body in the basement?"

Nujent gasped. Her eyes bulged and her mouth dropped open. "Other body?"

"There is a partially uncovered body of a woman who has been dead for many years."

Nujent was trembling with disbelief and bewilderment.

Crab tried to soften the question. "Do you know anything about that, Alvira?"

"No! No!"

Her eyes searched the room. "Maybe one of the patients from the institution? It was discovered that Stephen had euthanized a number of patients. Maybe he buried them down there."

"You think there could be more bodies in the basement?"

Nujent's eyes flared. "I don't know. I didn't know Stephen was doing that until later."

She looked down and started muttering in a whisper, "Penitence wrapped in sad regalia, buried in its penetralia."

Morrison leaned forward. "I'm sorry, what?"

Crab touched his arm. "It's from the letter. I'll explain later."

He stood. "Thank you, Alvira. If you think of anything that might help us, you know how to reach us."

Out of respect, Crab tugged on Morrison's sleeve and quietly slipped out of the room leaving her whispering over and over, "Penitence wrapped in sad regalia, buried in its penetralia."

In the hallway, he stopped to get White Feather's take on it. "What do you think?"

White Feather opened his eyes and declared, "She didn't do it."

Morrison raised an eyebrow. "She's not off my list yet."

Chapter 42

Weisman's Granddaughter

Frank, Ruth, Albert, Monty, and Ralph stepped out of the elevator on the first floor just as White Feather, Chief Crab, and Deputy Morrison walked up. Frank blurted out, "Chief Crab, we were looking for you." He glanced nervously at his friends.

Albert took over. "We find it interesting that there are still sounds coming from Elizabeth's room that sound like someone stirring around in there."

Crab looked at Morrison. "Let's go check it out."

Ruth suggested, "You'll need a key. The doors are locked."

Morrison replied, "We were on our way to talk to Mrs. Barkley now."

White Feather accompanied Chief Crab and Deputy Morrison up to Mrs. Barkley's office. While everyone else exchanged pleasantries, White Feather was snooping around the office examining knick-knacks on the shelves, book titles, pictures, plaques, and certificates on the wall. He caught Morrison's attention and pointed at a picture on the wall behind Barkley's desk and then her diploma. Morrison recognized the picture of Stephen Weisman.

"Nice picture."

Edith Barkley's eyes betrayed her surprise. She took a quick look at the picture and then shifted in her chair glancing over the papers on her desk as if the answer might reside in one of the stacks. "Uh, yes, yes it is . . . a previous administrator."

"Is it the administrator of the institution that was here before the hospital?"

Barkley appeared concerned. "Yes, when it was the Institution for the Insane."

Chief Crab stared at the picture as if admiring an old piece of history. "Dr. Weisman, right?"

Barkley's lips tightened, her brow furrowed into a scowl. Starting to speak and then stopping short, she turned her eyes to the undersheriff, and then tilted her head to one side. "Yes. I believe so."

Chief Crab commented, "He is turning out to be quite controversial."

Mrs. Barkley forced an uncomfortable smile. "Controversial?"

Crab explained, "His name keeps coming up. Alvira has a picture of him on her credenza. She claims to have worked for him years ago at the Steelworks Clinic and then here at the institution."

Barkley was getting nervous. "Yes, it was on her application."

White Feather had worked his way behind Mrs. Barkley making her very uneasy. White Feather faced Morrison and nodded toward the plaques and certificates mounted on the wall behind her desk and pointed to the name on her college diploma. It read "Edith Stephanie Weisman."

Morrison glanced back at the picture of Weisman to notice that the picture was not a studio picture. It was a smiling young man holding a drink, standing outside in what appeared to be a backyard.

Barkley was eyeing White Feather. "Would you like to sit down?"

White Feather ignored her, crossed his arms and walked around to stand behind Morrison. Morrison remarked, "I see your maiden name was Weisman. Any relation?"

A tear trickled down her cheek. "Grandfather . . . Stephen Weisman was my grandfather."

Chief Crab choked on his coffee. "Your grandfather?"

Barkley gathered her poise, interlocked her fingers, rested them on the desk in front of her and explained, "My father was his son by his first wife. They divorced when my father was four and grandfather moved to Colorado after that. My father hardly knew his own father. The controversy at the asylum happened when he was only six or seven."

"They live here in Colorado?"

"No, they lived in Boston before Grandfather and Grandmother divorced and then he moved out here. My father stayed with his mother in Boston. Not long after his father left, he lost his mother."

"What happened to her?"

"She mysteriously disappeared. That's when my father went to live with Grandmother's sister."

"Any ideas what happened to her?"

"Auntie despised Grandfather and always believed that her sister had gone to Colorado and was killed by Grandfather. She continued to believe that even after Grandmother's car was found in Lowell, Massachusetts. Her body was never found.

"Family believed that she had gone to Colorado to try to reconcile with Grandfather. There was an investigation, but law enforcement here claimed that they never found any evidence that Grandmother was ever here."

"Where was the car found?"

". . . at the University of Massachusetts Lowell in one of the student parking garages. Police there suspected she was having an affair with one of the professors, but could never prove it. There was a rumor that the affair had prompted their divorce. It always amazed me that Father never seemed more curious about it. He wouldn't talk about his father or his mother."

Barkley sipped on her coffee. "Would you like a refill, Buster? Deputy Morrison?"

The two stunned men declined. White Feather prompted her. "You were curious?"

Barkley walked over to a small table to refill her cup. "Not until I was much older ... right after my divorce. I needed to get out of Boston and away from my ex. I decided to escape to Colorado and maybe learn more about my grandfather."

Morrison prompted her. "What did you find out?"

"I learned that he had died at the asylum in Pueblo many years ago. They said that he was just a mental vegetable those last years. He didn't know anyone."

She snatched a tissue off her desk and blotted her eyes and nose. Tossing the crumpled tissue in the waste basket, she added, "I learned that my father had once visited him. I guess he was curious after all but never mentioned it because he was ashamed of him. And my great aunt once said that Grandfather had never tried to contact any of the family. Of course, if he was in the sanitarium ..."

Crab was curious. "What made you take a job here?"

"It was like a fluke really. I drove over here to look at the place," she looked at Crab, "you know, just to see what it looked like. There were cars in the parking lot, the front door was open, and so I went in.

"It was still being renovated and they were interviewing applicants for this job. So, when I walked in, they understandably thought I was there for an interview. I didn't even realize what was going on at first. I assumed they were just asking questions to tactfully find out why a stranger had walked into the old building.

"When they asked me for my resume, I was dumbfounded. I don't even know what I said, but I just remember suddenly wanting the job. I was really intrigued by what they were planning to do here. They took down my information and told me they would call. I put together a resume that night and faxed it over. Two days later, they called me with an offer. I was confounded but I really didn't want to go back to Boston. I wasn't happy at my old job. And I wasn't happy about the possibility of running into my ex from time to time. The thought of starting over and being independent was exciting. Like I said, I was intrigued by the plan for St. Jude so I took the job. And here I am."

"Did you know ... about Elizabeth's and Nujent's connection to your grandfather?"

"Connection? I knew that Elizabeth was a resident of the Institution and I often wondered if she was here when my grandfather was here, but we never discussed it. I didn't find out about Alvira working here until I looked up her resume recently."

"You had never seen her resume before?"

"No, she was hired by the board, same as me, same time as me."

"When did you pull her resume?"

"About a week ago, Alvira came to me about bringing in her daughter. When I saw her name, Diana Elizabeth Nujent Meyer, I laughed and joked about our other resident named Diana Elizabeth. I was shocked when Alvira told me that it was no coincidence. That our Elizabeth is her daughter's birth mother."

Barkley checked Buster and Morrison for their reaction.

Crab wondered if she realized that this information put her on the list as a suspect. "What did you think when you learned that Diana Elizabeth was your grandfather's daughter?"

Barkley dropped her coffee. "My grandfather's daughter?"

Crab jumped up to help clean up the mess. "You didn't know?"

Barkley shook her head and placed her hand on her forehead. "My grandfather was married to Elizabeth?"

Morrison responded, "No. I don't think they were ever married. Nujent told us that Elizabeth got pregnant while a patient at the Institution."

Barkley looked off into the distance. Morrison inquired further, "You didn't tell Nujent about your relationship to Weisman?"

"No. She doesn't know about that."

Crab gave her a moment and then asked, "Did Alvira say anything to you about her relationship with your grandfather?"

Barkley was clearly shocked. "Alvira? My grandfather?"

Crab again gave her a moment to absorb the shocking news. Finally, Edith recovered and asked, "What was their relationship?"

"She worked for him back then and, well, I think she may have had a crush on him."

Now Barkley was clearly curious. "Did she say why she was raising Lizzie's and my grandfather's daughter?"

Crab shrugged. "I'm sorry, Edith, we told Alvira we wouldn't say anything."

Barkley shook her head. "The more I learn about Grandfather, the more of an enigma he becomes."

Crab responded. "I would have to agree with that, Edith."

Morrison got to the point. "Where were you Saturday night?"

Barkley's eyes widened. "Me? Well, I was at the party until around eleven. After I kicked off the party, I went around and visited with everyone and helped Birdie with drinks and hors d'oeuvres. After the party, I helped the staff clean up. Then I went home."

"Did you ever leave the party?"

"Am I a suspect?"

Morrison shifted in his chair. "It is just routine, Mrs. Barkley. We like to eliminate anyone involved."

Barkley looked up at the ceiling. "I did go up to my office around eight-thirty to finish some paperwork that was due. I went back down around ten, I think."

"Did anyone see you in your office?"

Barkley dropped her head and rubbed her forehead and replied, "No. The administration floor was quiet."

"Can anyone confirm when you got home?"

"No. I live alone." She was clearly shaken. "Should I think about a lawyer?"

Crab glanced at Morrison and then smiled. "Oh, no, I don't think so, Edith. We just have to ask these things."

Morrison closed his notebook. "Can you put together a list of who was at the party?"

Barkley nodded slowly. "Of course."

"We would like to look in Elizabeth's room."

Barkley blinked and shook her head as if trying to break from a trance. She opened a desk drawer and pulled out a ring of keys, stood and said, "Shall we?"

They found Frank, Albert, Monty, and Ralph in a raucous standoff with Ruth, Mary, and Kate. Ralph seemed to be at the heart of the argument. All parties seemed grateful for the opportunity to break it off.

Mrs. Barkley curtly nodded to the residents and then unlocked Elizabeth's door. When she opened it, a gust of cold air escaped. Morrison warned, "We'll need everyone to stay out for now."

They found a window broken with a chair lodged precariously half in and half out. On the vanity, the pages of a thick catalog blew back and forth making a loud ruffling noise. Morrison remarked, "The sound everyone was hearing, no doubt."

Barkley questioned, "So she was never in here?"

Ruth asked, "How did the door get locked?"

Morrison demonstrated how the door could be locked and then pulled shut. White Feather pointed to a crumpled piece of paper on the floor. Crab picked it up and handed it to Morrison. "The letter."

Morrison accepted it and bagged it.

Barkley glanced around at the room that was in shambles. "Oh, dear."

Ruth touched her arm. "We can clean all this up, Edith.

Morrison objected. "This is part of the crime scene. Please don't touch anything for now."

Crab guided everyone away from the room as Morrison locked the door behind him. Crab doubted they would find anything to help the case in her room, but it was proper procedure.

Barkley asked, "What about the broken window? What if it snows again?"

"They will cover it when they come up to investigate."

Crab and Morrison shook Barkley's hand. "We can find our way out."

Morrison checked his watch. "CBI team could be here by now."

"Let's go check."

White Feather hung back and whispered into Mrs. Barkley's ear, "Lawyer up."

Barkley gasped and grabbed her mouth as White Feather strolled away.

Morrison and Crab waited for White Feather at the elevator. On the ride down, Morrison inquired, "What do you think?"

Crab shook his head. "I like Edith. I don't think she would do something like that. But, man, what a bombshell."

Morrison looked at White Feather. Even though he was in his familiar stance with arms crossed and eyes closed, he seemed to sense Morrison was looking at him. "She didn't do it."

Morrison took a deep breath and shook his head. "Pretty suspicious, if you ask me. We need to know who the other body in the basement is. Who dug her up and why. There must be a connection."

The elevator stopped and after a long pause, the doors opened and they stepped out. Yellow crime scene tape had been placed to prohibit entrance to the basement. Morrison said, "I want to talk to the crime scene investigators."

"I need to get back to the office. If you need any help with interviews, I could send over Jacobs," Crab offered.

Morrison answered, "Yeah, that would be great. Agent Smiles coming over?"

"Working on a drug case in Pueblo. You're on your own."

Morrison smiled.

Chapter 43

Interviews

MORRISON CAUGHT UP WITH the CBI crime scene investigation team. "Got anything for me?"

"Well, no prints on the letter opener. It appears it was originally in the chest of the other victim. There is a hole in the sternum that would match the blade of the opener. And the opener appears to be of the right age to have been used in the first murder. Footprints around the grave and the recent victim suggest a petite woman."

Morrison was making notes. "So, you're saying the person in the grave was murdered, too?"

"It would appear so. We have extracted DNA from both bodies. We may be able to extract DNA from the opener, but there are no finger prints or any other evidence from the murderer."

The bodies were carried out of the basement in body bags and loaded into hearses to be transported to the Colorado Springs morgue. Morrison watched from the reception room. Naomi approached and reached out her hand.

"Good afternoon, Deputy Morrison. I'm Naomi Johnson, the receptionist here."

Morrison shook her hand. "Yes, Naomi, I remember."

"Mrs. Barkley asked me to put together a list of the residents that were at the party Saturday night and work with you to arrange interviews." She handed him a typed list.

"Thank you, Naomi, I appreciate this."

"You may use the northeast reception area like last time if that works for you."

"Yes, that's perfect. I'm expecting Deputy Jacobs to help me. She should be here any minute."

"Oh, yes, Sydney. I'll show her back there when she arrives. If you like, I will contact the first five on the list now. Then I will call the next five when you've finished with the first group."

"That would be very helpful. Thanks."

Naomi looked up. Well, there she is now! Good afternoon, Sydney."

The reserved deputy forced a smile but quickly returned to her serious demeanor. Morrison smiled and waved her over. "Naomi has typed up a list of residents that attended the party Saturday night—the night Elizabeth was murdered. The first group is coming down shortly. We will be interviewing them in the northeast reception area."

As they walked back to the room, Morrison added, "I want to take their statements about what they saw and especially anything they witnessed of an argument between Elizabeth and Nurse Nujent and her daughter Diana Meyer. I also want to know if they saw Mrs. Barkley at the party and if she ever left. Try to nail down the times."

Jacobs made notes of the key points to be covered. "Copy that."

"We should also ask them what they remember about Elizabeth's demeanor leading up to Saturday and anything they might know about her visiting the basement or her interest in the basement."

"So then, Meyer is Nujent's daughter and not our missing person."

"Actually, Sydney, we have just learned that Meyer is Dawson's daughter."

"What? Lizzie's daughter?"

"I need to catch you up on what we've learned so far . . .."

Frank was standing by the pool table in the second floor rec room when he noticed White Feather slip in and find a corner to stand and wait. Ralph and Monty had challenged him and Albert to a game of eight-ball. Only Ralph was really interested in the pool match. Everyone else was anxious to hear from White Feather.

Albert called "corner pocket" and hit the cue ball with a delicate stroke into the eight ball knocking it into the specified pocket. Ralph was devastated and threw a hissy fit while his friends joined White Feather.

White Feather commented, "Smooth."

"Thank you, White Feather. We have been anxiously awaiting your report."

In his usual style, the elder summed up the interviews with Nujent and Barkley with brief efficiency. The incredible stories mesmerized everyone except Ralph who was still pouting in a chair across the room.

Frank inquired, "So, is Mrs. Barkley the prime suspect?"

White Feather responded, "Probably."

Albert shook his head. "She is such an unlikely suspect."

White Feather pronounced, "She didn't do it."

Frank's face screwed up. "How do you know?"

White Feather only responded, "Humph."

Frank back peddled. "Oh, I didn't mean to imply ..."

Ralph shocked his friends with a comment. "My money's on Nujent."

Frank asked, "What about the other body?"

"Very old. Probably from the institution. Murdered with same weapon as Dawson."

"You mean the murderer pulled the letter opener out of the dead woman's chest to stab Elizabeth?"

"Appears so."

"Bizarre."

"Footprints indicate a woman."

Ralph blurted out, "That takes us off the hook."

Naomi stepped into the rec room. "Gentlemen, Deputy Morrison wants to interview everyone that was at the party Saturday night down in the northeast reception."

Ralph complained, "Why us? A woman killed her."

Naomi frowned. Albert countered, "They need all of our testimonies, Rudolph, to establish the whereabouts of everyone."

"We were at the party, so we're on the list?"

Albert huffed in frustration. "We'll go right down, Mrs. Johnson."

Naomi smiled sympathetically. "Thank you, Mr. Stein."

Frank asked, "Will we be using the library next door to listen to the interviews again?"

Everyone nodded affirmatively. When interviews had been conducted in the Cook case, the Sleuthkateers had been able to secretly listen in from the library.

As Chief Crab entered the sheriff's office, he found Deputy Melton receiving an update from the phone company for the location of Agatha Phillip's phone. It had not moved from the previous day. "The ping is consistently across highway 96 from St. Jude."

"May not be accurate."

"No, but the fact that it is consistently not St. Jude makes it more likely she is hiding out in one of those housing developments."

"I think you're right. We know that she is not one of the new residents at St. Jude. We have confirmed the identity of one of them and the other doesn't match the description. What did you learn at the Dome?"

Melton replied, "I talked to the bartender and it was very enlightening. First, he was able to confirm that Frederick Geisendorff had indeed been at the Dome Saturday night and left staggering drunk.

"But second, and more interesting, John Phillips was also at the Dome that night with a drunk lady friend hanging all over him. He was confronted by a young man that someone identified as John Phillips' son and they had an argument before the young man stormed out."

The Chief nodded. "Seth."

Melton grinned. You're gonna love this. John Phillips was there while I was talking to the bartender. Agatha's husband was sleeping off his latest binge at one of the tables in the back. I woke him up and learned that he had not heard back from his wife. Of course, I wonder how he would know if she had returned home if he was spending all of his time at the bar."

Crab acknowledged. "Good point. So, the son may be back in town?"

"I'm looking into that. And I think I have an idea why Agatha disappeared."

Crab was interested. Melton proposed, "I think the son caught his stepdad carousing with another woman and sent pictures to his mother."

Crab stated simply, "She got angry and left him."

"Looks that way."

"So, we just need to confirm that Mrs. Phillips is okay and we can close the case."

Wednesday

Excluded from a proud society,
like ghosts who've lost their ubiety.

Chapter 44

Status of Affairs

Frank was a little late joining his friends for breakfast. His brain had toiled all night over the death of Elizabeth. He yawned broadly as he put down his tray. "Good morning." He managed.

Albert seemed in good spirits. "Good morning, Franklin. Glad you could join us."

The other members of the Sleuthkateers nodded. Frank wanted to share something that had kept him awake through most of the night. "Why would anyone else be in the basement?"

Albert tried to offer his take. "There must be someone else that is concerned about or has a secret hiding down there."

Monty found it simple. "S-Someone knew about the b-body buried down there."

Frank agreed. "Do you think that the holes we found down there were actually dug by the person looking for the body instead of by Elizabeth?"

"Unless L-Lizzie was the one l-looking for that b-body."

Frank continued, "Interesting point. So it could be that Lizzie found the body and that is why she was killed."

Albert added, "I wonder why the other body was not covered back over?"

"Or wh-why didn't they b-bury L-Lizzie?"

Ralph replied, "Ground is too hard below the surface."

Frank was not sure. "What do you think, White Feather?"

"Ground too hard."

Ralph beamed. "Settles that. Let's play some pool."

Frank begged off. He was not in the mood for pool or for even being around friends. His grief for the loss of Elizabeth Dawson was consuming him.

Sheriff Bailey had called a staff meeting to discuss the pending cases. "Bill, you want to update us on the missing person case?"

"You're suspicion about Geisendorff was correct. He had been at the Dome getting plastered before he drove back down Hardscrabble. He should never have been driving. The hospital can confirm that his blood alcohol level was too high. He is due out of the hospital tomorrow and I plan to meet him at the door."

Bailey was frustrated. "I need to go over to the Dome and review their policy. They should have taken his keys away."

Melton continued, "Guess who was there. John Phillips was passed out at one of the back tables. That's why we haven't been able to reach him. He's been spending all of his time there. But even more interesting, the bartender was pretty sure Seth was there Saturday night. Phillips was drinking and ... flirting with some lady and evidently Seth confronted his stepdad. I think that Seth took a picture of his stepdad making out with the floozy, sent it to his mom, and then got into a fight with his stepdad before leaving."

Morrison's eyes lit up. "If he called his mother and sent a picture, might explain why she took off."

Melton nodded. "Exactly."

Bailey asked, "So that puts Seth back in town?"

Melton responded, "Yep. I went out to the Phillips' place yesterday but there was no sign of anyone there. I went by Hagen and Madden's place but they claimed they hadn't seen him. I learned from Hagen that the reason Seth had left for Oklahoma in the first place was to avoid paying child support to the Watkins girl. I visited her and she swears she hasn't seen him since he first disappeared."

"Why do you think he came back?"

Melton shrugged. "I don't believe her. I think he came back to see her or maybe his baby daughter."

Bailey raised his eyebrows. "Interesting. You ought to keep an eye on her place."

Melton gave a thumbs up. "I've got Calhoun out there now. Chief Crab told me that Agatha is not at St. Jude. I've been talking to some of her friends. None of them were aware she was missing." He shrugged. "I believe 'em. I'm trying to find out if she has any friends living over in that development across from St. Jude."

Bailey summed it up. "If we can confirm she is okay and it's just a marital dispute, I would say we can close the case."

Melton nodded.

Bailey rubbed his hands together. "Okay, let's hear about the murder investigation."

Morrison shifted in his chair and picked up his notes. "Here's what we know so far. It looks like Elizabeth surprised someone digging up a body in the basement. The body was of a woman around thirty-ish who had been murdered by a puncture wound to the chest. It is probably the same letter opener used to kill Mrs. Dawson."

Bailey was surprised. "Really?"

"Yes, the perp probably pulled the letter opener out of the dead body and stabbed Mrs. Dawson. Footprints in the dirt indicate our suspect is a woman with small feet. However, there does not seem to be any other evidence that might help identify her. It does appear that she returned to try to bury Elizabeth, but below the surface the ground is hard as a rock. She must have given up."

Bailey interjected, "So, the murderer may still be around?"

"Pretty sure of it. No one is missing from St. Jude including the staff. Of course, she might not be a resident or staff member at St. Jude."

Bailey was curious. "Any suspects pop out in the interviews?"

Morrison pulled out his phone. "Before we even started our interviews, I got a message from the crime scene investigators. They had found ten recent distinct footprints in the basement that do not include Buster's or mine. They sent me pictures and we examined the shoes of the people we interviewed."

Bailey was confounded. "Ten people have been in the basement recently?"

"We have tentatively identified all but the murderer's prints. Of course, Mrs. Dawson had been down there numerous times.

Our friends, the famous Sleuthkateers, were down there last Friday night snooping around. Barkley was down there with four engineers to look at where the new furnace is going to be installed. They were the ones who found Elizabeth."

Bailey was counting on his fingers. "Okay, the five Sleuthkateers, Barkley and the four engineers is ten. Elizabeth and the murderer makes twelve."

Morrison checked his notes. "Oh, that's right, only three of the Sleuthkateers actually ventured down to the basement floor. Ralph Jacobs and Walter Montgomery waited in the corridor."

Bailey shook his head. "Why on earth were they down there?"

Morrison chuckled. "Investigating Mrs. Dawson. They were working on a letter full of riddles found in Mrs. Dawson's room when she disappeared last week. They thought that there were clues that indicated Mrs. Dawson might have secrets buried in the basement."

"Clues?"

Crab jumped in. "I have a picture of the letter on my phone. It seems that Nujent gave Elizabeth a love letter from Weisman from years ago. The man had an incredible vocabulary and the letter is filled with two-bit words no one understands including poor Lizzie."

"Provide any clues to the murder?"

Crab shook his head. "Naw, I don't think so. According to Mr. Stein, it's a love letter expressing remorse over the controversy at the Institution. However, there is one line that Lizzie quoted recently. Let me see. Here it is, Penitence wrapped in sad regalia, buried in its penetralia."

Bailey smiled and shook his head to indicate confusion. Crab translated, "Mr. Stein thinks it refers to Lizzie's stillborn baby that she thought was buried in the basement. White Feather and the gang found a way to get to the basement to determine whether Elizabeth read it to mean that something was actually buried down there or if it was referring to memories buried down there."

Bailey summed it up. "Okay, so the ten people we have identified are definitely not the murderer."

Morrison hesitated. "Well. Although wearing different shoes, Barkley's foot size is close."

Bailey shrugged. "Okay, but is she a suspect? Why would she want to kill Mrs. Dawson? The fact that she was a pain to deal with doesn't seem like motive enough."

Morrison looked up. "Well, I'll get to that in a minute. This case is similar to the prior Cook case. Like Mr. Cook, Mrs. Dawson had plenty of enemies. But the interesting thing to me is the number of people who knew her well before her current living arrangements. It turns out that Nurse Nujent worked with Mrs. Dawson at the Steelworks Clinic and then was a nurse at the institution when Mrs. Dawson was admitted there.

Bailey shook his head. "You don't say."

Crab had to jump in. "It is quite the sordid tale, Sean."

Morrison continued. "The short version is that when inspectors showed up at the Institution, Weisman ordered Nujent to hide Dawson who was pregnant with his baby in the basement. The physical exertion of taking the stairs induced Lizzie's labor. Weisman did a C-section, pronounced the baby stillborn, and threw it into a metal box for burial. But when Nujent went back down to the basement to bury it, the baby was alive. She slipped it out and raised the baby herself."

Crab added, "She's the new gal at the Center, Diana Elizabeth Nujent Meyer."

Bailey stopped them. "Wait a minute. Who's the father?"

"Weisman."

Bailey smoothed his hair back. "Wow."

"Nujent tried to introduce her daughter to Elizabeth at the party Saturday night and that was what the fight was about. Elizabeth has believed all these years that her baby was buried in the basement in that metal box."

Bailey rubbed his forehead. "Man!"

Crab added, "Yeah, it's an amazing story, but why would Nujent want to kill Lizzie?"

Bailey hypothesized. "Maybe it was self-defense. Maybe Elizabeth attacked Nujent and she ...."

Morrison nodded. "Yeah, it could be something like that but we have to understand why Nujent would be in the basement and what connection she might have had with the other body. Besides, her feet appear to be the wrong size."

Bailey was not convinced. "Foot size might be pretty difficult to nail down. The prints are in dirt. Plus we know they were in a heated argument ..."

"That's true so we can't rule her out completely."

Morrison picked up his stack of papers and went to the second page. "This one will shock you. That Dr. Weisman? He's Mrs. Barkley's grandfather."

Bailey's eyes widened. "Grandfather?"

"Wait 'til you hear this, Sean," Crab shared.

"Weisman moved here after he divorced his first wife. Mrs. Barkley's father was their son. Barkley came out here after a contentious divorce to get away from her ex-husband and decided to visit the old building where her grandfather had worked. By coincidence, they were interviewing for an administrator for the new St. Jude and she landed the job."

Bailey shook his head. "That is bizarre!"

"Definitely. That makes Meyer the daughter of Barkley's grandfather."

"Suspect number two."

"Yeah, except it appears that she didn't know about that until we told her."

"I wouldn't take her off the list, though."

"Agreed. With different shoes, maybe ... same with Nujent. Now get this. Lizzie's best friend here at the Center was her case worker after she left the Institution."

Bailey tilted his head to one side. "What would her motive be."

Morrison shrugged. "She may have learned Lizzie's secrets and if she happened upon Lizzie while she was digging up the body ..."

"Okay," Bailey said. "I see where you're going with that."

Morrison added, "But, her feet are definitely bigger than our murderer's.

Morrison set down his papers. Bailey leaned back. "Anything more?"

"No, but I don't think we've really gotten to the bottom of it. Things are not adding up yet."

Bailey asked, "What's next?"

"I think we wait for the lab results. Hopefully there's more evidence there."

Chapter 45

In a Funk

FRANK SAT ALONE on the bench by the pond. The weather in Wet Mountain Valley could be sunny one minute, blustery the next. This moment was sunny and calm but cold enough that he could see his breath. With each exhale, Frank was reminded of Lizzie's ghosts.

His heart ached for her. White Feather had told them Nujent's story and Barkley's story and he remembered the story they learned from the museum archivist. It was no wonder that Lizzie could be scary crazy sometimes. He never thought he would miss that, but now he did.

The revelation about Meyer made him see her differently now, too. Looking closely at her face, he could see the resemblance. Sometimes, when she caught a glimpse of him staring at her, he could see Lizzie's fire in her eyes. Her head movements, her walk, her gestures were just like Lizzie's. It was curious because she could not have picked up those things by being around her mother since she never was. She had picked up Lizzie's characteristics just by being her daughter. It was genetics. No doubt, Meyer was what Lizzie would be like if she could have had a different upbringing. Meyer was Lizzie raised with love and encouragement instead of grief and tragedy.

Sadly, it appeared that everyone in Lizzie's early life had tried to put her down or take advantage of her. She was a beauty but her crude manners deceived people into thinking she was dumb or slow. That quirky combination had made her vulnerable and misunderstood. It was actually amazing that Lizzie had not been crazier than she was. She must have had incredible survival instincts.

He felt privileged to have seen the soft, hidden side of her at the party, the Lizzie that could have been. For that brief time, she was like Meyer—refined, sophisticated, and graceful. For that brief time, Lizzie's softer side, her loving side came out and snatched Frank's heart right out of his chest.

A tear released and froze on his cheek. Did she still hold his heart in her chest? Could he ever love again the way he had that night? Would he ever feel that thrill, that all-consuming desire for someone? It was that feeling he had experienced as a young man and that he had assumed could not be felt by an old man. And yet, that was the intense passion he had felt for Lizzie. He covered his face with his hands and sobbed.

Suddenly, the bench shifted. White Feather had joined him. Frank swiped the tears from his eyes and tried to cover his grief. They sat in silence. White Feather with folded arms and eyes shut. Frank was at first resentful of White Feather's intrusion into his wallowing grief. But over time he felt the quiet closeness of friendship. He felt support and respect from this strange man who had been so enigmatic. Just by White

Feather sitting with him was making Frank feel his concern and feel connected.

It was like with Lizzie. White Feather was scary in his own way. But now, in this instance, he seemed warm, loving, and supportive. In this moment, White Feather was a friend.

White Feather spoke, "You saw inside her."

His words surprised Frank. They were powerful and unequivocal. Yes, he had seen inside her. "Maybe her facade opened up to let me in."

"Hmm."

This was not his usual caustic "Humph"; it was more reassuring, perhaps affirming. It made Frank feel that maybe for the first time he had impressed the wise man. For a brief time he felt like White Feather's equal instead of the neophyte.

Frank's tears returned.

After the updates, Morrison was keyed-up and full of energy. He found himself in back of the Sheriff's office pacing. He was even feeling bold enough to call Samantha.

"What is it, Sam?"

"Oh! Are you at work?"

"Well, yes, it is a workday."

Morrison's heart sank and his energy was immediately deflated. "I'm so sorry, Sam, I, I can call back tonight."

"It's okay. What do you need?"

Morrison resumed pacing. "I, well, I just wanted to talk."

Samantha was quiet. He stopped to look up into the clouds

feeling, once again, like a total fool. Samantha answered softly, resignedly, "Maybe this is not the time."

"Yeah, sure, I mean, of course ... can I call tonight?"

After a pause, she responded in an almost whisper, "Yes, I guess so," and hung up.

Frank drew back and started to hurl his phone but caught himself. "Dammit!" he shouted as the back door of the sheriff's office opened and Chief Crab stepped out.

The two men stared at each other briefly, and then Morrison turned around shaking his head and stuffed his hands into the pockets of his jacket. Crab walked up to stand beside him. They gazed across the parking lot at the Search and Rescue building. Crab decided to break the silence with, "She still mad at you?"

Morrison kicked a rock. "I don't know, Buster. I think so. I caught her at work and she didn't want to talk. She said I could call her tonight, but it didn't sound like she wants me to."

Crab put his hand on Morrison's shoulder. "Man, I'm sorry. But she'll come around, Sam. Just be patient."

"I don't know, Buster, it may be over—really over."

"You can't give up, my man. It may take time. She loved you once and ...."

"Once, maybe. But I've screwed this up so badly ...."

Crab shook his head. "Just don't give up yet. See how it goes tonight. Keep your chin up."

He gave Morrison a moment, and then said, "Bailey brought up a good point. The killer may try to run at some point if she thinks we're getting too close. He thinks we should consider keeping an eye on the place."

Morrison added, "Of course, if it's Barkley or Nujent, we would have to watch their houses at night.

Crab glanced over at his forlorn deputy. Fact is, I can't spare the manpower. I'm thinking about deputizing the Sleuthkateers."

When it sunk in, Morrison snapped his head around to glare at the Chief who burst out laughing. Morrison couldn't help it. He punched the Chief on the shoulder and allowed a moment of levity for himself.

Crab regained his composure. "Hopefully, we can narrow this thing down more after CBI finishes their investigation. Until then, maybe we keep in touch with White Feather."

Morrison nodded. No humor this time. Crab confided, "Seriously, I have asked my cousin Naomi to try to keep an eye on things and let me know if anyone disappears or doesn't show up for work."

Crab patted him on the shoulder and turned to go back inside. "Keep your chin up. Things have a way of working out."

Frank spent his afternoon walking around the compound. He stopped to read a few of the tombstones at the old cemetery on the hill beyond the pond. He wondered what sad histories were buried there. Albert had said that it was once a family plot but that there were many graves added from the institutional years, patients without families. Soon there would be a new headstone bearing the name Diana

Elizabeth Austin Dawson. It seemed fitting that she be buried near the place that had become so much a part of her life.

He discovered a crumbling stone wall around the back perimeter of the grounds. There was a foundation where a small house or barn may have once stood. Nearby a cistern was slowly falling down. The roof had already dropped and some of the stones had broken off. He sat down on the foundation. The site provided a grand view of the valley south of the compound. A vast pastureland was sectioned off by barbed-wire fences and dotted with ranch houses. It was speckled with grazing cattle and a herd of antelope had collected near one of the many ponds. The Sangre de Cristo Mountain Range extended like a mountain wall along the west side of the valley. It was touted as the longest, straightest continuous mountain range in the Rocky Mountains. It ran from the Arkansas River about fifty miles north all the way south to Santa Fe, New Mexico. The smaller rounded peaks of the Wet Mountains guarded the east side of the valley. Many of those mountains were scarred by deserted silver mines. Wet Mountain Valley was home to around five thousand residents, but it had retained a feeling of open almost vacant grassland. It was a beautiful place to spend your final years. Frank wondered what it would have been like growing up in the valley. If he had grown up here, would he be taking this glorious view for granted?

The wind was picking up and Frank was getting chilled. He reluctantly returned to his room and retired for a nap.

Chapter 46

Heartache

MORRISON RAISED THE REMOTE control and clicked off the news. A front was moving across northern New Mexico and would cause a snowstorm all across southern Colorado. Working the valley in a snowstorm was tough. Tomorrow would not be fun.

He checked his watch; it was seven o'clock. He crumpled up the paper littering the couch and stuffed it into the sack. He found one last French fry, popped it into his mouth and carried the sack to the kitchen trash can.

Samantha liked to eat at six o'clock so his ex and kids would likely be finished with dinner. He had stripped to his underwear when he got home, but now, with the sun down, it was getting nippy. He turned on the gas fireplace and went upstairs to don his heavy robe. The picture of Samantha on his night stand caught his eye. He picked it up for a closer look and sat on the bed. It was his favorite picture. Her auburn hair was long and hung down off her shoulders. She was wearing a serious expression, which made her look strong and self-assured. Of course, she was that. But her beautiful amber eyes were soft and nonjudgmental and reached out like a beacon beckoning him.

Her hair was shorter now, but she had not really aged since this picture. He felt like he had aged much more. His hair was streaked with white. The wrinkles on his face were getting deep and long. He rubbed his face as if trying to smooth it.

His stomach was queasy. It was time to call her but he did not feel he had the courage. Dread, piles and piles of dread weighed on him. He tried to reassure himself that it was unfounded. Samantha was such a kind person; she could not be mean to him. But, it did not help.

He dropped his cell phone into the pocket of his robe, put on slippers and headed downstairs. He dropped into the recliner, pulled down the lever, and reasoned that he should be comfortable and relaxed now. He fished out the phone and pushed the emergency icon on the screen. He had programmed her number for his emergency contact. It was dialing. He panicked. He released the lever on the chair, jumped to his feet, and started pacing. It rang and rang and rang. Would he have to leave voice mail? This was no time for voice mail. He might not have the courage to try again.

"Hello, Sam."

Her voice was soft and unemotional. He felt like a minor bother. He tried to put forth a cheerful voice. "Hi, Sam. Did I catch you at a bad time?" He worried that he had sounded too hopeful.

"No, this is fine."

"Did you have a good day?"

"Oh, I suppose. You?"

"Mostly worked on the homicide out at St. Jude."

"Hmm."

He flinched. Why was he mentioning that? It just brought back bad memories for them. "We're supposed to get snow tonight."

"Yes, I saw that. I guess we need the moisture."

"Yeah, may make it tough getting around tomorrow." *Damn, not work again!* "How are the kids?"

"Oh, they're fine. Jerry has been busy with football. He's trying to turn his fat into muscle, so spending a lot of time in the weight room. Tammy is a cheerleader this year and plans to play volleyball."

"She still dating David Ludwig?"

"Oh, yes, they're still an item . . . going steady as we used to call it. I don't know what they call it these days."

"She's really growing up."

"Humph. She thinks she IS grown up. And sometimes, she acts like it."

Morrison chuckled. "She thinking about college?"

"Sort of. I don't think she really has her heart in it. She wants to go to CSU."

"Why CSU?"

"That's where David goes."

"Really? What is he studying?"

"Law enforcement."

Sam paused. He thought he might have read some disgust in her voice. "What would Tammy study there?"

"She's not sure, maybe nursing."

"That would be good."

"I guess."

They both got quiet. They had covered polite conversation. Morrison took a deep breath. He did not feel that Samantha had softened any. She was still cold and aloof. "Sam, I just wanted to apologize for how I have behaved."

Samantha did not respond. He tried another approach. "I just want us to be friends . . . to get along."

She was still quiet. "I've made a lot of mistakes and I don't know if you can ever forgive me. I have no right to ask you to. But, if we could just get along, you know?"

Still no answer. He had to force the issue. "Do you think we could be friends?"

"I thought we were."

Sam swallowed hard. What did that mean? "Well, I did, too, but the other night ...."

He could hear her sigh, but she did not speak. "Do you think we could forget the other night and start over?"

"What do you want from me, Sam? Do you think that by coming to Rockcliffe, everything can just be forgotten and we can start over?"

"No. No, of course not. But, I was hoping we could ... I don't know, try."

"Try to what?"

Sam held the phone back, whispered a curse word and then admitted, "I don't know."

Samantha got quiet again. Sam felt the opportunity slipping away. "You asked me what I want. I want to turn back the clock. I want a second chance. I want to make up for not fighting for you."

"Why didn't you fight, Sam? Why didn't you at least tell me then what you wanted?"

"I was stupid. I was, I don't know, shocked. I was hurt. I didn't realize anything was wrong. I didn't know what to say ... or what to do."

"So you just did nothing? Did you think it would just go away if you ignored it?"

Sam shook his head. She was right, absolutely correct; he had tried to avoid the issue. "Honestly, Sam, I don't know what I thought. I admit that I was too self-absorbed, too deep into my job to think about anything else. But I see it now. I completely understand why you did what you did. I hate myself for how I reacted."

Samantha sobbed quietly, but he could hear her. His heart crumbled into little pieces. "Oh, Sam, I am so sorry. I don't deserve ..."

He broke down into tears. "What can I do to make it up to you, Sam? I will do anything."

"I don't know. You hurt me. I can't forget that."

She was quiet for a moment. Sam feared the worse. "I don't hate you, Sam. I should hate you, but I don't."

He waited. Finally she said, "I just don't know where it goes from here."

"Okay. That's fair."

He heard her sigh and blow her nose. She was trying to regain her composure. "I want you to continue to be in the kids' lives. I want you to go to the football games and spend time with them. They need you. They need your presence."

"Of course. I want that, too. I will be as much a part of their lives as ...."

"I know you do. Let's just see how it goes. The first game is next Friday night. Can you pick us up around five-thirty?"

"Absolutely. Want to have dinner first?"

She paused before answering, "No, Jerry will probably have to be there early. I don't know. Not this time."

"Sure, okay."

Sam wanted to shout and celebrate. "Thank you, Sam. Thank you."

She hung up.

Frank awoke from his nap and checked his clock. He was late for dinner. He rushed to the dining room not expecting his friends to still be there, but they had waited. As he set down his tray, Albert greeted him, "Welcome, Franklin. I was just about to go up and check on you."

"Sorry. I was taking a nap."

Monty added, "M-Must have been a sh-short one. We saw you out by the pond."

Frank's brow wrinkled. "That was this morning."

Ralph challenged him. "No it wasn't. It was just now."

His friends giggled. Frank was confused. Albert added, "We think you have been avoiding us, Franklin. Every time we see you, you duck and run."

"When was that?"

Ralph answered, "Up at the pool room."

Monty added, "In the hallway."

"I don't know what you are talking about. I went for a walk around the compound and then came back for a nap. I haven't been to the pool room."

White Feather suggested, "Doppelganger."

Albert put on his serious face. "You think so, White Feather?"

Frank frowned and then smiled. "Oh, I get it."

"M-Must be if it w-wasn't you."

Ralph suggested, "Maybe you were sleepwalking."

Albert quizzed him. "Yes. Have you ever sleepwalked, Franklin?"

Frank was getting irritated. "No, I don't sleepwalk."

"G-Guess it m-must have b-been a d-doppelganger."

His friends snickered again. Frank had had enough. "Yeah, sure." He began shoveling down his meal.

Monday

Love's inheritance in rapturous gestation,
fouled by a feckless ablation.

Chapter 47

DNA and Doppelgangers

THE COLD WIND WAS rattling the windows and blowing snow sideways as Morrison sat at a computer working on reports. Chief Crab rushed in and as he shrugged off his heavy coat covered with snow, he declared sarcastically, "I hear it might snow today!"

Morrison smiled. "Wind could blow, too."

Crab was rubbing his hands together vigorously as he approached his friend. "How did it go last night?"

Morrison grinned and gave him a thumbs up. "I'm taking the family to the football game next Friday."

Crab slapped him on the back with one hand and a thumbs up with the other. "Great news." He shuffled off to the break room for his coffee.

Morrison opened up his email. There was something from CBI. The lab results dropped another bombshell on the investigation. Morrison choked on his morning coffee. He looked at it again and then pushed the print button. "You're not going to believe this, Buster."

Crab came out of the break room clutching a steaming cup of coffee. "Whatcha got?"

Morrison pulled the first page off the printer and handed it to Crab. "What am I looking at?"

"DNA. The body from the basement is a relative of Edith Barkley."

Crab examined the report closely. "I'll be a son of a gun."

"You know what this means?"

Crab looked up, "Yes," then his face turned somber. "Well ..."

"Yeah, actually, I don't either, but remember she told us that her grandmother disappeared?"

"Right, but they found her car in Massachusetts somewhere, didn't they?"

"Lowell, I think."

"So how did her body wind up in the basement of St. Jude?"

"Edith told us that her grandmother's sister always believed that her sister had gone to Colorado to make amends with Weisman. What if she came to Colorado but they got into an argument and Weisman killed her?"

"Then he buried her in the basement and drove her car back to Lowell?"

The two were excited at first but then grew quiet. Morrison's mind was spinning. What did it have to do with Mrs. Barkley?

"Maybe Barkley suspected something and came here to search for her grandmother? Maybe she found her grandmother's body and Elizabeth surprised her?"

Crab rubbed his mouth. "I think you may be on to something, Sam."

Crab dropped his fist on the desk. "Damn. I guess you better bring her in. Too much of a coincidence."

"Not enough for an arrest."

"No, but enough to bring her in for questioning. Who knows, she might confess."

Morrison was looking at the other reports. He handed Crab another page. "The DNA on the letter opener."

Crab took the page. "Says unknown."

Morrison sidled around the desk to see the form better. "That's curious. What do they mean when they say 'current/previous match?'"

Crab scratched his head. "Beats me."

Morrison studied it for a moment. "Does this mean that Barkley didn't do it?"

"Good question. Do you think it may mean there are two samples. One is unknown and the other is a match?"

"I see what you mean. I guess we better call CBI for clarification."

"You do that, Sam. I'll call Edith. It might sound better coming from me."

Crab went to his office as Morrison sat down at the large work table to phone CBI but it bounced to voice mail. He left a message for a call back and explained the reason for his call then joined Crab.

"Like I say, Edith, it's routine. We need to get some things cleared up, okay? ... Okay, thanks, Edith."

Morrison reported, "CBI didn't answer. I left a message."

Frank had slept through breakfast. When he awoke, someone was stirring in his room.

"Who's there?"

The tall thin man moved closer. "Sorry, I didn't mean to startle you."

It was his doppelganger. "What are you doing in here?"

"We need to talk."

"About what?"

"About the time warp."

Frank rubbed his face in disgust. His double pleaded, "I think we should discuss how we approach it, don't you?"

"Why? What's to discuss?"

The man glanced about as if trying to decide how to put it. "Well, you know that when White Feather comes for you, you won't be able to deny him."

Frank still did not understand what the man was leading up to. He was right, though, White Feather was not a man you could turn down.

"So, I was thinking, what if I go instead?"

"You?"

"Yeah. Think about it. I've already been back. I know what to expect. I know ... I remember when I was you how scared I was. I remember how much I resisted."

"I'm not scared. I just don't believe any of this stuff."

"You have to. How do you explain me?"

Frank was getting frustrated. This was not real. He was sure it was not real. It was another dream and he would soon wake up.

The man backed away. "Look, I'm sorry; I'm not trying to make you angry. Just think about it, okay?"

The doppelganger turned and opened the door, peeked out, and then left closing the door behind him. The sound of the door closing startled Frank and he sat up blinking and rubbing his eyes. He consoled himself. "It WAS a dream. I knew it was just a dream."

Frank found his friends in the pool room. Ralph spotted him first. "You back already?"

Frank frowned, "What?"

Albert chimed in, "You were just here, Franklin. You looked in and then left. We thought you might still be angry with us."

His friends were grinning suspiciously. "Oh, right, the doppelganger."

They laughed. Frank protested, "You guys can drop that. It's not funny anymore."

Ralph snapped back. "Us? You're the one sneaking around pretending to be the doppelganger."

Frank sighed, "Okay, okay. Anything new?"

He looked at White Feather who was giving him one of his omniscient looks. "Not you, too, White Feather."

White Feather raised his eyebrows and turned his head away as if to say, "I don't know what you mean."

Frank wanted to sock him on his nose, but, of course, knew better than to challenge him to a physical fight. Albert answered his question. "They called in Mrs. Barkley for questioning."

"Mrs. Barkley?"

"We think she must be the prime suspect."

Ralph quipped, "They're gonna lock her up."

Albert shook his head. "We don't know that, but we are very worried for her."

Frank found a chair to sit on. "Wow! I can't see Mrs. Barkley being the killer."

White Feather agreed. "She didn't do it."

Ralph tossed his pool cue onto the pool table and headed for the door. "Lunch time."

Albert stood and addressed Frank, "Are you joining us, Franklin? Or are you the doppelganger?"

His friends found Albert's comment hilarious. Frank did not.

Chapter 48

Barkley's Interrogation

LUNCH HAD BEEN PRETTY quiet. Frank assumed everyone was concerned about Mrs. Barkley's questioning. He could see why she might be a suspect, but he could not believe someone as nice and caring as Mrs. Barkley could commit murder. He looked across at White Feather. "Why don't you think Barkley did it?"

The creases on the bridge of White Feather's nose deepened. "Was surprised by second body." With that he resumed eating.

Frank was a little disappointed. "That's it?"

"Humph."

Apparently, that was enough. Now Birdie, the head cook, walked up. "You sleuths hear about Miss Edith?"

Albert answered for them. "We heard that she had been called in for further questioning."

"Can you believe that? Why, that woman couldn't hurt a fly."

Frank asked, "Have you heard anything on Lizzie's funeral?"

Birdie waved her hand. "Ain't got nobody. Still at the morgue in the Springs but it's been decided to bury her here in the little cemetery on the hill. Mrs. Meyer is her only living relative as far as anybody knows. She thought it'd be real nice for her to be buried here. She ain't got nowhere else, don't ya know."

Birdie patted Frank's shoulder. "I'm sorry, Frank, I knows you thought a lot of Miss Lizzie." As she turned to leave, added, "Ya'll keep ya'lls fingers crossed for Miss Edith."

Crab could read horror in the eyes of Edith Barkley as Morrison led her into the interrogation room. It was a cold, intimidating room, which was, of course, its purpose. He would play the good cop. Bailey, Melton, and Jacobs watched through the one-way window that was directly opposite the chair of the person being interrogated.

"Please have a seat, Edith. May I get you something to drink?"

Barkley hesitated, glanced around the room to get her bearings and then requested a cup of warm tea. Morrison motioned toward the single chair on one side of the table. He and Crab would sit opposite her. She looked at herself in the mirror and a tear trickled down her cheek. She straightened her hair.

Morrison opened the conversation. "I know this is kind of scary, Mrs. Barkley, but we need to ask you some very serious questions.

"About the murders?"

"Yes, ma'am."

Morrison clicked on the recorder and stated the names of the persons present and the purpose of the interview.

Chief Crab stepped in with a steaming cup of tea and a small bowl with sugars. "Anything else, Edith, before we get started?"

Barkley cupped her hands around the hot cup and shook her head. She appeared to be distant and distracted. Morrison asked her to state her full name for the record and then proceeded. "I'll get right to the point. We got lab results from the CBI in Colorado Springs. The DNA from the victim in the grave is a close match to your DNA."

Barkley frowned. "What does that mean?"

"The victim is a relative of yours."

She gasped. "A relative of mine? How could that be?"

Crab stepped in. "We think it may be your grandmother, Edith."

Barkley appeared to have an eureka moment. "Oh!"

They waited for it to sink in. She appeared to think out loud. "But that would mean . . ." She appeared to be struggling with the implications.

Morrison continued, "You mentioned that your grandmother's sister was convinced that your grandmother had come to Colorado to speak to your grandfather, Dr. Weisman."

Barkley nodded. "She always believed that she did. She hated grandfather and was certain he was behind her disappearance."

Crab commented, "She may have been right. It appears she may have come out here, perhaps argued with your grandfather and he stabbed her with a letter opener."

Barkley put her hand over her mouth. "Oh, dear!"

Morrison gave her a moment and then pressed on. "We think you may have known about the body. We think that you may have come to Colorado to look for your grandmother and took the job at St. Jude so that you could investigate the possibility she came out here and never went back."

Barkley began to sweat and responded, "No! I had no idea. Like I told you before, I came out here to get away after my divorce and maybe learn more about my grandfather. The job at St. Jude just fell in my lap."

Morrison persisted. "We think you found your grand-mother's body and were surprised by Elizabeth."

Barkley was shaking her head profusely. "No! No! I had no idea. I never even considered the possibility."

Morrison pressed. "You never considered the possibility that your grandmother came to Colorado after hearing your great aunt insist that was what happened for all those years?"

Barkley's eyes darted back and forth. "I guess I should have. Auntie did insist that was what happened. But, honestly that was not why I came out here. And that has not. . .."

Crab stepped in. "It must have crossed your mind, Edith."

Barkley looked down and began to wring her hands in her lap. "I guess it did cross my mind from time to time, Buster, but I never acted upon it. I wouldn't know how to research it. There are no records from that time. They were all sent to Denver and sealed."

Morrison leaned forward. "So, you did look into it?"

Barkley gasped. "No! I learned that from having to fill out forms and needing information on the building."

"What kind of information?"

"You know, like when the current boiler was installed, when the electrical was modified, stuff like that."

"That sort of stuff would be at the county. Only the personnel records would have been sent to Denver."

"No. Diagrams and building forms were all sent to Denver. Wet Mountain County has very little on the building."

Crab took over. "Edith, in talking to the residents that were at the party, they claim you were gone for most of the evening. No one saw you between eight and ten."

Barkley took a deep breath and tried to focus. "Well, like I said, I went up to my office to do some paperwork. I wanted the residents to enjoy themselves and not feel like they were being chaperoned."

Morrison flipped a page in his notes. "We estimate the murder took place sometime between 9:30 p.m. and 5 a.m." He looked into her eyes. "You are unaccounted for between eight and ten and after midnight."

Barkley broke down. Crab pushed the tissue box over to her. She snatched a few tissues and sobbed.

They gave her some time and then Crab said, "Edith, it will go so much better for you if you cooperate."

Barkley looked at Crab through red, tearful eyes. "I didn't do it, Buster."

Crab looked at Morrison and nodded toward the door. The two excused themselves and stepped out to chat with Bailey and the others.

Crab was not feeling good about the interrogation. "She really should be told she needs a lawyer, Sean."

"You recommending we arrest her?"

Crab threw out his hands. "I don't know. My gut says she didn't do it. What do you think, Sam?"

"The D.A. would tell us the case is weak. She doesn't have an alibi, but we don't have any concrete evidence to tie her to the scene either."

Bailey looked at Melton and Jacobs. Jacobs shrugged. Melton suggested, "Gotta cut 'er loose."

Bailey admitted, "I think we've gotta cut 'er loose, guys, unless you want to sweat her."

Crab grimaced and rubbed his face. Morrison looked back through the one-way glass. Barkley was trembling and sobbing at the same time. "You know, Sean, I have busted plenty of murderers during my years at Denver P.D. Barkley does not fit the usual profile. But every once in a while, they don't."

"What do you want to do?" Bailey asked.

Morrison looked at her again. "If she's guilty, Buster, I worry she might run."

Crab pondered the possibility. Did he know her well enough to vouch for her?

Bailey made the decision. "Okay then, cut 'er loose. Jacobs, why don't you go home and get some sleep and then stake out her place tonight. Morrison . . ."

Morrison did not need to be told. "I'll watch her after she leaves. Sydney, can you relieve me say at midnight? We'll need to use our personal vehicles."

Morrison unzipped the Walmart insulated grocery bag and peeked in. Just having the bag sitting there made him hungry, or at least made him crave something to eat. He pulled out a small bag of Lays potato chips and then poured himself more coffee.

Barkley had gone straight home after the questioning. She had been in the apartment now for two hours. He was pretty sure she was not going anywhere tonight.

He opened the chips and settled in for a long night.

Tuesday

Penitence wrapped in sad regalia,
buried in its penetralia.

Chapter 49

White Feather Comforts Barkley

NAOMI JOHNSON WATCHED MRS. Barkley pull into the parking lot. She glanced at the clock. She was running late for her, but she knew that Edith had been taken into the sheriff's office the day before.

Mrs. Barkley dragged into the reception room with a red face, runny nose, and swollen eyes hiding behind a wad of tissues. Naomi showed concern. "Are you okay, Miss Edith?"

Barkley shook her head. "I thought I could do it, Naomi, but I just can't. I'm going home for the day."

Naomi touched her arm. "Of course, there's nothing pressing today."

"Okay, well, I'll see you tomorrow. I'll be home if you need anything."

Naomi pointed to the couch on the north side of the room and whispered, "White Feather wants to see you."

Barkley looked over to see the old man sitting with his back to her. She whispered, "Damn. Do you know what he wants?"

Naomi mouthed, "No. Wouldn't say."

She took a deep breath and joined him. "You wanted to see me, White Feather?"

White Feather opened his eyes, touched her shoulder and looked deep into her eyes. "The interview went well."

Barkley shook her head. "It went very badly; it was terrible."

He persisted. "Went well; you were released."

Staring at him, she asked, "What do you mean?"

Closing his eyes, he took a moment to respond. "New evidence turn up?"

"Yes. How did you know?"

"Reason to bring you in for questioning. Lab result?"

Barkley blew her nose and searched in her purse for another tissue. White Feather produced a box from the end table and waited patiently.

Barkley said, "The DNA from the other dead woman ..." She stopped midsentence to address a new tide of tears.

White Feather finished for her. "Your grandmother?"

Barkley was surprised. "Yes. How did you know that?"

White Feather remained quiet as if the answer were obvious. "Sorry about your grandmother."

"Thank you. So, you knew that was her?"

"No."

"When did you find out?"

"Just now."

Barkley stared at the strange wizard. "What should I do?"

"Go home. Rest. You're in the clear."

Barkley was amazed how much better she was feeling. White Feather seemed so certain and so supportive. She wondered why. They had never been particularly friendly. Especially after he had pointed out her diploma to Deputy

Morrison. She respected him but they had never talked, really talked. She felt very close to him at that moment.

"Do you think my grandfather stabbed my grandmother?"

"Probably. Was definitely involved."

"Why do you say that?"

"Hid the car."

Naomi watched Mrs. Barkley pat White Feather on the shoulder and rise to leave. The old Indian remained seated as Barkley waved to Naomi and then exited the building. She watched her cross the gravel driveway, and get into her car.

Naomi approached White Feather. "What did you say to Mrs. Barkley? She seemed to be feeling better when she left."

White Feather paused thoughtfully, and then answered, "She didn't do it."

Naomi huffed. "Of course she didn't do it!"

White Feather explained, "Needed to be told."

White Feather stood and looked out the big windows at the front lawn. Naomi turned to see what had caught his attention. A green subaru pulled into the parking lot. A lady got out of her car, straightened her dress, and started for the building. At first, Naomi thought it was the new resident, Mrs. Meyer. But, as she got closer, she could see that it was someone else.

The lady entered, crossed the room and stopped at Naomi's desk. "I'm here to see Mrs. Rommel."

Naomi was shocked. Maire Rommel was supposedly a recluse. "Maire doesn't normally see people."

The lady laughed. "Oh, I know. She'll see me. She left me a message on my phone to come see her. Where may I find her?"

"Could I get you to sign our register?"

Naomi watched the lady sign. "You have pretty handwriting, Mrs. ... Phillips."

"Thank you."

She waited. "Oh. Well she is on the third floor ..."

White Feather had magically appeared. "I can show you."

Startled, Mrs. Phillips jumped back, grasped the collars on her blouse with one hand and pinched them together. "Oh, dear! Who are you?"

"It's okay, Mrs. Phillips. This is White Feather, one of our residents. He is offering to show you to Mrs. Rommel's room if that's okay with you?"

Phillips regained her composure. "Well, yes, I guess that would be all right. Thank you ... White Feather is it?"

On the ride up in the elevator, Phillips tried to make conversation. "Have you lived here long?"

"Not long."

Phillips cleared her throat and shifted slightly. "It seems like a nice place."

White Feather replied, "Humph."

The elevator shuddered and after a pause, the doors opened. Phillips nervously observed, "Oh! Well. Here we are."

White Feather led her down the corridor and stopped at the first hallway. "First room on left."

Mrs. Phillips acknowledged his directions with a nod. "Well, thank you."

White Feather waited as the stocky, well-dressed woman knocked on the door. "Go away."

"Joyce? It's Agatha, dear."

The door opened and the woman entered. White Feather moved closer.

Deputy Morrison pulled up beside Deputy Jacob's car parked discretely at the base of the hill beside the road leading up to St. Jude. He got out and joined Jacobs in her car. "She go in?"

"Yep. I just don't see it. There's something missing."

Morrison agreed. "There's definitely a piece missing. Maybe we should go back and interview everyone again. Maybe someone is holding back."

Jacobs pushed her unruly hair off of her face. "What about the recluse?"

"The recluse?"

"Remember? Grampa said there were two new residents. Mrs. Meyer and we know all about her. But there was also a new resident that has some phobia and stays in her room. I didn't see any paperwork on her interview."

"Ding, ding!" Morrison pronounced. "She wasn't on the list!"

"Why?"

"It was a list of people that were at the party. And I am sure no one went up to her room. And she certainly never came down to be interviewed."

Jacobs offered. "Want me to interview her?"

"No. I can do it while I'm watching Barkley today." Then Morrison looked up in time to see Barkley leaving the building.

Jacobs cranked her car. "Is she running?"

Morrison opened the door. "I'll get this. You go home and get some rest. Call me when you get up tonight." Morrison headed for his car.

Jacobs rolled down her window. "Want me to interview the recluse? I don't mind."

Morrison wanted to do the interview, but it was not fair to Sydney to have her follow Barkley. Besides, what if Barkley was about to run? He should handle that. Barkley was backing up. "No. We can get her later. You need to rest for tonight."

He jumped into his car not giving her a chance to protest. They circled around. Morrison found a side road to hide and watched Barkley pass and turn onto Highway 69 heading south . . . probably headed home.

Morrison let her get down the road and then pulled out to follow her. He had only gone about a mile when Jacobs phoned him, "Just passed the Phillips' car."

"Green Subaru?"

"Yeah, the plates match. I've turned around and I'm on her tail."

"Better let Melton know."

"Roger."

Morrison's head was spinning. Everything was happening at once. As he was passing the Beckwith Ranch, his phone buzzed again. It was Jacobs. "She's gone into St. Jude."

"St. Jude? Really?"

"Yeah, it's definitely her. She signed the register. Naomi says she's here to see the recluse whose name is Rommel."

"You're kidding? Did you call Melton?"

"Yeah, he's on his way. Told me to keep an eye on her."

"Thanks, Sydney, keep me posted."

Naomi led Deputy Jacobs out of the elevator on the third floor and turned left. "Her room is on the left at the next hallway."

They turned the corner and Naomi stopped. "It's the door White Feather is standing beside."

Naomi turned to head back to the reception desk. Jacobs saluted the snoopy old resident and whispered, "Afternoon, White Feather. You on a stake out?"

White Feather nodded. "Rommel's about to run."

"How do you know?"

"Planning to slip out north exit."

Jacobs glanced down the corridor. "Down the stairs?"

White Feather nodded.

Jacobs asked, "You think she murdered Lizzie?"

White Feather nodded again.

Jacobs unsnapped the strap over her pistol. "Okay, I got this."

White Feather remained in place. "It's okay, White Feather, my backup is on the way."

White Feather remained steadfast.

Chapter 50

Runners

MORRISON FOLLOWED BARKLEY TO her home and parked a block down the street. He watched the visibly distraught woman climb the stairs to her apartment on the second floor. If she were about to run, he figured she would soon be coming out with a suitcase.

His mind was on St. Jude. Why was Phillips visiting the recluse? What connection did she have? His mind began to speculate. They had to be just friends, just a quirky coincidence. But he did not believe it. He had passed Melton at Copper Gulch Road a couple of miles outside Rockcliffe. Checking his watch, he figured that Melton should be close to St. Jude by now.

"On the floor!" Jacobs commanded from behind the pistol she held in Phillips' face. Phillips was stunned and just froze.

"Face down on the floor, now!"

Phillips fell to her knees, then to her hands, and finally onto her stomach. Jacobs turned her gun on Rommel. Rommel raised her hands. "Face on the floor, now!"

Rommel leaned forward as if obeying her command. Jacobs shook her head in disgust at the lack of mobility these old ladies possessed. She holstered her gun and dropped down to cuff Phillips. Rommel made a dash for the stairway with White Feather in pursuit.

The door across the hallway opened and Frank peeked out. Ralph came ambling into the corridor from his room. "Sydney?"

As Sydney raced for the door she shouted, "Grampa! I need you to keep an eye on her."

Ralph rushed over and threw himself on top of Phillips. "No, Grampa, just watch her."

Jacobs could not wait. Rommel was getting away. She rushed through the door to the stairs, leaving her grampa wrestling with a very angry woman. Frank wanted to help, but had no idea what to do. "I don't think you have to hold her down, Ralph."

Sydney raced down the three flights of stairs and burst outside in time to glimpse White Feather disappearing into the woods. She sprinted after him.

Back on the third floor, Deputy Melton stepped off the elevator to find an old man rocking back and forth holding his ribs with another old man kneeling beside him. Melton strolled up with his hands in his jacket pockets. "What's wrong with him?"

"That lady kicked the crap out of him."

"Lady?"

"The one Sydney handcuffed."

Melton looked around. "Where is she?"

"She ran through there." Frank pointed to the stairwell at the north end of the corridor.

Melton calmly walked over to the large window and looked out. He could see Sydney disappearing into the woods north of the building. Then a woman in a skirt and high heels with her hands cuffed behind her staggered out of the building and looked around trying to get her bearings.

He shook his head and turned to Frank. "You call anyone about your buddy?"

Frank shook his head. Melton pulled out his cell phone, but Frank interrupted him. "We have a nurse."

Melton put his phone away. "Can you call her?"

"Yes sir."

Melton strolled over to the elevator and pushed the down button.

Sydney found White Feather holding Mrs. Rommel by her arms. She was struggling, but no match for the stronger man. Sydney grabbed her and dropped her to the ground as she reached for her cuffs. "Damn!" Her cuffs were gone. She stood and raised the lady to her feet and started dragging her toward the parking lot as she explained her rights.

As they exited the woods, the Phillips woman came stumbling up. "What's going on?" she shouted.

Jacobs read her her rights as well. "What are you arresting me for?"

"You're an accomplice."

"Accomplice to what? I'm just giving my friend a ride home."

"Your friend is a suspect in the murder of Elizabeth Dawson. I think she was trying to flee."

"Hogwash," Rommel retorted.

"Murder?" Phillips questioned. "Joyce, what is going on?"

"There's been a mistake!"

Jacobs countered, "Yeah, you got caught."

Jacobs noticed Deputy Melton coming across the lawn toward her. She waited for help. Melton nodded toward White Feather and then studied the two ladies. "You Agatha Phillips?"

"Yes, who are you?"

"I'm Deputy Melton. I've been looking for you."

"What for?"

"John reported you missing. He's been very worried about you. He thought you might have been kidnapped."

"Pshaw. That dirt bag should've thought about that before he hooked up with that floozy."

"So, you're okay?"

"Of course. But I'm not going back to that low life."

Melton nodded. "So, how do you know Mrs. Rommel?"

"I'm a friend from the Steelworks Museum. Joyce is the historian. She left a message on my phone that she needed a ride."

Melton handed Jacobs his cuffs and addressed Rommel. "Where were you going, Mrs. Rommel?"

"The tiny woman straightened and tilted her chin up. "I have been staying here for some well-needed rest. I asked Agatha to help me get home."

"Weren't you going to check out?"

"Of course, but your deputy here stuck a gun in Agatha's face."

Melton glanced at Sydney. Sydney explained, "They were trying to run."

Melton nodded. "We're going to need for you ladies to accompany us to the sheriff's office for some questions."

"We haven't done anything!" they protested as they were escorted to Melton's SUV.

"Sydney, you been up all night?"

"Yes, but I'm all right."

"I can take care of this." He looked at White Feather. "My friend can ride with me. We'll be fine."

Sydney was feeling tired. "I'll follow you to the office."

Morrison checked his watch again. He felt that if Barkley were going to run, she would have come out by now. He slouched down in the seat and laid his head on the headrest. It was probably going to be a long day. He pulled his thermos from his bag and poured hot coffee into the cup.

His thoughts turned to St. Jude, the recluse and missing person. Something was strange about that connection. He tried to come up with some tie-in to the murder, but was totally at a loss on that one.

He had finished answering emails on his phone when it buzzed. It was Deputy Jacobs. "Sydney, what's happening?"

"I think we have our murderer."

"Phillips?"

"No, Rommel. I caught her trying to run. Phillips was there to give her a ride."

"Rommel's the recluse?"

"That's the one."

"She confess?"

"Of course not. She claims she was just staying at St. Jude to get some rest and was ready to go home."

Morrison waited for more, but that was Sydney's report. "Well, what makes you think she's the murderer?"

There was a long pause. "Well, why would she be running?"

Morrison was growing concerned. "What if she's telling the truth?"

"Then why did she run when she saw me? She ran out of the building and was trying to hide in the woods. An innocent person wouldn't do that, would they?"

Morrison wanted to be supportive, but had grave doubts. "Probably not. Where are you now?"

"Melton and White Feather are transporting them to the office for questioning. I'm following for backup."

"White Feather?"

"He helped me apprehend Rommel."

Morrison chuckled and shook his head.

Jacobs remembered. "What about Barkley?"

"She's in her apartment. I don't figure she's going anywhere."

"No, I guess not. She didn't do it."

Morrison frowned. "I don't know, Sydney. I think I'll wait to hear how the questioning goes."

Sydney concluded, "I think I'll sit in on it. I'll let you know how it unfolds."

Deputy Melton had invited White Feather along for more than just backup. He suspected that White Feather knew something about Rommel. "So, how did you get caught up in this, White Feather?"

"Helping Jacobs."

Melton glanced over at him. He had forgotten how hard it was to get White Feather to talk. "You just happened to be in the vicinity?"

"Saw Phillips come in. Escorted her to Rommel's room for Naomi."

"Okay. That's when Sydney showed up?"

White Feather did not answer. Melton was getting impatient. "Why don't you just tell me what happened and save us both some time?"

White Feather coughed. "I listened at door. Heard Rommel explain she was leaving. Wanted Phillips to give her ride. Jacobs arrived as they were leaving. Pulled gun on Phillips; Rommel fled down stairway. Jacobs was tied up with Phillips. I chased Rommel."

"Why were you so interested in Rommel?"

"Met Rommel at museum. She knew Dawson and Nujent. Was at clinic and asylum with them."

"Sydney thinks she's the murderer. What do you think?"
"Possibly."

Chapter 51

Phillips' Interview

MELTON HAD CALLED INTO dispatch, so Bailey and Crab were waiting when he drove up with his prisoners. Crab was anxious to share new information from the CBI. DNA under Lizzie's fingernails matched the DNA on the letter opener. Also, CBI clarified the meaning of the cryptic notes: The old DNA matched recent DNA on the letter opener.

Both ladies had calmed down and were quiet when they entered the office. Melton suggested they place Rommel in the secure interrogation room while they questioned Phillips at the conference table in the open area.

Crab immediately noticed the scratch marks on Phillips' forehead. Melton started the questioning. "Mrs. Phillips, can you tell us why you were at St. Jude?"

Phillips' lower lip stiffened. "Like I told you, I got a message on my phone that Joyce needed a ride home." She reached into her purse and handed Melton her cell phone. He confirmed the message.

"Did she tell you why she was staying at St. Jude?"

"Not until I got there. She said she had checked in for some rest and relaxation. That she was stressed."

"Did that sound right?"

"What do you mean?"

"I mean that St. Jude is a retirement center, not a rehab center."

Phillips shifted. "I guess it didn't occur to me. I'm not that familiar with St. Jude."

"Where were you going to take Mrs. Rommel?"

"I assumed to Pueblo. That's where her home is."

"You didn't discuss where you were going?"

Phillips looked away. "No. I just helped her pack her clothes. I asked her how she was feeling. She said she was feeling better but had had enough of St. Jude."

Crab asked, "Where did you get the scratches on your forehead?"

Phillips touched her forehead and looked at Deputy Jacobs. "When we stepped out of the room, your deputy poked a gun in my face, made me lay on the floor, and handcuffed my wrists behind my back. Then she foisted some old man on me. He jumped on my back and .... Well, in the fight, he scratched me."

Jacobs bowed her head. "I'm sorry, Mrs. Phillips, Grampa misunderstood. I just wanted him to watch you, not pin you down."

Phillips glared at Jacobs. "That's your Grampa?" she turned away in a huff. "Well, I'm sorry I kicked him. I hope he's okay."

"You kicked Grampa?"

Melton held up his hand. "He's okay, Sydney. He'll probably have some sore ribs for a while is all."

Jacobs rubbed her eyes in disgust. Melton resumed his questioning. "So, why haven't you answered any of my phone calls?"

Phillips showed concern. "That was you? How was I supposed to know?"

"By answering your phone, I guess."

"I figured it was one of John's friends."

Bailey asked, "Did you know that John filed a missing person's report on you? We've expended a lot of resources looking for you."

Phillips face was drawn. "I'm sorry, Sheriff, I didn't know."

Melton asked, "You want to tell us why you disappeared?"

Phillips looked down and shook her head. "John had gone to the Dome for his Saturday night binge. I didn't like it, but sometimes it is nice to get him out of the house so I can get some writing done. It must have been around midnight when I got the message from Seth. It was a picture of John grinning stupidly, and I recognized Florence draped over him, nibbling on his ear.

"I was so shocked and upset that I threw the phone across the room. I'm surprised it still works.

"I called her all kinds of names to myself and then ran to the bathroom and threw up. After a good hurl, I paced through the house angrily trying to decide what to do. At last, I decided that I had to confront him. I had to scratch Florence's eyes out. I threw on some clothes, grabbed my keys, wallet, and phone and stormed out.

"At first I drove fast and reckless, but the closer I got to Rockcliffe, the more confused I became. As I slowly cruised by the Dome, my eyes filled with tears. In the end, I did not want to stop; I did not want to see him with her; I did not want to believe it.

"So, I headed out of Rockcliffe on Highway 96 toward Wetmore where my sister lives. But as I headed up the hill that passes the turnoff for the development Cristo Vista, I remembered that my sister was on vacation. I just kept driving. Then some drunk almost crashed into my car and ran off the road. I drove down to check on him. He was dazed and hurting so I helped him get out and took him to the hospital.

"After I took him to Pueblo, I spent the night in a motel. Next day I didn't want to go home, so I went to stay with my good friend here in the valley."

In a private conference, it was the consensus that Phillips had really done nothing wrong. She was not intentionally helping a fugitive. She had disappeared of her own free will and was not in any danger. They had invested a lot of their time and energy into the investigation, but sometimes that just comes with the job. Their priority was the safety of the public and it served the public no good to continue the case.

Mrs. Phillips was informed that the missing person case would be closed and she was free to go.

"What about Joyce? Should I wait?"

"No, Mrs. Phillips," Bailey said. "We have some questions for her. We will make sure Mrs. Rommel gets to where she needs to be."

Chief Crab left the room for a moment and returned with a deputy to take Phillips back to her car.

Chief Crab invited Sheriff Bailey, the deputies, and White Feather to join him at the conference table. "We received some new information from the Springs. The DNA from skin and blood underneath Dawson's fingernails do not match Mrs. Barkley's DNA. That was why I asked Phillips about the scratches on her forehead. I am satisfied with her answer and, besides, as you could see, the scratches were fresh. We are looking for a wound almost a week old."

Bailey commented, "Might even be healed by now. Any match on the DNA?"

"No, I think we need to swab Rommel. They did confirm that the old DNA is a match with the new DNA on the letter opener."

Bailey put it together. "Are you saying that the person who killed the lady in the grave is the same person who killed Dawson?"

"It looks that way," Crab replied. "I'm going to call Sam and have him come in for Rommel's interview."

Melton leaned forward to share his information on Rommel. "White Feather has informed me that he has met Rommel before. He and his geezer buddies at the Center went to the Steelworks Museum last week to see if they could find out anything about Dawson's past. Rommel is the historian at the museum. They learned that Rommel worked with Dawson and Nujent there."

Surprising everyone, White Feather added, "Also worked at asylum."

Crab shook his head and joked. "Am I the only person who DIDN'T work at the steelworks and the old asylum?"

White Feather continued, "Nujent mentioned pregnant file clerk named Joyce."

"I don't remember you being in the room Mr. Feather, but she did say that." Then Crab rifled through some papers and stated, "Rommel's full name is Maire Joyce O'Quin Rommel."

Bailey questioned, "What exactly are those papers?"

"St. Jude resident list from Naomi."

"See if you can get Morrison in forthwith."

Bailey decided to let White Feather hang around. Although he tried to get Jacobs to leave, she refused and he felt she had probably earned a right to stay. "We need to check Rommel for an old scratch wound."

Frank spent part of his afternoon helping Ralph get to the clinic to get his ribs wrapped up. In Frank's opinion, Ralph had been a big baby about the whole thing. He had squealed every time Nujent had touched him in the examination. The X-ray had been clean—no cracked or broken ribs, but listening to Ralph, he had thirteen broken ribs. Nujent prescribed a mild pain killer and explained, "We don't wrap rib injuries anymore. It stifles recovery."

"It hurts when I breath!" he cried. So, she wrapped his chest to appease him.

Frank had helped him back to his room and poured him a glass of water to wash down the pill. Ralph had looked at the glass and asked, "What is this?"

"Water."

"The wine is in the cabinet."

"You're not supposed to take wine with medicine."

"Who says?"

"Everyone knows that, Ralph."

"Bull pucky. It's right over there, top shelf."

Frank shook his head and looked at the bottle of pills. They were probably sugar pills. He poured Ralph some wine and handed it to him. As he was leaving, Ralph demanded, "Where you goin'?"

"I'll come check on you later. You'll be fine."

"Thanks a lot," Ralph scoffed.

"You're welcome."

Frank closed the door behind him and shook his head. Out of spite, he headed for the pool room, Ralph's favorite pass time. Monty and Albert were in the middle of a game. Albert was shooting, so Monty saw him first. "F-Frank!"

Albert stood and smiled. "Franklin! How is Rudolph?"

"We'll need to change his diaper in about an hour."

Monty showed concern. "His d-diaper?"

Frank waved his hand. "He is the biggest baby I've ever known."

Albert laughed. Monty frowned and then got it. Frank sat down and updated them. "He's going to be fine. No cracked ribs or anything, but he whined until Nujent wrapped his chest anyway. He complains that his sides hurt when he breathes."

Albert shook his head. "Rudolph may be a pain in our sides for a while, too. Heard from White Feather?"

Frank replied, "No, not yet. I think he accompanied Deputy Melton to the Sheriff's office with the two ladies.

Albert pushed on for more details. "So, you were there. What happened?"

Frank began to share the morning's sequence of events. "Well, I was in my room and heard Jacobs shout 'on the floor' or something like that. When I looked out, she had her gun right in the one lady's face. That lady got on the floor and then Jacobs turned her gun on the other one and told her to get on the floor. She bent over like she was cooperating and so Jacobs dropped down to cuff the first one. That's when the other one took off running. She headed straight for the stairway and White Feather took off after her."

Frank cleared his throat and then continued, "That's when Ralph came flying around the corner and Jacobs ordered her grandpa to watch the lady on the floor while she took off after the other one. Ralph did a swan dive on top of the lady on the floor."

Monty and Albert started laughing. Frank continued amidst his own sniggering. "Poor Ralph was no match for that woman. She managed to roll him off her, stand and then started kicking the crap out of him."

Monty covered his mouth. "O-Oh, no!"

After a good laugh, Frank was feeling exhilarated. "Let's play pool. How often do we get the chance to play without some grumpy guy giving us fits?"

Ralph strolled in. "Rack 'em."

Chapter 52

Joyce's Interrogation

WHILE THEY WERE WAITING for Morrison to return, Bailey ordered Detention Officer Terry Kruger to do an informal body search of Rommel with instructions to mainly look for scratches and to do a DNA swab. Kruger reported faint marks on her wrists and palms.

Morrison and Melton were chosen to do the interview. Crab joked that it was unfair to have two bad cops. In good humor, Melton volunteered to be the good cop.

After turning on the recorder, Morrison started the interview with a tired, restless, and angry woman. "Please state your full name."

"Maire Rommel."

"Who is Maire Joyce O'Quin Rommel?"

Rommel squirmed. "That would be me."

"Are you currently employed at the Steelworks Museum in Pueblo?"

"No."

Morrison glared at her; she glared back. Morrison won the stare down. "I volunteer."

"In what capacity?"

"Archivist."

"Can you tell us why you were living at St. Jude?"

"I wanted to get away for a while. I've had some stress in my life lately."

Melton smiled and asked, "What kind of stress?"

She seemed surprised by the question. "Just some bad news."

"Family member?"

"Not really."

"Care to elaborate?"

"No."

Morrison took over. "Mrs. Rommel, this is a murder investigation. We need your complete cooperation."

"It is none of your business."

"We'll be the judge of that. Answer the question."

Rommel's eyes searched the surface of the table. "I was looking at some old documents in the archives that brought back sad memories."

Morrison decided to take a chance. "About your time at the clinic or the institution, perhaps?"

Rommel looked up with fire in her eyes. "How do you know about that?"

"I understand you knew the victim, Mrs. Dawson, back then. You worked with her at both the clinic and at the Institution."

Rommel began to rub her hands. Morrison noticed the red, swollen marks on her wrist and palms. "Yes, I knew Lizzie then."

Melton tried to put her at ease. "I understand that Elizabeth was involved in an experiment that went badly."

Rommel scrutinized Melton closely. "You've been talking to those old geezers, haven't you?"

Morrison took over. "Do you remember the experiment?"

"Oh, yes, it was quite tragic. Steve ..." she blushed and then quickly corrected herself, "Dr. Weisman gave her LSD hoping to make her smarter so he could win a bet with Dr. Howard. It blew her mind and she took a dive off the clinic roof."

Morrison filled in more details. "That is when she was admitted to the institution in Pueblo. Shortly after that, Weisman took the administrator's job at the Wet Mountain Institution and transferred Mrs. Dawson over there. We know that he transferred several people from the clinic as well. Were you one of them?"

Rommel seemed resistant but answered. "Yes, just Nujent and me."

"In Nujent's testimony, she mentioned a 'pregnant Joyce.' Was that you?"

Rommel rubbed her hands and shifted in the chair. "Yes."

"Was Weisman the father?"

"Why do you need to know that?"

"Was he?"

"Yes."

"What happened to the baby?"

Rommel touched the corner of her eye. "I lost her."

Melton leaned forward. "What happened?"

"I just don't see how this is any of your business."

Morrison pressed on. "Were you aware that Elizabeth was also carrying Weisman's baby?"

"I suppose."

"How did that make you feel?"

Rommel's lips began to tremble and her eyes started to glisten. She did not answer.

Again, Morrison decided to take a chance. "Did Weisman perform your abortion?"

Rommel's forehead appeared to be getting moist. Melton decided to pour on a little sugar. "It must have been a very difficult time for you."

A tear raced down her cheek. She lowered her head and nodded.

"Did he do it at the institution?"

She was slow to answer. "There was a secret operating room in the basement."

"I think it is still there, isn't it?"

She remained quiet.

Morrison attacked. "How did you get those marks on your wrist?"

Rommel quickly moved her arms from the table to her lap. She peeked at her wrists and then answered, "Must be from the handcuffs."

"It looks like the sores have been there for a while."

She rolled her head. "I don't know." She began to sob.

"We found skin and blood under Lizzie's fingernails. I expect the DNA will match yours, Mrs. Rommel."

Tears were streaming now.

Morrison gave her a minute. "Why were you in the basement?"

She shook her head. He pressed her, "You were looking for the body, weren't you?"

Melton pushed the tissues over to her. She pulled one out, folded it neatly and then blew her nose. Then she pulled another and another. She was shivering. "It's cold in here."

Melton stood to leave. "I'll get you a blanket."

Morrison resumed. "How did you know about the body? Were you there when Mrs. Weisman showed up?"

Rommel's eyes bulged. "How do you know about that?"

"DNA."

Rommel dropped her head into her hands. "Oh, Lord." She burst out crying.

Melton returned and draped the blanket around her shoulders. He patted her shoulders. "It's time to come clean, Joyce."

She dropped back in the chair resignedly. "Stephen and I were going through the old secret surgery files in the basement."

"Secret files?"

"Stephen stashed his notes in that basement surgery location regarding abortions, sterilizations, and other forbidden surgeries, experiments, and reports. The numbskull documented all of the illicit surgeries and left them in file cabinets in that basement dungeon."

"Were you pulling the files to destroy them?"

"No, not at that point. That would come later when the inspectors showed up. I know. It's crazy."

"Anyway, that is when we heard someone coming down the steps. No one was allowed to go down there without Stephen's approval. Steve closed the file drawer and headed toward the stairs. I'm not sure why, but I feared the worst and grabbed a letter opener that was lying on the cabinet. I heard Steve say, 'Eydie?'

"I didn't recognize the name at first. When he said, 'What are you doing here?' I knew he was talking to his ex-wife Eydith.

"She claimed she was there to try to reconcile with Stephen but they quickly started shouting at each other. It was clear to me that she had gone through the settlement and wanted to get more money out of him. I was proud of him for standing firm and denying her demands."

Joyce leaned forward, put her elbows on the table and put her face into her hands. "She became furious and attacked Stephen. She started slapping and kicking him ... that's when I reacted and jumped in front of Stephen and plunged the letter opener into her chest. She immediately went limp and fell to the ground."

Joyce began to sob into her hands.

"The look in his eyes! ... The world began spinning around me ... I must have fainted."

They gave her some time to pull herself together and then asked, "Is that when you buried her?"

Joyce dabbed her nose with a crumpled tissue. "When I woke up, I was on the dirt floor. I lay there for a while trying to understand what had happened. I heard Stephen and looked over to see him shoveling dirt on a pile. I called to him asking, 'What are you doing?' He dropped the shovel and turned to me all out of breath. He told me to go home and pack some things for a four-day trip. I asked him where we were going and he insisted I leave right away and told me that he would pick me up in an hour."

Joyce pulled another tissue and continued, "Stephen showed up at my house about forty-five minutes later in Eydith's car. He informed me that I was to follow him to Massachusetts. We stashed her car at UM at Lowell in a parking garage. Stephen tossed her purse into an ally nearby and then we returned. On the drive back, Stephen told me that he had buried Eydith in the basement 'in a place no one would ever look!'"

"But you knew where?"

"Oh, yes. I found the shallow mound by the north wall, dug down enough to find the body and uncovered it enough to ..."

"Why did you dig her up?"

Joyce shook her head. "I don't know. I guess I thought I could move the body. I was afraid they would find it while putting in the furnace."

"Why did you wait for so many years?"

"Oh, I tried to go down there when it was vacant but couldn't get in. Then I went there when it was converted to a hospital, but that was a twenty-four hour operation."

She turned a pitiful look to Melton. "When they closed the hospital, I thought I was finally in the clear. I didn't know until last Friday that it had been reopened."

Joyce covered her eyes and sobbed. Morrison gave her time to recover.

"Lizzie surprised you."

"I panicked. That night ... well, I was horrified. It had not been like Eydith, you know, instant, easy? Elizabeth had fought back ... I had to force the letter opener in and then she started pulling it out. I had to shove it in and hold it until ...."

Joyce broke down. "What did you do after she, well, finally passed?"

"Like I said, I was horrified. I ran back to my room in a daze . . . in shock, I guess."

Joyce stared at the table. "I didn't know what to do. Before I knew it, it was morning and people were stirring around so I had to stay in my room. I decided that I would sneak back down after dark and bury Elizabeth. I found the shovel and started digging a grave next to Eydith's."

Rommel shivered. "She was already starting to smell. The ground was soft on top, but hard as a rock underneath. I gave up trying to dig even a small portion of the grave. Exhausted, I dragged myself back to my room with the intention of resting and then coming back. But I passed out and wasn't able to go back down until the next night. That was Tuesday night. When I opened the door to the stairway, the smell was overwhelming. I had to run outside and throw up. There was just no way I could force myself to go back down there again.

"I wrestled with what to do the rest of the night. Then, the next day ... well, they found the body. I panicked and packed my bags and was planning to escape that night until I realized that if I ran, it would call attention to me. Never mind having to explain to my ride why I was sneaking out in the middle of the night."

Joyce put out her hands. "So, I just decided to hunker down and wait for the inevitable."

She looked at Melton. "When you didn't question me with the other residents, I thought maybe I was in the clear. Anyway, last night, I decided I couldn't wait any longer, so I called Agatha."

Morrison glanced at Melton and then stood. "Joyce, I am arresting you for the murder of Elizabeth Dawson and Eydith Weisman. You have the right to remain silent ...."

Chapter 53

Time Quake

FRANK, ALBERT, MONTY, AND Ralph arrived at the dining room early hoping to find White Feather. Albert had buzzed Naomi in reception earlier so they knew he had been dropped off already. Naomi shared that White Feather had looked dreadfully tired, and she suspected he had gone to his room to rest. The plan was to wait for him in the dining room since not even Ralph was brave enough to go knock on his door.

So, when White Feather dragged in, they were all elated. Albert greeted him. "White Feather, we have been waiting with bated breath for your report."

White Feather turned up his glass of water and emptied it. Frank offered to refill it if he would wait for him to return before giving his update. He did.

"They let Phillips go."

"Albert clarified. She was the missing person that Sydney was looking for."

Frank was curious. "How did she get mixed up in this?"

"Knew Rommel from Steelworks Museum."

Frank snapped his fingers and pointed at White Feather.

"That's it! That's where I heard the name. Joyce Rommel, right?"

White Feather was not impressed, but Albert and Monty were. Ralph commented, "I never liked her."

White Feather stopped to eat a few bites before continuing. "Rommel called Phillips for ride home. Phillips knew nothing about murder or Rommel's intent."

Frank questioned, "Intent?"

"To run."

Ralph chimed in, "Wasn't much of a runner if YOU caught her."

"Humph. Then White Feather continued, "Rommel confessed to everything."

Frank asked, "She murdered Elizabeth?"

"She murdered both."

"Both? How is that possible?"

"Other corpse was wife of Weisman. Came to asylum, argued with Weisman, Rommel stabbed her."

The shock allowed him time to grab a few more bites. "Came back to move body."

Frank got it. "She was surprised when we told her that St. Jude was in the old Institution's building, remember? She rushed back to her office."

Albert was curious. "I wonder why she didn't do that long before now."

White Feather shared, "Tried numerous times. Building was closed or occupied. When hospital closed, thought she was safe."

Albert shook his head. "I'll be darned."

White Feather shared the irony of the murders. "Both killed with same weapon by same woman."

With another case solved, the Sleuthkateers ate quietly lost in their own individual thoughts until suddenly the table began shaking. Monty threw up his hands and shouted, "Wh-What's that?"

Ralph answered calmly, "Earthquake."

Albert challenged him. "How do you know, Rudolph?"

"I'm from California, remember?"

Frank asked urgently, "What do we do?"

Ralph put down his spoon, blotted his mouth with his napkin, stood and suggested, "Perhaps we should go outside before the next tremor."

Frank jumped up and announced, "Earthquake! Everybody outside, quickly."

The dining room was instantly turned into chaos with screaming old ladies and shouting old men. White Feather grabbed Frank's arm and steered him to the back of the building while the mob headed out the front.

"Where are we going?"

"Time quake. Pick a time in your past to return to."

Frank struggled to free himself. "No! I don't want to go back!"

White Feather grabbed his arm again. "There's no time. Must hurry."

Frank dug in his heels. "No! Wait. The doppelganger!"

White Feather stopped and glared at him. "Doppelganger?"

"Yes. Yes. He said he would go back instead of me. We have to find him."

White Feather stared at Frank for a moment and then doubled over in uncontrolled laughter.

Frank was completely confused. "What? What is it?"

Suddenly, Albert approached him followed by Monty and Ralph. All were overtaken by laughter. Ralph managed, "Gotcha!"

Albert gained control first. "We did get you, Franklin."

Now Frank was getting angry. "What do you mean?"

"Actually, it was White Feather's idea."

Ralph complained, "I thought of the doppelganger."

Albert admitted, "Oh, yes, that's right, Rudolph."

White Feather had regained his composure and stood to lead Frank over to the bench. Frank was fuming. White Feather explained, "I was concerned. Too much grieving."

Albert joined in. "We were all concerned about you, Franklin. White Feather suggested that we needed to do something to take your mind away from your grief. Ralph suggested the doppelganger. We all agreed to tell you we had seen the doppelganger every time you came around."

Monty added, "I-It s-seemed to be w-working."

Albert agreed. "It did seem to be taking your mind off things. We were a little worried when you started getting angry, so we sort of backed off. Then White Feather had this great idea about the time quake."

Frank was confused. "How did you know there would be an earthquake?"

White Feather admitted, "I kicked the table."

Morrison could see in his headlights that the snow had started up again. It would be cold in the bleachers. Atypically, he switched off the engine without revving it up first. For some reason, he wanted to be quiet and not draw attention to himself. Closing the door without slamming it, he stepped lightly onto the porch and hesitated before ringing the bell. The breeze was icy, whipping around the corner of the house.

He heard quick heavy footfalls and the door flew open. "Hey, Dad! We're about ready, I think."

Jerry turned to look behind him.

Sam could see the lights switching off in the back of the house. Tammy dashed past her brother in colorful coveralls and fluttered her fingers at her dad. Jerry followed his sister out the door. They ran to the car and then pushed and shoved each other as they crawled into the back seat.

Another light switched off leaving the house dark. Samantha emerged, bundled up and pulling on thick mittens. She glanced up and smiled warmly, "Brr. It's going to be miserable tonight."

She struggled to pull the door shut. Sam reached around too late to help. She bit the tip of a mitten to pull it off and retrieved keys from her purse. Sam reached out to assist but she had the key in the lock and door secured in one motion. Dropping the keys back into her purse, she pulled the mitten back on and turned toward the car. Sam hurried to get the door, but the kids had left it open. Samantha brushed snow off the edge of the seat and slid in quickly allowing him to shove the heavy door shut.

As he trudged through the accumulated snow to the driver's side, he was thinking about the warm smile he had just received. It was not the indifference he had experienced at his last visit. And she had actually looked into his eyes briefly. Maybe ....

As he dropped into his seat, Samantha was fussing with Tammy and Jerry. "You two need to behave, please. You're acting like three year olds."

Tammy whined, "He shoved me into the car."

Jerry countered, "It's cold. You were taking too long."

Samantha insisted, "ENOUGH!"

Sam sheepishly started the car. Everyone was quiet now as he backed out and started down the snow-packed street. Only the crunch of the tires and the rumble of the engine entertained them as they watched the snowflakes getting larger and thicker in the headlights. Sam decided to pick on the easy target. "So, Jerry, you've lost some weight?"

"Not really."

Samantha glanced back and then added, "He's bulked up."

Jerry laughed, "I haven't bulked up, Mom."

Samantha huffed. "Well, I mean you haven't lost weight. It's just muscle now, right?"

"Yeah."

Sam decided to try to change the subject. "You excited about cheerleading this year, Tammy?"

Tammy didn't answer. Samantha scolded, "Your father asked you a question, Tammy."

As if breaking out of a daydream, she responded, "Oh. I was."

"Not now?"

"It's going to be freezing out there."

Sam and Samantha laughed. And Samantha added, "You should have thought about that before signing up."

"It was summer then."

Jerry punched her. "Wimp."

Tammy punched him back. "Will you shut up! Leave me alone."

Samantha shook her head. "Stop, both of you."

Sam smiled. It was just like old times. It felt good.

Aftermath

Immure me in your heart,
So that we shall never be apart.

Chapter 54

Buried Treasures

FOUR SOMBER MEN SAT quietly at the table unable to eat. The fifth man, Ralph Jacobs, gobbled his food with his usual enthusiasm. White Feather had just informed them that Rommel had been indicted on two counts of murder, resisting arrest, and conspiracy. Frank shared, "Can you imagine trying to live with that all those years knowing that the body could be found at any time?"

Albert added, "With all of the renovations and repurposing, it is quite extraordinary that it wasn't found before now."

Monty was patting his fingers together. "Y-Yes, a-amazing."

Ralph commented, "Wonder what else is buried down there?"

The other Sleuthkateers stared at him. Frank was the first to speak. "What else would be buried down there?"

Ralph held up his hands, wiggled his fingers and made his eyes bug out. "More bodies maybe?"

Monty gasped. "Y-You th-think?"

Albert contributed. "Actually, there could be. The administrator before Weisman was accused of all sorts of atrocities.

The graveyard out on the hill behind the pond has dozens of Institution patients buried in it." He paused. "Now Elizabeth will be joining them."

Frank observed. "If he buried them up there, what would be buried in the basement?"

White Feather responded. "Rommel's abortion."

Everyone gasped.

Since Elizabeth had never made any arrangements for her funeral and had no family left except for Diana Meyer, it was decided to bury her in a complimentary plot in the St. Jude Methodist Cemetery up on the hill overlooking the pond. The cemetery was now owned and maintained by the Methodist Church. It was suspected that there were institution residents secretly buried there since many of the graves were unmarked. Ten marked graves had German names, suggesting an old family plot, probably a ranching family from the late 1800s.

The Sleuthkateers sat together on the back row. Frank sat next to Albert on the end of the row. He wondered if there were any in attendance that felt as sad as him about the crazy old lady. Her daughter, Diana Meyer, sat in the front row with Alvira Nujent. Mrs. Barkley sat next to Alvira and Lizzie's three best friends occupied the other three chairs.

A retired Methodist preacher who lived in the valley volunteered to do the service. Brother Parker also held services every Sunday morning in the second floor parlor, so he knew Elizabeth.

"As we all know, Mizz Elizabeth possessed mysterious powers and it appears that whatever powers she had left were used to produce this beautiful day. It is not often for this time of year to be calm, sunny, and mild."

The congregation politely laughed.

"I doubt that many of us knew the hard life that Lizzie lived that has been revealed recently in the investigation of her demise. It is fitting that she be buried here where so much of what molded her life transpired."

Frank shook his head thinking that all of that guilt he had felt for not attending Sunday services had been for naught. This guy was as nutty as Elizabeth. He glanced down the row and was not surprised to find Ralph nodding off, White Feather sitting with eyes closed, Monty studying a bird warbling in a nearby tree, and Albert playing with the crease in his pants. Fortunately, the service was brief.

Heading back from the cemetery, Frank found himself walking beside Nujent. Something that White Feather had said was churning in his head. He heard himself address Nujent. "Do you find it strange that Weisman would send that letter to Lizzie knowing she wouldn't understand it?"

Nujent jerked her head around as if startled by Frank's presence. Then she looked down and shook her head. "He didn't send it to her."

Frank was surprised. "She made it up?"

Nujent cackled. "For Heaven's sakes, no!"

She looked at Frank as if deciding whether to explain. "I gave that letter to her."

"You wrote it?"

"No. Goodness no. I didn't understand any of it. You see, I visited Stephen in the hospital, or the institution rather. I think I was the only one of his infamous girlfriends that did. I thought I loved the bum. He handed me that letter and asked me to deliver it to Joyce, of all people."

Nujent kicked a pebble. "The scum loved Joyce, not me ... not Elizabeth. I wasn't about to give the letter to that ... woman. When I got home, I opened it and read it. I just had to laugh. What a bunch of crap.

"Later, when I landed the job here at St. Jude and found Lizzie living here, it broke my heart that she was still pining over that scoundrel. Being back here in this building had stirred old memories, I guess. I ran across the letter while I was unpacking and decided to give to her. I don't know, I thought it might mean something to her."

Nujent glanced at Frank. "I mean sentimentally, not the words."

She looked back down at the trail. "It meant everything to her, but she was devastated because she couldn't understand a word of it."

Nujent shook her head. "Me and the girls tried to help her translate it and I think it helped some, but she always thought that there was some hidden message in it. She thought that the line about something buried in its penetralia referred to her daughter. I should have told her about Diana then, but I felt I needed Diana's blessing first."

"I guess she had been looking for her baby's grave when she surprised Rommel."

"Imagine what she would've thought if she would've stumbled onto the body!"

Frank and Monty were stretched out on their backs on the dirt floor gasping for air and creating mud dots around their heads with oozing sweat. Ralph and Albert were taking their turn in the shallow pit. White Feather sat cross-legged in an apparent trance. Ralph's shovel scraped something solid.

Frank and Monty sat up. "Find something?"

Ralph began to scrape dirt away from the solid object. "Duh."

Albert squatted down over the object to shine light on it. "Looks like a rectangular metal container of some sort."

Frank stood and picked up a shovel to help Ralph dig it out. When they lifted it out, they discovered that it was a sealed metal container roughly twelve inches by fifteen inches by eight inches deep. Frank handed it over to Albert while he and Ralph stepped out of the shallow pit.

White Feather's eyes opened and he reached up to take the container from Albert. From somewhere, he pulled out a mean-looking Bowie-style knife and began working on the lid. Frank and Albert focused flashlights on the task. The metal lid grated and squeaked against the point of the knife occasionally cracking and popping but not giving way to the pressure.

At last, White Feather gave up. "Rusted shut."

Ralph bragged that he could open it.

Frank was indignant. "How?"

"I got stuff. I'm a construction engineer, remember? Done it lots of times."

Chapter 55

Fire in the Hole!

THE BULKY METAL BOX was getting heavier with each step. Frank's shoulders were aching from the load. He followed Ralph through the bushes and trees to the west side of the St. Jude property.

One last push through the brush put them in a large clearing. A six-foot stone fence defined the western border of St. Jude. An old and rotting wooden door set ajar inside a three-and-one-half foot gap in the fence. About fifteen feet from the gate, an old cistern made of the same stones sat crumbling. What was once the roof lay broken and rotting. Warped planks lay across the rounded top to cover the abandoned well.

"Set it down there," Ralph demanded pointing to the center of an old foundation in the center of the clearing.

Albert, Monty, and White Feather crowded around to watch the querulous ex-construction engineer unroll two wires wrapped around a simple control box roughly the size of a sandwich. He plunged the firing caps into the soft doughlike substance he had used to line the rim of the lid of the can.

"What is that, Silly Putty?" Frank asked.

"C4," Ralph matter-of-factly answered.

Frank's face grew red. "I've been carrying a box lined with plastic explosives?"

Ralph was walking away stringing the wire behind him. "It's harmless without the blasting caps."

His four friends scurried away from the box.

Albert challenged his cantankerous colleague, "What are you planning here, Rudolph?"

Ralph had reached the end of the fifteen-foot wire and was facing the metal box and holding the control box. "I'm going to blow the lid off the damn thing." His friends gasped. Frank stated the obvious, "You'll blow us all up."

Ralph was contemptuous. "You don't know anything about C4, do you?"

Frank snapped back, "Do you?"

"Trained on it in the military."

Frank, familiar with military training, was not satisfied. "Ever actually use it?"

White Feather cautiously directed his friends behind the old stone cistern. Monty was concerned for his friend. "B-Better g-get behind s-something, R-Ralph."

Ralph huffed. "Not a problem. C4 will direct the explosion toward the surface of the box. I'm perfectly safe." And with that, he flipped the switch on the control box. KABOOM!

The four men hit the ground behind the cistern. Although expecting a loud explosion, they were not expecting to feel the concussion of the blast from C4. It left their ears ringing loudly.

Frank peeked over the top of the cistern and was engulfed in the concentrically unfurling black cloud of smoke. When it cleared, he saw that the box had vanished. "You blew it up, you idiot!"

Ralph's shirt and pants were shredded, revealing his undershirt and underpants. His body was smoking and his hair singed. They ran up to him and discovered that the front of his body was black with soot. "Ralph! Are you all right?"

The smoldering, crooked old man coughed black smoke out of his mouth. White Feather proclaimed, "Here it comes."

He was staring into the sky. The others looked up to watch the smoking metal can hurtling toward the ground. The Sleuthkateers naturally ducked before realizing that the can was falling outside the rock fence.

They followed White Feather to the gate. He unlatched the dilapidated gate and pushed. Instead of swinging open, the old door fell flat. The Sleuthkateers rushed through and scrambled west toward where the box had dropped. Frank was in the lead when he stopped abruptly and threw out his hand, palm facing his friends. He had stumbled upon the edge of a deep ravine about twenty feet deep and seventy-five feet across.

His friends rushed up and stared curiously into the ravine except for White Feather who pointed across the ravine at a tall fence wearing a crown of curling razor wire. Inside the compound, Albert recognized the significance of the long, rounded green houses and dozen or so large water tanks. "A grow site."

Monty was confused. "G-Grow what?"

Ralph trudged up and declared, "Wacky weed."

Frank asked, "Marijuana?"

White Feather put his hands on Frank's and Albert's shoulders and whispered urgently, "Get down."

Six rough-looking men in camouflage fatigues raced to the center of the compound and surrounded the crater where the box had impacted. One started shouting and pointing at the old men. The others pulled assault rifles off their shoulders and pointed them at the shocked Sleuthkateers.

White Feather, the only one who had faced an enemy on the battle field, took charge and gave the command, "Run!"

The wobbly old men gave their best imitation of running as they scurried back to the safety of the stone wall. White Feather stood watch at the gate while his friends lay gasping on the ground behind the stone barrier.

Albert was the first to try to size up their situation. "Must be an illegal grow site. We must call the sheriff."

White Feather replied firmly, "We must not speak of this again."

Albert was confounded. "What do you mean, White Feather? We have to report it the authorities."

White Feather kept his eyes trained to the west. "How will you explain the box?"

Ralph got it. ". . . and the illegal C4?"

White Feather pulled an old gourd rattle out of his belt and started bouncing slightly, shaking the rattle and chanting. The others did not understand Cherokee, but clearly understood the significance of his prayer.

They would not speak of it again except to say, as if sharing a secret, "Penitence wrapped in sad regalia, buried in its penetralia," and then break into nervous guilty laughter.

Sneak Peek:

The Columbine Caper

A White Feather Mystery
by Courtney Miller

THE DIRECT RAYS FROM the sun made the snowcapped Sangre de Christo mountains sparkle while puffy but shadowy, subdued clouds perched over them. The dining room mood was gloomy matching the heavily filtered light from outside.

Ralph Jacobs had been focused on his meal. Albert Stein sat thoughtfully engaged with his newspaper. Frank Roberts picked at the crusty corner piece of his meatloaf. Walter Montgomery had paused to study the curious newcomer sitting alone in the corner.

Ralph loaded his mouth with mashed potatoes dripping with brown gravy, glanced at the empty chair at their table and asked, "Where's the Injun?"

Albert continued to read his paper but replied, "White Feather has gone to ride the Royal Gorge Express today, Rudolph."

"What's that?" Ralph countered.

"The train over in Canon City."

Ralph swallowed and reloaded with corn, "Where's he going?"

"Well, to ride the train, as I said."

"Where?"

Frank got it, "It doesn't go anywhere, Ralph, just up through the Royal Gorge canyon and then back to Canon City."

Ralph paused and stared at Frank, "Why? They forget something?"

Frank was exasperated. Albert continued reading. Walter asked, "Why do you think he's so sullen?"

Ralph cut off a piece of meatloaf with the edge of his fork, "Probably, because he didn't get nowhere."

Walter looked at Ralph bewildered. Frank glanced over at the newcomer in the corner. Walter was right, the elderly man looked sullen and defiant sitting all alone. "What do you know about him, Albert?"

Ralph stuffed the meatloaf in his mouth, "Yeah, he gonna stay on or get off?"

Albert closed and folded the paper and set it beside his plate. "Not much. Birdie thinks he may have been the sheriff in Wet Mountain Valley years ago."

Ralph reached for his glass of tea, "Not likely them ranchers would let an Injun sheriff 'em."

Walter frowned. "Injun? You think he's Native American?"

Ralph managed, "Duh!" before placing the glass to his lips.

Walter shook his head. Frank commented, "Doesn't look Native American, does he?"

Albert chuckled, "It seems you gentlemen are not on the same page."

Ralph set down his tea, "Duh!"

Albert smiled at Ralph, "We're talking about the new

resident sitting alone over there, Rudolph. You are still hung up on White Feather."

Ralph jerked his head around. "I thought you said he was in Canon City?"

Frank was frustrated, "White Feather IS in Canon City. We're not talking about White Feather!"

"He ain't ridin' that train?"

Ralph, Walter and Albert looked at each other and then burst out laughing. Ralph glared at them, threw down his fork and stormed out of the dining room.

"Ralph!" Walter pleaded, "Wh-What's wrong?"

Albert touched Walter's arm, "Let it be, Walter, he'll calm down. We can straighten things out when we join him in the pool room."

"It's a shame," Frank mused.

"Wh-What?" asked Walter.

"Ralph is the one of us that has the guts to approach the new guy and find out about him."

They laughed and nodded their heads. Then Frank remembered, "However, we shouldn't forget who he brought over last time!"

"Oh! Harold Flambeau!"

"Poor White Feather. He's stuck on the train with him today."

They looked at each other again, nodded and headed for the new guy's table. The man seemed unaware of their approach until Albert reached out his hand. "Good morning, I am Albert Stein and these are my friends Walter Montgomery and Frank Roberts."

The man squeezed their hands a little too firmly and nodded reluctantly not offering his name or any sort of greeting.

"We just want to welcome you to St. Jude."

He gave no response.

"May we join you?"

He motioned for them to sit but was not welcoming. Monty tried to start the conversation, "Wh-What b-brings you t-to St. Jude?"

Frank and Albert winced and the man's glare suggested he agreed that it was an improper question. Everyone at St. Jude was there because they had no other option. It was a home for the indigent.

Albert tried, "Are you from the Wet Mountain Valley?"

The man shrugged, "Yeah, you?"

"Monty is; I came here from Denver; Frank via Canon City."

The large man leaned back, took a deep breath and began his story, "Moved to the valley in 1945. Worked on a ranch and later leased a place of my own. Was sheriff for ten years until I got shot in the shoulder."

Albert commented, "I think we've met. I may have interviewed you when I was researching a story. I was an investigative reporter for the Denver Post."

"Yeah, maybe. I was interviewed pretty often about one thing or another. Part of the job."

Frank asked, "You play pool? We were about to go up for a game or two."

The sullen man looked down at his plate, tilted his head to one side. "Why not."

As they left the dining room, Mrs. Barkley approached. "Good morning, gentlemen. I see you've met Mr. Slade."

Albert admitted, "Well, we haven't been formally introduced."

"Oh, well, Cody Slade, this is Albert Stein, Walter Montgomery, and Frank Roberts."

The men nodded but remained aloof. They were reluctant to shake this man's hand again. Mrs. Barkley tilted her head slightly. It was an awkward moment, so she addressed Frank, "How is your new room, Frank?"

"Great! Oh, I need help turning on the little refrigerator.

"I'll have TJ stop by."

"You have a refrigerator in your room?" Slade asked.

Frank shrugged shyly, "I just moved into a new room. It has a small apartment-style refrigerator but it is turned off. I thought it might be nice to store a carton of milk in it."

His friends laughed. Slade frowned. "Milk? Needs beer if you ask me."

Frank was embarrassed. He was relieved when the elevator doors opened.

Albert handled introductions. "Rudolph, this is Cody Slade, a new resident. He wants to join us for a pool match."

Ralph was still angry with his friends, but was always in the mood for pool. "Me 'n him'll take Frank 'n Monty."

Albert smiled kindly at Slade. "Okay with you Mr. Slade?"

Slade shrugged, retrieved a pool que and chalked the tip rigorously. Ralph had already racked the balls so he placed the cue ball on the table and took out all his anger on the break. The balls exploded and bounced around the table. A striped ball dropped into the corner pocket. Ralph chalked the cue tip and leaned over for his next shot.

Slade asked, "You fellows lived here long."

Ralph pulled back his cue and turned to glare at the rookie. Albert interceded. "Ralph does not like for us to talk while he is hitting."

Slade glared back at Ralph. "Sorry, go ahead."

Ralph leaned over again to take his shot. He pulled the cue back and rocked it back and forth several times before making his shot. Frank answered, "I've only been here about a year."

Ralph lunged forward striking the cue ball off center sending it spinning into the side pocket. Ralph exploded into a tirade of expletives and started swinging his cue stick like a baseball bat with intent to behead Frank.

With lightning fast reflexes, Slade grabbed the cue stick and jerked it away from Ralph leaving the angry man and the spectators in shock.

"There's no need for violence gentlemen." The ex-sheriff proclaimed calmly.

Monty pulled the cue ball out of the pocket and suggested Ralph replay the shot. Slade handed Ralph the cue and nodded his head toward the table. Ralph replayed the shot but missed the shot slightly leaving the target ball beside the pocket.

Monty stepped up to take his turn while Ralph quizzed the new guy. "Who are you?"

Albert replied, "Mr. Slade was once the sheriff of Wet Mountain Valley."

Slade added, "Among other things."

Monty did not make anything, so Slade stepped up to the table.

"Like what?"

"Ranching mostly. What'd you do in your previous life?"

He aimed at the cue ball and sent it zinging across the table to knock in the green fourteen ball. The cue ball banked and rolled back to line up on the nine ball.

"Construction engineer."

Slade popped the nine ball into the side pocket putting backup on the cue ball to line up on the fifteen into the corner. Now the old men got quiet to watch Slade run the table putting Ralph into a joyous and triumphant mood. Slade became his temporary best friend.

Ralph asked, "You know about that big raid?"

Slade squinted. "What do you know about it?"

"Five cartel hoodlums got away. I saw 'em in our kitchen last night."

Frank, Albert, and Monty gasped. Slade was interested. "In the kitchen downstairs here?"

"Yep. I was down there ..." he paused to glance at his friends and then continued in a more confidential tone, "I was hungry and went down to raid the refrigerator. I heard something and saw two of 'em by the drink carts and then heard the other three in the kitchen fumbling around."

Slade cocked his head to one side. "What'd you do?"

"Got a ham 'n cheese and returned to my room."

Albert, Monty, and Frank could not help laughing, but Slade gave him a look that said he was unconvinced. Ralph must have realized how unbelievable his story was, so he voluntarily explained. "I was in Vietnam and have been diagnosed with PSTED so I thought I was just having one my spells."

"PSTED?"

Ralph got defensive, "Whatever they call shell shock these days."

Slade nodded, "Oh, PTSD."

"So, anyways, I thought I was reliving an episode from the war. But when Sydney told me about the raid, I realized it was real."

Slade was getting impatient. "Sydney one of your imaginary friends?"

"Sydney is my granddaughter. She's a deputy for this county."

Slade raised an eyebrow. "Sydney Jacobs is your grand-daughter?"

"Yeah. She comes by to see me all the time. She was here last night."

"So, you think they may still be here?"

Frank answered, "I saw them up on cemetery hill yesterday morning. White Feather and I checked it out and they were headed north."

"How do you know that?"

"White Feather is a Cherokee shaman and he read their tracks."

Slade shook his head. "You guys are real jokesters aren't you. You must think I fell off a turnip wagon."

This clearly raised the dander on Frank and Ralph. Albert stepped in to try to save the peace. "As strange as it may seem Mr. Slade, I must say that these two are not trying to pull your leg. Rudolph did serve in Vietnam and his granddaughter is Deputy Jacobs and I did see her here last night. White Feather is a resident of St. Jude and was a Cherokee medicine man in his younger days."

Slade studied the comical looking man whose resemblance to Woody Allen was uncanny although his demeanor seemed quite refined and intellectual. Albert detected that he was still not convinced, but was also curious why his interest in their stories.

Slade turned back to Frank. "I would like to see these tracks."

Frank shrugged, "Sure. Come with me."

About the Author

Courtney Miller is the multi-award winning author of the seven-book series, *The Cherokee Chronicles*. He is considered an expert on ancient Native American culture and incorporates that knowledge into his writing. He has written over 200 articles on the art, archeology, astronomy, culture and history of ancient Native America for Native American Antiquity and other online ezines. *The Cherokee Chronicles*, has received multiple awards and widespread praise from the Cherokee community for its authenticity.

In his new series, *The White Feather Mysteries*, Miller once again shows his award-winning talents bringing to life fresh characters with a twisting plot and surprise ending.

Courtney lives in the Wet Mountain Valley, where the White Feather Mysteries are set, with his wife, Lin. He enjoys playing golf, is active in the local Rotary club, and volunteers as a star guide for the Smokey Jack Observatory.